A SEASON FOR MURDER

"God, this was a beautiful kill."

Another man with his back to Sandy held up a paw he had cut off the animal. "Here, Benson, now you got a mitten."

They all laughed, but Sandy had seen enough. She edged out of her cover and then took off running, keeping her body in a crouch.

"Hey, someone's back there," she heard one of them say.

She had made it to a fairyland of birch and aspen when a shot rang out. She plunged ahead as another shot pierced the air. Her legs pumped faster. . . .

Blood Ties

BLOOD TIES

ALEXA BRIX

DIAMOND BOOKS, NEW YORK

This book is a Diamond original edition, and has never
been previously published.

BLOOD TIES

A Diamond Book / published by arrangement with
the author

PRINTING HISTORY
Diamond edition / June 1992

ISBN: 1-55773-718-5

Diamond Books are published by The Berkley Publishing Group,
200 Madison Avenue, New York, New York 10016.
The name "DIAMOND" and its logo are trademarks
belonging to Charter Communications, Inc.

PRINTED IN THE UNITED STATES OF AMERICA

10 9 8 7 6 5 4 3 2 1

**To
Lynda and Gaylon,
who suggested a Minnesota vacation**

1

SANDY Wilson peered through the tiny glass window of her mailbox for a moment before depositing her grocery bag on the tile floor. A lumpy envelope inside the box intrigued her.

Certainly more interesting than the parade of junk mail that usually passed through here, she thought. She worked the combination and pulled out the envelope, glancing at the return address:

> Skaar's Taxidermy Shop
> 219 Central Avenue
> Northlake, Minnesota

What would a taxidermist in Northlake be sending her? she wondered. A stuffed vole?

She smiled to herself. She wasn't particularly sure what a vole was. She had it kind of loosely categorized as a small furry creature, but that was the extent of her knowledge. Nature wasn't exactly her thing.

Her fingers ran across the lump which distended the center of the envelope, trying to guess what was inside. She wanted to prolong the mystery instead of ripping right into the envelope and satisfying her curiosity. She thought drily how desperate she was for any kind of excitement.

"Northlake," she murmured, closing the mailbox. She'd been through there only once, a long time ago when her stepfather decided that her six-year-old brother was old enough for a "camping experience." He'd zeroed in on a state park just west of Northlake, dragging her along. She still didn't know why he and Jerry hadn't gone alone, since it was supposedly for her brother's benefit. To his credit, Willis Cochran had really tried to bond with them when he first married into the family; she guessed that had been the trip's purpose.

However, sixteen had been the wrong age for her to develop a passion for the outdoors; she was far too interested in her friends, makeup, and parties to appreciate being trotted off to the boondocks without the basics, like telephone, shower, and electricity, in that order of importance. But not only had Willis disregarded her protests, he'd brought her mother, who dragged her heels about the trip, too.

Northlake. It was odd how clear the whole memory was. The whole family had set out from Minneapolis on a day which held a lot of promise. Bright sun, blue sky.

But promises are hard to keep. The first clouds began to appear from the west shortly before they pulled into a primitive campsite. Erecting the strange tent had been like putting together a plastic model with no instructions. Willis had barked out orders, but even he was obviously baffled. As they struggled, the wind came up, catching the canvas, making it even more difficult to tame.

By nightfall, there'd been a cold, insistent drizzle threatening to turn to snow. Although they'd been in the tent by then, enveloped by a faint smell of mildew, the sharp night air had sneaked in, chilling them to the bone. The rain on the canvas made white noise that discouraged any conversation, but that was okay with Sandy. What did she have to discuss with them anyway? They were adults and didn't have a clue about what was important to her. She'd lain on her sleeping bag feeling sorry for herself.

By morning a fine mist penetrated the sodden canvas, and water was seeping in through the floor seams. They'd done something wrong, Willis admitted, but he wasn't sure just what. Sandy's mother had been acting out of sorts the entire time, so when Willis admitted he didn't know all there was to know about camping, she'd insisted on calling it quits. They'd fled back to civilization and Sandy's beloved curling iron and telephone. After that, Willis and Jerry had confined their camping to Scout father-son trips.

Northlake. Sandy had a vague recollection of driving through the town itself, a long main street flanked by businesses. Very frontier. Very on the edge of nowhere.

She glanced again at the return address: Skaar's Taxidermy Shop. The name rattled something in her memory, but it was a long time ago and a long way from Washington, D.C.

As Sandy spun the mailbox lock a half-turn to secure it, the outer door of the apartment building opened, and she was joined in the small vestibule by her elderly neighbors. Esther Purvis was a spry octagenarian, and her face crinkled up in a smile when she saw Sandy. Her husband, William, doffed his corduroy golf cap in greeting and drew his wiry gray eyebrows down till they brushed across the top of his wire-rimmed bifocals; then he turned to the inner door to the stairs. Sandy always thought he looked a little like Oscar the Grouch.

"Here, let me get that," Sandy said, dropping the

envelope into her grocery bag and digging in her pocket for her keys.

The old man flicked his wrist at her. "I've already got my key out," he said, then punctuated his sentence with a "dammit!"

Surprised, Sandy stopped abruptly at his exclamation and looked up, wondering if he was angry at her. But he was looking at the door.

"What is it, dear?" Mrs. Purvis asked, trying to peer over his shoulder.

"This damn door wasn't even locked. That's the third time I've found it like this. You move to an apartment where you think you won't be murdered in your bed, then the damn security door doesn't work." He clicked the lock several times, then bent over, adjusted his glasses, and peered at it. "Maybe someone's been tinkering with it."

"Don't get in a dither, William," his wife said. "He gets so upset about things," she told Sandy, "and it's not good for his blood pressure. It runs high anyway. We just came from the doctor's. Dr. Henderson over in—"

"Well, don't just stand there," he said to the two women. "Come on, get on in here before some drug dealer drives by and shoots you."

Constant access to cable news was having an ill effect on him, Sandy thought, picking up her groceries and hurrying to get through the door before William Purvis' wrath had the chance to turn toward her. The crime rate in their little northern Virginia neighborhood was really pretty low, and she hadn't seen any visible signs of drug-dealing nearby, but the D.C. statistics had people on edge.

"Was anything wrong?" Sandy asked Mrs. Purvis.

"Wrong?"

"You said you've been to the doctor?"

The old woman nodded. "Oh, that. No, it was just a

routine visit. We get our blood pressure checked once a month.''

Sandy followed her up the narrow stairs with William bringing up the rear.

''I'm going to call the building owner about this,'' he mumbled. ''I'm fed up. Either he needs to get someone out here to fix it or find out who's tampering with it.''

''What are you grumbling about back there, dear?'' Esther was slightly hard of hearing.

At the top of the flight Sandy slid past the elderly woman and went over to her own door, where she put down her bag of groceries to search for her key. ''Have a good evening, you two,'' she called across the hall.

But the couple didn't reply. Mr. Purvis was repeating his tirade so his wife would catch it all, but she was talking at the same time. ''What good will it do?'' she asked. ''The owner's not here to catch someone.'' They went into their apartment, still arguing.

With a sigh, Sandy went inside, locking the door behind her. At least they had someone to talk to. Her companion for the evening was the television. She quickly unloaded the frozen foods and milk from her grocery bag, then left the rest and went into the living room, stepped out of her shoes, and curled up in an easy chair to open the tantalizing envelope.

The lump turned out to be a roll of exposed film wrapped in a piece of paper. She unfolded it and glanced down at the signature.

Well, wonder of wonders, she thought drily. A letter from my little brother. This might be a first. She couldn't remember a time when he'd ever written to her. Usually his cries for help came by phone.

She toyed with the paper a moment, reluctant to read it, certain that it *would* be a cry for help. Jerry-initiated communications with her had always meant trouble. The first had been when she was teaching English at a high school in Minneapolis. The principal had called her out of class one afternoon because her brother had been caught red-handed setting off a smoke bomb in the teachers' lounge. He'd been suspended for three days, and she'd covered for him at home.

Another time, Sandy had gotten a call for help when Jerry'd been picked up for possession of marijuana. He'd needed bail money. And when he'd gotten a girl pregnant, he'd asked for money to pay for an abortion.

Then there was the time—but she could go on and on. He had needed picking up often, and she'd been there to help, always feeling a little sorry for him. Their real father—Forrest Ahlgren—had abandoned them before Jerry was even born. If Jerry was irresponsible, well, it wasn't solely his fault.

Sandy had been nine, going on ten, when Forrest had walked out. She remembered her mother's frequent crying jags, weekends when she wouldn't dress, wouldn't fix meals. It was a wonder to Sandy, looking back on it and considering the woman's emotional state, that her mother somehow managed to get a job when Jerry was six weeks old, then held onto it. Apparently she'd kept her emotions in check at work, lapsing into depression once she got home, allowing Sandy to take over.

Sandy's own grief at losing her father was somehow tempered by having a new baby to take care of. It was as if Jerry was hers, not her mother's.

When Sandy was fourteen, Pauline had married Willis. He was a nice guy, but Sandy had resented him. They'd been making it okay without him.

She had long since talked to him—apologized really—about those early feelings and how she had tried to subvert

Jerry's growing attachment to his stepfather, but those days had shaped her whole life. And Jerry's.

Jerry was still acting like a little boy, and Sandy carried around a lot of guilt for coddling him too much. But she hated to see him suffer.

She'd last seen him six months earlier when he'd come to Washington and dropped in unannounced at her office. Her initial pleasure at seeing him had turned to embarrassment as she introduced him to her boss, Senator Mattingly, and then Troy Gunderson, his top aide, whom Sandy was dating. Jerry barely acknowledged them before he started bragging about his accomplishments as a free-lance photographer.

She'd looked at him skeptically. He'd had a succession of jobs and was now working in a video store in Duluth, if they didn't fire him for taking time off to come to Washington. She knew nothing about his working at free-lance photography. She suspected Jerry was in fantasy land, but she kept quiet.

Then he'd asked if he could visit privately with the senator.

At the next available opportunity, she had apologized to the Senator.

Jim Mattingly had brushed the apology off with a wave. "Listen, Sandy, I have relatives, too. Don't worry about it. Besides, maybe I can help him. Who knows? He is one of my constituents, after all." He winked at her. "Constituents" covered a wide range of people who wrote, called, and strayed into the office. Jerry was mild by comparison with some. The only trouble was he was related. She had the same feeling she'd had when the principal called her out of her classroom—a sinking sensation in the pit of her stomach.

Help him what? she had puzzled over the Senator's words. But Jim Mattingly's press secretary had interrupted just then, so she didn't get to ask him, and Jerry had left for Minnesota that morning, so she didn't pursue it with him either.

So now her will-o'-the-wisp brother was in Northlake. Was he living there, or had he just passed through? For a brief moment, Sandy wondered if he had moved there permanently. No, Jerry didn't understand the word *permanent.*

She sighed and rather reluctantly began to read the note.

> Dear San,
> Hold on to this film for me. It's important and needs to be in a safe place. Don't tell anyone about it or it might be over for me. You've always been my insurance.
>
> Love,
> Jerry.

The whole thing was written in a barely legible scrawl and took some major deciphering on her part.

Over for him. She grimaced and gripped the paper and felt a prickle of fear dot her scalp, then pushed the feeling back. What in the name of God was he up to? And what right did he have to involve her in it? It was just like him to drop something like this on her, then tell her not to mention it to anyone.

She put down the letter and fingered the roll of film, wondering what was on it. What hot potato had her irresponsible brother stumbled onto? His words suggested blackmail.

The last line—*you've always been my insurance*—surprised her. He seldom said anything that smacked of self-revelation. And yet it almost sounded as if he'd been putting things in perspective. But no, she thought pessimistically, the sentence was probably calculated to turn her screws. He knew precisely how to do that.

She crumpled the envelope and tossed it across the room toward the wastebasket, making her shot.

"Two points for me," she mumbled. Surely Jerry was just being overdramatic, caught up in his own world of exaggeration. She felt slightly foolish for her first reaction of foreboding, picked up the letter and started to toss it in the trash too, then changed her mind. She stared at the logo at the top of the page and her apprehension returned. What did Skaar's Taxidermy Shop have to do with Jerry? Had he just taken a piece of their shop's stationery? Or did the origin of this letter have more significance? And why did that name prick her memory?

She laid the film on the end table, pushed herself out of the easy chair, and headed for the kitchen phone with the letter.

She'd just give the shop a call and get to the bottom of this.

2

BUT no, Sandy couldn't call Skaar's Taxidermy Shop. What if Jerry was in real trouble? What if this wasn't just some skewed perception of his overactive imagination? Could she ever forgive herself if she ignored his request? He had warned her not to mention it to anyone, and *anyone* certainly included the taxidermist, whom she didn't even know. Was this Skaar person friend or foe?

Again she found herself feeling a little foolish for thinking in terms of an enemy.

She hesitated a moment, then removed the telephone receiver from its hook and dialed information in northern Minnesota and asked for Duluth. There was no listing for Jerry there, so she asked the operator to check Northlake. Same answer. No listing for Jerry Cochran. It figured. He really couldn't afford a phone bill on the kind of money he'd earn at a video store. Now blackmail? That was something else. She shook her head and replaced the receiver on its cradle.

No sooner had she done so than the phone rang. The sound made her jump.

"You must have had your hand on the phone," a male voice said.

For the shortest moment she thought it was Jerry, but then she recognized Troy Gunderson's warm voice.

"Hi, Troy. I'd just hung up. How was the trip?" She was a little surprised, but glad that he had called her. They'd decided a few weeks earlier to put their relationship on hold, but hearing his voice made her realize how much she'd missed being with him. She was awfully lonely.

"Excellent. Just fine. I think we made some headway in negotiations with the Koreans. At least we made some good contacts."

"Was the Senator pleased?"

"Yes. He's feeling optimistic. Then we stopped in the Cities on the way back and he had a productive meeting with the staff there."

"That sounds good. How was the weather in Minneapolis?"

"Definitely autumn. Leaves were just beginning to turn. The Senator had some personal business to take care of, so I took my mother to see *I Do, I Do* for the tenth or eleventh time."

"At Chanhassen?"

"Yeah. Say, Sandy, may I come over?"

His voice held a sudden softness, a warmth that made her feel vulnerable, and she hesitated, wondering if it was a good idea. "Sure, I guess." At least, he would be a good diversion from worrying about Jerry and would keep her from talking to the walls.

"Do you mind?"

"No, of course not, it's fine," she said, still not too sure. "Have you had dinner? I can fix something." She stopped speculating about his motivation and began mentally going through the freezer and cupboards.

"How about if I pick up some cashew chicken?"

She laughed. It was her favorite and he knew it, but she'd just had Chinese food the night before. "No, just bring yourself. I have some spaghetti sauce and stuff for a salad. Bring wine."

She laid the letter from Jerry on the end table with the film, then went to the bedroom, *to get into something more comfortable,* she thought wryly.

She pulled a pair of brown knit slacks off the back of a chair, examined them for wrinkles before putting them on, then found a coordinated cotton pullover and slid it over her head. She fluffed her chin-length hair a bit, then studied herself in the mirror, hesitantly drawing the fingers of one hand across her cheek, then down her neck till her index finger rested in the indentation at the base of her throat. She blinked hard several times and flashed herself a fake smile to try to erase the waiflike look worry gave her; then she headed for the kitchen.

The spaghetti sauce was simmering by the time there was a knock on the door.

"How'd you get in downstairs?" she asked Troy when she let him in.

"It wasn't locked."

She made a face. "I think there's something wrong with the lock. My neighbor thinks someone's tampered with it."

"Something smells good," he said, handing her the wine.

"Oregano," she said. "I still have to cook the spaghetti and throw together a salad, then dinner will be ready. Are you starving?"

He wrapped his arms around her, planted a kiss on her lips, then began to nibble at her neck. "We could have a little appetizer."

"A drink," she said. "Just a drink. Or maybe you've had one. Or two." She quickly pulled away. He seemed more laid back than usual. Apparently she hadn't been imagining the nuances in his voice over the phone.

"Why do you think that?"

She shook her head and smiled. "You seem awfully mellow."

"I've just been missing you. What do you mean, anyway? Am I not a mellow guy?"

She gave a snort. "Troy, when they thought up that Type-A personality stuff, you were the model."

"Aw, c'mon, Alexandra. Give me a break." He took her arm and pulled her toward him.

"Don't 'Alexandra' me," she said, pulling away again, flashing him a smile. Early in their relationship, he'd advised her that she would rise to the top faster if she used her formal name, and she'd told him dating the boss's right-hand man was probably just as effective. Since he was worried that others in the office would find out about them, calling her Alexandra was the closest he came to a pet name for her. He was afraid of slipping up at work with a *honey*.

"Have a seat," she said, eager to get away. She needed to keep this under control, until she could figure out what direction she wanted it to go. "I'll get you a Scotch and you can read the paper while I make the salad."

She mixed his drink and took it to him. He had taken off his jacket and loosened his tie, and was settled into the easy chair. The newspaper sat in his lap unopened.

"Thanks," he said, taking the drink.

"It'll just be a few minutes. Can you occupy yourself?"

He flashed her a political smile, the one he could turn on and off at will; the one that didn't extend to his eyes. "Sure." He unfolded the paper and held it up in front of him. "Are you satisfied?"

"I just don't want you to be bored."

"Don't worry. I'm fine." He took a sip of his drink and turned to the paper in earnest.

When she reached the kitchen door, she looked back at him. He sat slumped in the chair, long legs stretched out on the ottoman. His conservative haircut didn't cover the silver-dollar-sized bald spot at the crown of his head, but that was his only physical flaw. It certainly didn't detract from his good looks, but any imperfection was one too many for Troy. Lately he'd been talking about hair weaving. His other assets included a good job, intelligence, and ambition.

It was comfortable having him there. Funny how just having another person in the house made things okay.

She went back to the kitchen, feeling less lonely than she had in several weeks, and tackled the salad greens. The only thing missing with Troy was the breathlessness of new love, and that wasn't something on which to base a long-term relationship; she knew that from experience.

She'd met her ex-husband, Charlie Wilson, standing in a lunch line at the University cafeteria where she'd been chattering with a friend and had accidentally bumped his tray, sloshing iced tea onto it. After her apology, they'd struck up a conversation, which ended with his following the two women to their table and joining them for lunch. Even at that first encounter, her heart had felt as if it were swelling up and would burst out of her chest cavity. She couldn't breathe. She wondered now if maybe that feeling was something reserved for the young.

So why not a Troy Gunderson who only excited her passion with the lights out and a fantasy in her mind, but could provide her with companionship and security? It sounded very reasonable.

After a pleasant dinner, she put some coffee on to perk, then stacked the dishes in the sink, deciding to leave them for later. When she returned to the living room, Troy was standing by the easy chair, thumbing through *Newsweek*. "Do you want to watch television?" she asked.

He looked up, closed the magazine, and put it on the end table next to the exposed film and Jerry's note. He picked up the film. "Did you decide on a camera?"

For months she'd been poring over leaflets and articles, trying to make a decision about which camera to buy. "No. Still haven't decided. My brother sent me that." She hesitated, her uneasy feeling about Jerry returning. "Read that letter," she said.

Troy read it and frowned, then refolded it and put it back on the end table.

"I don't know what to do," Sandy said. "I guess I'll take the film down tomorrow and get it developed. See what he's up to. I just can't imagine—"

"Don't," Troy interrupted.

She looked at him, puzzled. "What?"

"I said, 'Don't.' If he's doing something illegal, you'll be putting yourself in the position of being an accessory."

She hadn't thought of that, but Troy was probably right.

"I don't like this—his involving you." He sounded angry. He stood up and paced across the room.

She felt protective of Jerry, but pleased, too, that Troy cared enough to get upset.

"Why would your brother do this, put you in this kind of position?"

"It's probably nothing. He exaggerates everything. It's okay."

But Troy was hot now and he ranted some more, displaying his Type-A behavior.

"Troy, it will be okay, I just won't do anything."

"Well, please don't. I just can't—"

"Troy," she said. "Relax."

He stopped himself, visibly calming. "You're right. I need to relax." He spread his palms and made several little pushing gestures toward the floor, then smiled and came toward her, taking her in his arms. His voice softened. "How about dessert?" he said, nuzzling her neck.

"I don't have anything. But the coffee's probably ready."

"I had something else in mind," he said as he nibbled at her jaw line and moved toward her mouth, finally stopping there. He kissed her tentatively once on the lips and she knew the next kiss would be more insistent. She turned her head away.

He kissed the other side of her face. Again she turned away. This time he got the message. "What's the matter?"

"I don't know." She made a face and stepped out of his arms. "I'm not in the mood. I guess it's talking about Jerry. It upsets me. He's always in trouble of one kind or another. He's a walking time bomb, set to go off and send shrapnel my way." She shook her head and picked up the *T.V. Guide*. "Listen, how about television? Surely there's something on." She flipped the pages to the listings for Wednesday.

Troy glanced at his watch. "I haven't been home for a week. I think I'll call it a night, if you're sure you aren't—"

She shook her head and smiled. "I'll probably regret it."

"Well, then—" He took a step toward her, a smile lighting his face.

She held up her hand like a stop sign just as the phone rang.

3

SANDY's mother was on the other end of the line. As she and her daughter got the preliminaries out of the way, Troy mouthed a thanks for the dinner, gave a wave and let himself out.

So, he'd just come for dinner and sex, acting out some hormonal imperative, she thought glumly. Didn't even stay for coffee. So much for her great personality.

As soon as the thought occurred, she mentally kicked herself. An assumption that it was a female responsibility to make relationships work was an albatross she was trying to get off her neck.

"You seem distracted," her mother said. "Am I interrupting something?"

She *was* distracted and she apologized. "I had a dinner guest and he was letting himself out."

"He? Who was it?"

No one would ever accuse her mother of being subtle. "Troy Gunderson. He's—"

"Oh, yes. He's the man from work. I thought you two had called it off."

"Not exactly. We're kind of having a time out, but that

doesn't mean we can't be friends.'' Or did it? "He and the Senator just got back into town and he called, so I invited him over for dinner.''

"Well, my goodness, I'm sorry if I broke something up.''

"No, you didn't. He was leaving when the phone rang.''

"Oh—well, we've had a little excitement here.''

"Really? What happened?''

"Our house was broken into last night.''

"Oh, Mom, I'm sorry. Were you out of the house—I hope?''

"Yes. We were bowling. When we got home, the place was a wreck. Things thrown everywhere. It was awful.''

"Well, I guess so. What did they take?''

"We couldn't find anything missing, so the police think it was just vandals. Probably hopped up on drugs or something.''

Sandy frowned. "That's scary enough, isn't it?''

"Yes. We stayed at Aunt Sara's last night—till we could get the glass fixed beside the front door—that's where they broke in. Knocked the glass out, then reached in and opened the door. I'm kind of uneasy about tonight.''

"I'm sure it will be okay.'' She didn't feel as certain as her words. "Two nights in a row—that never happens.''

"I guess not, but''—the telephone made an impatient little beep, blotting out Pauline's words—"my Call Waiting. Hold on a minute.''

Sandy smiled. Her mother had Call Waiting, Call Forwarding, everything the phone company could provide to ensure Pauline didn't miss something. This was a social woman.

A minute later she clicked back in.

"Do you need to go?'' Sandy asked.

"No. That was Mildred Hale. We're working on the

church bazaar together. I told her I'd call her back. Remember? It was her son who visited you.''

Oh, yes, Sandy remembered. Dave Hale was a limnologist—he studied the life in lakes and ponds—with the U.S. Fish and Wildlife Service. She'd shared two rather boring meals with him.

Sandy's mother continued. ''She wonders if you ever hear from him.''

''Not since he was here.'' The mothers had put him up to calling on her when they heard he was coming to Washington on business.

''I guess you two just didn't get along.''

''Oh, it wasn't that. He was okay, but I don't know—who wants a long-distance relationship?'' *Okay*, she'd stretched it a little. Dave had seemed kind of like an overgrown Boy Scout to her, tall and lanky, a triangular-shaped face with a weak chin—a beard could have helped that—ears that stuck out. Not that looks mattered that much. Her ex-husband, Charlie, hadn't been particularly handsome, but Dave Hale had simply lacked the fire to kindle her interest. He'd spent the evening telling her about the study he was doing on some kind of mussels that were threatening the ecological balance in the Great Lakes. His work was ultimately important, she understood that, but he made his life sound deadly dull.

''Mother, you sound so hot to get me married off.''

''I just don't want you to be lonely like I was after''—she hesitated—''before I met Willis.''

Pauline had been more than lonely, Sandy thought. ''Well, don't worry about me,'' she said, ''I can take care of myself.''

''Oh, I'm sure you can, but I can't help but worry. Up there alone. Last night really brought that home to me. I hope you get this out of your system and come back to

Minnesota. Not that it's any safer," she said. "By the way, Dad saw Steve yesterday."

"Charlie's brother?"

"Uh-huh. He said Charlie is in an alcohol rehabilitation program."

"That's good."

"Uh—Steve wondered whether maybe you could call Charlie and talk to him, encourage him—you know."

"Mom, you know I can't do that. Besides, I was probably part of his problem."

"That's what I told Willis, but he told Steve he'd tell you. Just in case."

"You understand, don't you, Mother? I don't want to confuse things. I've closed that chapter of my life, and I just can't go back and open it up again. It would be too painful." Not to mention confusing.

"Well, Willis said he'd tell you, so I'm telling you."

"Okay. You've done your duty." I'm *not* going to get sucked into calling Charlie, Sandy thought, gripping the phone tightly. She'd given him all of her life that she could. She'd stuck with him through a lot of hell, all because of that breathless feeling, thinking it was enough, that it could save their relationship. But in the end she had to save herself.

"You know best," her mother said, then abruptly switched subjects. "Honey, have you heard from your brother? He's always so good about calling me, and I haven't heard from him in several weeks."

"Uh—I haven't talked to him since he was here in the spring," Sandy said, sticking to the literal truth.

"I just feel uneasy, as if maybe he's in trouble."

The maternal antennae were tuned in. "Mom, I'm sure you're worrying about nothing." She was reminding herself with her words. "Jerry's a big boy. He can take care of himself." She decided to fish a little. "Is he still in Duluth?"

"As far as I know." Pauline's voice sounded suspicious as she asked, "Why?"

"I just wondered."

"When I didn't hear from him, I called every video store in Duluth, looking for him. That was Monday."

"And?"

"I finally found the one he used to work for. Used to. He hasn't been there in several months."

"And he never told you?"

"No. So do you think he might have left there? Why did you ask if he was still in Duluth?"

"No reason." She certainly couldn't tell her mother about the note from Northlake. Her brother would have contacted their mother too if he'd wanted to.

"When he called, he never said he wasn't calling from Duluth. I just assumed— He always calls from a pay phone, so I don't have any way to reach him."

"Did the people at the video store know anything? Maybe he just changed jobs. You know he was trying to be a free-lance photographer."

"No, they don't have a clue."

"You don't have an address?"

"Just a post office box in Duluth."

"What do you think he's up to, Mom?"

"Up to? What do you mean, Sandy?"

"Nothing. I just wonder why you haven't heard anything."

"I just don't understand it. He's usually so good about calling."

"Well, I guess we need to remember that he's an adult. I know it's hard to think of him as grown-up, but it's true. He's almost twenty-five."

"I know, but—" A long, audible sigh. Sandy imagined she could feel the air from it, filtering along the line all the way from Minnesota. "I wish he were as responsible as you are."

This time Sandy changed the subject, asking her mother what she and Willis had been up to—before the excitement of the break-in. Pauline told her about a trip they'd taken up to the Brainerd area.

"Willis bought one of those new one-step cameras and took lots of pictures."

Sandy was glad to be on a neutral subject. "I've been shopping around for a camera. He'll have to tell me how he likes his when I come at Thanksgiving."

Pauline snorted a laugh. "Oh, he'll like doing that. How's your job?" she asked, then quickly changed the subject back to the break-in when Sandy had barely told her anything.

Sandy listened patiently, worried because her mother was worried. Before she'd left Minnesota the two of them had been fairly close. They'd lived only three miles apart, and Pauline's place was on the way home from the school where Sandy taught. It was easy to drop by and visit after her teaching day, before it was time to start dinner for Charlie. But her new life was alien to her mother, and their common ground was slipping away. They were becoming loving strangers.

When she said goodbye a soft feeling like remorse blanketed her. She had lost everyone. Her real father, Charlie, Jerry—even her mother seemed distant. An emotional gulf lay between her and everyone to whom she'd ever been close. It made her wonder if she should grab onto Troy. There was still time for a family of her own. A fleeting desire for a baby came over her, but she knew it was illusory. Babies grew up. Jerry had grown up. It didn't help.

After she put the dishes in the washer, she flopped down on the couch to watch television, enervated by the mild sadness that had slipped over her. Later, as she started to turn off the lamp, she noticed the film and letter on the end table. She picked up the letter again and reread it.

Jerry. She conjured up a mental picture of a time when he was a toddler, pear-shaped in the bulky overnight diaper under his stretchy sleeper, standing in his crib crying. Her mother had come home from work and had shut herself in her bedroom as she often did, so it was up to Sandy to check on Jerry to see what was wrong. He'd lifted his arms at the sight of her.

"What's wrong, baby?"

"Bears git baby," he'd said through his tears, his lower lip puckering.

"What bears?"

"Tree bears."

She had frowned. Tree bears. What were tree bears?

Then she remembered she'd played him an audiotape of *The Three Bears* the evening before.

"No tree bears are going to get Jerry," she'd said. "I'll always take care of you." And she'd pulled him up over the crib rail, the sound of his disposable diaper crinkling inside his sleeper, and had held him in the rocking chair till he settled down, thumb in mouth, and drifted off to sleep.

Tears pooled in the corners of her eyes, just remembering. Lord, how she had loved that little guy. Why couldn't they stay little and easy?

She put the film and letter back on the table and turned out the lamp. *I'll always take care of you.* Always was such a long time.

4

MID-MORNING the following day Senator Mattingly came across the hall to Sandy's office. He spoke to the two other legislative correspondents, both of whom were relatively new, then came over to Sandy's desk and sat down on the edge with his cup of coffee, legs extended.

Sandy had always thought his looks played well for a senator. He stood half a head taller than most men, carrying just enough weight to make him look formidable. And it didn't hurt that his hair was beginning to gray at the temples. His gray-blue eyes looked honest, made a person want to trust him.

When she'd joined his campaign back in Minnesota as a volunteer she'd only known the hype, but it had turned out to be true. He had intelligence, a strong backbone, and enough scruples to make him an oddity in Washington. She admired him. He was "presidential," in the best tradition of the word. Maybe in a few years he'd be ready to make such a bid. And she kind of hoped she was around to help get him there when he did.

"How are you?" he asked, blowing on the coffee.

"Fine, thank you." Sandy stopped mid-sentence on the

letter she was drafting, and sat back in her secretarial chair. It responded with a squeak. Travel never seemed to slow the Senator down. Some people would have returned looking tired, but he seemed energized. "Troy said your trip was productive."

He nodded. "Very satisfactory. I think we can work out a good deal. Speaking of Troy, he mentioned that you were upset about your brother."

Sandy frowned. She'd thought she could trust Troy not to say anything. "Did he tell you why?"

The Senator shook his head.

"I received this rather odd letter from him."

"Odd? In what way?"

"For one thing, it's practically the first letter I've ever gotten from him—I mean, this kid doesn't write. That's odd in itself, don't you think?"

Jim shrugged and took a sip of coffee. "Not enough to get worried over."

"Well—" She hesitated, making sure the other women were occupied, then continued in a softer tone. "There was also some film and he told me to hang on to it for safekeeping. Then he—" She closed her eyes and put her hand on her forehead.

"What's the matter?"

"He told me not to mention it to anyone or it might be dangerous for him. I've already told Troy, now I'm—"

"Sandy, you know you can tell me anything and it won't go any farther. Sometimes it helps to tell someone. What was the film?"

She shrugged. "I have no idea and Troy told me I'd probably better not get it developed. He said I should stay as uninvolved as possible."

Jim Mattingly rubbed his cheek. "Good advice, but I can see why you're worried."

She smiled lamely. "This is probably just one of Jerry's dramatic gestures."

"You think so?"

She nodded. "Probably. I just never know what he's up to."

"He really pulls your strings."

"I know."

"And you just can't quit being a rescuer, can you? First Charlie, now your brother."

He had it backwards, and it had all started before that—with her mother—but Jim Mattingly had entered her life in the midst of her domestic problems. She'd signed on to help Jim with his campaign in the final year of her marriage and she'd flung herself into it with zeal. Some people used an affair to get out of a marriage; she'd used a cause.

The long hours she'd spent organizing volunteers for phone banks and door-to-door canvassing brought her to the candidate's attention, and she found herself part of his inner circle of strategists in the Twin Cities. Their meetings had frequently lasted into the early morning hours. And after the work was done they had talked. And talked. Had she been single at the time, she and Jim, a widower, would have probably slid into an affair—they had come very close, had even talked about it—but there were too many scandals associated with politics at the time and Jim Mattingly didn't deserve to be part of one. When her divorce was final—well, the moment had passed.

The Senator had offered her a job in Washington as a legislative correspondent. The offer had been a lifesaver, so he was in no position to talk about rescuers.

Mattingly glanced at his watch. "Well, I've got to get over to the Capitol," he said, standing up and patting her on the shoulder. "Take it easy."

The rest of the day passed in monotonous routine. At first she'd found it exciting just to be in Washington, but after a while, it was merely a job. She did still get a thrill when she went over to the Capitol. The massive corridors, the echoing footsteps—it made her feel part of something important. When the job began to get to her, she would take her lunch outside and look at the dome of the Great Rotunda, and at the Washington Monument and the Lincoln Memorial, all of the venerable buildings surrounding the Mall. She would return to work charged up again.

She didn't do that today, and by the time she got home she felt drained.

Ray Champion, her smarmy downstairs neighbor, was standing in the vestibule when she came in. If Ray were a food, he'd be a marshmallow, she thought.

"Oh, hi, Sandy," he puffed. "You look super today."

"Thank you, Ray," she said, barely glancing at him. She had to be careful about being friendly or he wouldn't leave her alone. She opened the mailbox and drew out an envelope. No surprises today.

Ray lived by himself and was obviously lonely. At first her heart had gone out to him. Big mistake. Within a week of her moving in, he was making a nuisance of himself, dropping by at strange hours. And he seemed a little odd.

Once he'd even shown up at the office and had hung around until Troy spoke to him and ushered him out. Later, Troy told her to avoid Ray.

"I checked up on him. They threw him out of the service on a Section Eight and the police have hauled him in a few times for harassing women."

"That figures. How did you find all this out?"

"I have a friend in *your* police department. How does your weird buddy manage to pay his rent? He doesn't have a job, according to my friend."

"My neighbor says his mother pays it. She takes care of her boy." Sandy felt a twinge of guilt, but let it go. Jerry was irresponsible, but was no Ray Champion, no matter what he did.

Now Ray sidled up close to her and looked at the bill she was studying.

"You use a credit card? I don't believe in them."

She gave a noncommittal, "Hmmm." If she'd said, "You don't?" he'd spend five minutes telling her why.

"Are you doing anything this evening, Sandy?"

She nodded, folding the bill and putting it back in the envelope. "I have some things to catch up on."

"What kind of things?"

"House kind of things."

"I was just going out to get a hamburger."

"Have fun," she said.

"You want to go, Sandy? My treat?"

"No, thanks, Ray. Not this time."

"Why do you keep saying that?" His voice held an edge. "Not this time. It's such a stupid thing to say when you never mean to go with me."

She didn't know why she said it. He was right; it was stupid because she never intended to go out to eat with Ray Champion.

She opened her mouth to reply, but he interrupted.

"It's all right. I'm sorry I got mad there for a minute. You didn't do anything to deserve that anger."

Sandy started digging for her keys to the inner door, eager to get away from him

"It's open," he said, and he held it while she went through. "See you later."

I hope not, she thought, making sure the door locked behind her. Trouble was, Ray had a key. So, were the crazies locked out or in?

She went up the stairs slowly, thinking about what a nuisance he was, still looking for her keys. There, she found them. But there was no need. The door to her apartment pushed open when she barely touched it to put the key in the lock.

Sandy gasped. The apartment was a mess. Someone had ransacked it. She stood at the door, frozen. Last night her mother's place, tonight hers. It was uncanny. Burglaries were a fact of modern life, one that was so common among her acquaintances that she'd always known one day it would happen to her. But it didn't lessen the shock. Adrenaline shot through her as she backed away from the door, pulling it closed. Someone might still be inside.

She rapped lightly at the Purvises' across the hall, hoping they were home and that they would answer quickly.

She felt rather than heard a presence on the other side of the door as one of them probably looked out the peephole; then she heard the rattling of the chain and the click of the bolt.

I could be dead by now, she thought, glancing uneasily behind her at her own door.

Finally, the door opened. Esther Purvis stood there.

"Mrs. Purvis, someone has broken into my apartment. Please let me come in and call the police." She spoke quickly, pushing her way in.

Mr. Purvis had risen from his chair, the newspaper dangling from one hand. "A break-in, you say? I should have done something about that damn door."

"You go ahead and use the phone, dear," Mrs. Purvis said.

Sandy called the police, then stationed herself near the door so she could listen for anyone leaving her apartment.

The police buzzed the Purvises' apartment as Sandy had told them to, and shortly thereafter she heard them coming up the stairs. There were two of them. One of them looked like a young Burt Reynolds, moustache and all. His badge read "Sinclair." The other was older, graying hair showing beneath his cap, a spare tire beginning around his middle.

Sandy led them to her apartment. "The door was open when I came home from work," she said.

"You sure you didn't just forget to lock your apartment?" Sinclair asked.

"Take a look," she said. "It's been ransacked."

"You go on back inside," Sinclair said, motioning toward the Purvises', "while we have a look."

A few moments later, he came to the door. "The premises are clear, ma'am. You can come on in."

"Well, I really didn't think anyone was still in here," she said with a nervous laugh that held no humor. As she stepped into the hall, the old couple were right behind her. They weren't going to miss any excitement.

"You did right," the officer assured her. "You never know. And what you don't want to do is corner someone."

Which is what Mr. Purvis did to Officer Sinclair the moment he got into Sandy's apartment, telling him about the door downstairs and other complaints about security in the building.

Sandy could hear him, but she was in such a state of shock at the full sight of her apartment that she couldn't rescue the policeman. Her stomach felt queasy. The place was a wreck. Things had been swept off the tables onto the floor, including the lamps. She bent to pick one up.

"Just leave it there," the older policeman, Officer Rappaport, advised, "until we get the lab boys over here to dust the place."

The basket that held magazines had been dumped, its contents strewn around the room. The drawer in the end table had been emptied of poker chips, dice, playing cards. Books had been thrown out of the bookshelf.

Rappaport looked at Mrs. Purvis. "May I use your phone?"

"Certainly. It's on the wall in the kitchen." She gave a little flutter of her fingers in the general direction of her apartment. The woman wasn't about to show him and miss getting a good look at Sandy's apartment.

The kitchen was in worse shape than the living room. Every utensil Sandy owned had been dumped; the contents of the flour and sugar canisters had been strewn over the kitchen, although the ceramic canisters themselves hadn't been broken.

Mrs. Purvis was clucking her tongue at each new sight, and Sandy felt a blue funk settling over her. How on earth could she ever clean up all that flour and sugar? There was a fine dust of it over everything. And she'd planned a boring evening in front of the television, which was still possible. The TV and VCR were still in their accustomed places, about the only things that seemed untouched.

Sinclair had noticed that as well. "Considering that your TV and VCR are still here, it looks like vandalism," he said. He had extricated himself from Mr. Purvis.

It was just like at her mother's house—nothing seemed to be missing. Just a bizarre coincidence? Break-ins were rampant, but for vandalism? She ran her hand through her hair, twisting a strand of it.

"Can you think of anyone who's got it in for you?" Sinclair asked.

"No, I don't think so," she said, even as her mind darted to Ray Champion. Was he getting even with her for not ever going out with him? No. That was crazy.

Officer Rappaport rejoined them. "Notice anything right off that's missing?" he asked.

Sandy shook her head as they trailed down the hallway.

The bedroom had suffered the least. Several drawers had been emptied, others were standing open, but none of the items on the dresser top had been disturbed, and the closet looked intact. It looked as if the vandal had tired of his work.

"Jewelry?" Rappaport asked.

"I don't have much worth stealing." She went to the closet and pulled a bunch of her clothes to one side. A string of pearls and a heavy three-strand turquoise necklace were still there on a hanger. "Good," she said, "they didn't get these." She shoved the clothes back together. "I'm afraid it will take me a while to figure out just what might be missing in this mess."

"Well, let me get what I need for my report," Rappaport said. "You want to go sit down?"

She nodded, and they went back into the living room where he took down the information. While the policeman wrote, a lab technician arrived to try to pick up some fingerprints.

"You need to get someone over to take care of that door," Sinclair suggested. "The striker plate's broken out."

That wasn't all. The inside frame was splintered where the intruder had forced his way in.

"Did you folks hear anything?" Sinclair asked Mr. Purvis. "This was bound to make some noise."

"I'm a little hard of hearing, Officer," Mrs. Purvis said. "And he—he sleeps all afternoon. Turns on the television to soap operas and then goes to sleep."

"I don't watch those soaps. She does," Purvis said.

"Are there any other tenants on this floor who might have heard something?"

Mr. Purvis scowled from behind his glasses. "We have tenants who might have done it," he said sourly.

His wife glared at him. "Now, William, that's not a nice thing to say." She turned to the policeman. "Everyone up here is gone during the day except us," she said.

As if on cue, another neighbor, John Constantine, appeared just then. "What's going on?" he asked, sticking his head in the door.

"Someone broke in," Sandy told him.

Constantine, a stockbroker, kept to himself and Sandy barely knew him even though he lived next door. Somehow though, having the police there seemed to be an invitation for him to wander into her apartment. He walked over to the kitchen and looked in. "This is disgusting."

"Did you happen to be home today?" Rappaport asked.

"No, I left at seven-thirty this morning and I'm just now getting back."

Sinclair looked at Mr. Purvis. "Just who were you talking about?"

Footsteps pounded on the stairs as he asked the question and Ray Champion popped in. He was carrying a paper bag dotted with grease. "There are police cars outside and— migosh, what happened?"

Mr. Purvis glanced around at him, and Sandy saw Mrs. Purvis grab her husband's hand. Purvis looked back at Sinclair and worked his wiry eyebrows up and down a couple of times and rolled his eyes toward Ray. Nothing like being subtle.

"Are you a neighbor?" Sinclair asked Ray.

"I live downstairs."

"And did you happen to be home today and hear anything suspicious?"

Ray's eyes darted to one side and he said, "Yes, I was home today"—his knuckles turned a little whiter where he was gripping the greasy sack—"and I think I—yes, I did hear a loud noise. I thought Sandy had dropped something."

"But I was at work."

He shrugged. "I didn't know that, Sandy. If I had, I might have investigated. Here," he said, "I brought you a hamburger." He held the sack toward her.

She drew back as if it were poison. "I don't want it." That man! He infuriated her.

He shrugged and pulled his hand back.

Rappaport asked Ray some more questions, including his name, wrote it all down, then snapped the notebook shut.

John Constantine was standing at the edge of the group, and Sandy realized it was the first time she'd ever been together with so many of her neighbors at one time. There was nothing like a crisis.

"You need to get this door fixed," Rappaport reminded her. "You know anyone who can do it?"

Sandy shook her head.

Out came the book again and the policeman wrote down a name, tore the sheet out, and handed it to her. "He's a handyman—he'll be able to fix the lock and the frame to boot. Might be tomorrow, though," he said. "You got somewhere you can stay?"

"She can stay with us," Mrs. Purvis offered. "If she doesn't mind the couch."

Sandy smiled in thanks. John Constantine expressed his sympathy and left. Sandy looked around for Ray but didn't see him. Good, he was gone.

The lab technician was finished, and he and the two policemen left. Mr. Purvis wandered back across the hall with a "Got to catch the news."

Mrs. Purvis lingered. "Now, I mean it, Sandy. You come on over to our place and stay till you get this door fixed."

"I appreciate the offer, but I'll see if I can get someone

in to fix it this evening. And if I can't, I'll just drag that chair in front of the door. That should slow someone down long enough for me to call for help.''

''Well, I'll worry about you all night,'' Esther Purvis said as she left.

Sandy turned back to the mess around her and heaved a deep sigh. Where to start? She couldn't do anything dressed for success, so she headed down the hall to change.

She was shocked to see Ray Champion standing in her bedroom, fingering the lingerie in one of the open dresser drawers.

Weirdo, she thought. ''You startled me,'' she said aloud.

He let out a sharp laugh, withdrawing his hand and putting it behind him. ''I did?''

''Yes, you did.''

He moved toward her and she stood back, giving him ample opportunity to get around her and go on his way, but he didn't make a move. He just stood there, staring at her.

''Sandy,'' he said unctuously, ''I'm sorry I had to tell the policeman about that noise.''

She grimaced. ''Why are you sorry, Ray? If that's what you heard.''

He gave her a conspiratorial look, then finally moved toward the living room. She wanted to throw up her hands, but instead she followed him, just to make sure he left. Maybe she would take Mrs. Purvis' offer to spend the night after all, since Ray had probably overheard her say she'd be staying here.

''Are you sure you don't want this hamburger I bought for you, Sandy?'' He extended the sack he was still holding.

''No. I'm afraid I don't have any appetite.''

''I understand. You want me to help you here?''

''No, I think I'll have to do this by myself.''

''I'm just trying to be friendly, Sandy.''

"I know, but I need to be alone."

He giggled. "Okay." He touched the door as he left. "You'd better get this fixed, Sandy."

He was right about that. The door had suddenly become a bigger priority than changing clothes.

She went into the kitchen, blew a cloud of flour off the phone, and dialed the handyman Rappaport had recommended.

Sure enough, he couldn't come that evening, so she made plans for him to repair it the following day. She would ask the Purvises to watch for him.

She hung up the phone, stood there, and looked around her. John Constantine had called it disgusting, but it was more than that. She'd never expected to feel so personally violated by this invasion of her space. Now she could really sympathize with her mother. Suppose whoever it was had just broken the door down and made the mess as a diversion? What if he meant to come back for the television and the VCR tonight? What if it was that awful Ray Champion? She shuddered. *Better not think about it.*

But she couldn't get the picture of him standing with his hand in her lingerie drawer out of her mind. She went purposefully down the hall, gathered up all the lingerie in that particular drawer and put it to soak in the bathroom sink in some cold water wash. She wanted to get his greasy fingerprints off her clothes!

She tackled the mess in the living room, putting the lamps back on the tables, then picking up everything that went in the end table. A potted plant had been upset and the soil was spilling onto the carpet. She scooped up the root ball and packed some soil around it, but unfortunately she'd just watered that morning and a good bit of the damp soil would have to remain on the carpet till it dried enough to be vacuumed up.

She squatted down and picked up the books and stuck them back on the shelves haphazardly. She could arrange them later. For now, just getting things off the floor was her primary goal.

She moved over to the upended trash basket and began to replace its contents, trying to make sure she distinguished what was trash and what had been swept off her desk, although she thought drily, the distinction was arguable.

It was when she tossed the crumpled envelope from Skaar's Taxidermy Shop into the basket that she remembered the letter and the film.

She went over by the easy chair and got down on her hands and knees to search, first shoving the ottoman aside, then peering into the darkness below the chair. She ran her hand under it. There was no sign of the film or the letter anywhere. She sat back on her heels and looked around with a frown.

She went back to her cleaning, moving faster now, thinking perhaps the missing items would turn up.

It was midnight before she finished. She dragged the easy chair over in front of the door, and slumped down in it. Her fear of staying in the apartment had dissipated. No one would be coming back for the television and the VCR. Ray Champion was weird, but he wasn't the threat. The disarray, the confusion—it was just camouflage for someone who took the film and Jerry's scrawled letter. And they'd been to her mother's house for the same reason.

5

THE next morning Sandy made arrangements with the Purvises to oversee the repair work on her apartment, then hurried off to catch the Metro.

She'd been awake most of the night, reviewing the ramifications of the missing film. Now, sitting in the swaying car she went over it again. Someone had surmised that Jerry'd sent the film to her or her mother, knew where they lived, and had come to retrieve it, or sent their henchmen. With the film in their possession, Jerry's danger would escalate. She remembered his words, "might be over for me." What if his penchant for the dramatic was not unfounded?

"You look beat," the receptionist said when Sandy came in the outer door to the Senator's suite of offices.

Sandy made a face at her. "Thanks, Debby. I'll give you a compliment someday."

"Seriously, what's wrong?"

"My place was broken into yesterday."

"Oh, no, that's awful."

Angel, the other woman in the front office, stopped what she was doing, listened for a moment, then came over to

Debby's desk while Sandy told about coming home to the ransacked apartment.

"What did they take?" Debby asked.

Sandy shrugged. "Nothing of any value that I can tell. A roll of film that my brother sent me"—surely it wouldn't hurt to tell Debby—"and that's it."

Debby frowned. "That's strange."

Sandy nodded. "But it was one heck of a mess to clean up. I think I've ruined my vacuum with all the flour."

"Well, just be glad you weren't there," Angel said as she turned back to her desk.

Sandy's eyes met Debby's, and they both rolled them skyward. "Yes, there's something to be glad about in everything, I guess," Debby said. Angel was always such a Pollyanna—her name suited her. It made the rest of the staff want to gag.

Sandy poked her head into the door of the legal department and spoke to the assistants there, then went in her office. Her two counterparts weren't there yet. She stashed her purse in the bottom drawer of her desk, then went down the hall to the room that housed a couch and the coffeepot and poured herself a cup. One of the Senator's press secretaries came in for some coffee.

"Debby said someone broke into your place," he said.

The scheduling secretary came in. "What happened?"

"My apartment was broken into yesterday."

A small crowd was soon gathered around her, listening to her story. Several of them had also had break-ins over the years, and they told their tales before they dispersed to their various rooms and cubicles.

Back at her desk, Sandy dialed information in Northlake and got the number of Skaar's Taxidermy Shop. She was past caution and promises. After all, she no longer had the film and Jerry needed a warning.

The phone rang nine times before she hung up. She glanced at her watch. It was an hour earlier in Northlake, maybe the taxidermist was still at home. She dialed information again, but the only Skaar listing was for the shop. Maybe he worked out of his home.

When her two co-workers arrived, she told them about the break-in. Each time she related the story, her stomach went into a knot when she remembered the film and the letter. It was a sign Jerry was truly in trouble. She needed to go to Minnesota.

She went to look for Troy to ask for some time off. As she was asking the Senator's personal secretary where he was, the Senator came out of his office.

"I sent him up to New York yesterday for a meeting, and he won't be back till late tonight. What did you need?"

"You haven't heard my story? What's happening to the office grapevine?"

"Her apartment was broken into," the secretary piped up.

The Senator drew his eyebrows together. "Come on in." He ushered her into his office, then closed the door behind them.

"Sit down, Sandy," he said, settling into his leather desk chair. "I know that's a frightening experience."

She sank into an armchair across from him as he related a story about his own house being burglarized. Then he said, "Now, tell me what happened."

"When I got home from work yesterday, I found my door ajar. The place had been ransacked. It took me all evening to get it back together—"

"Did you call the police?"

She nodded. "The only thing missing was that roll of film my brother sent me. Well, that and his letter. I'm *really* worried about him now. I have some vacation days left—I was going to ask Troy if I could—''

''Take what you need, Sandy.'' His frown deepened. ''You said your brother is in Northlake?''

She didn't remember telling him that, but she nodded. Maybe she'd mentioned it yesterday and had forgotten.

''I think there's something I need to tell you.''

Sandy cocked her head questioningly, but kept quiet.

''I don't know whether this is relevant, but under the circumstances—well, I can't see that it would hurt, either.''

''What?'' She leaned forward. *Get to the point, Jim.*

''When he was here, your brother asked me to pull some strings and find out the last known address of your father.''

Sandy remained silent, but she felt a well of emotion forming in her chest. Jerry was looking for their father. Their real father.

''He had tried through Social Security, but his request didn't fit under any of their guidelines. I think he even tried the Salvation Army, but met a dead-end there too. So he asked me.''

''And?''

''I called in a favor and got him the information he wanted.''

She smiled slightly. ''You won't say who or where.''

He returned her smile. ''Right.''

''What did you find out?''

''That your father was last living in Northlake. I didn't find an address, just general delivery.''

''So that's what sent Jerry off to Northlake.'' She vaguely remembered Jerry asking her a couple of questions about their father on that visit. She'd brushed them off.

''I imagine so. You remember I have a summer house a few miles outside of Northlake. Why don't you stay there?''

She hadn't remembered and she started to protest, but he

insisted. "There's a fellow named Niles Benson who lives in another place I own, the neighboring property. He takes care of my house." He wrote the name on a pad. "When you get there, look him up and get the key." He was drawing a map. "See this?"

Sandy stood up and bent over his desk.

He was pointing to an *x* he'd made. "That's my place. There's a wrought-iron silhouette of a howling wolf at the entrance. Just keep on going past it. This"—he tapped another *x*—"is where Benson lives. It's a mile and a half down the road." He tore the sheet off and handed it to her. "I'll give him a call, so he'll be expecting you. There's bedding, towels, all that sort of stuff, maybe even a little food in the freezer." He smiled at her.

"This is kind of you," she said, folding the map and standing up.

"It's okay, Sandy. I understand."

She called the airline from her desk and made arrangements to fly out Saturday morning. Then she tried Skaar's Taxidermy Shop again. Still no answer.

She pushed down the cradle, hesitated a moment, thinking. It seemed foolish to fly clear to Minnesota and not visit her folks. She released her finger, listened for the tone, then dialed.

"Why didn't you tell me you were coming when I talked to you night before last?" her mother asked, sounding a little put out when Sandy announced her impending visit.

"I didn't know then. Something came up and Senator Mattingly said I could handle it." She marveled at the subterfuge offered by the judicious use of language. Her mother would assume she was coming home on official business. "I'll need to leave Sunday morning and go up to Duluth."

"Maybe you can look Jerry up." The mother's antennae again. "I'm really worried about him."

"Well, yes, since I'll be in Duluth, maybe I can."

When she arrived home that evening the lock and the frame on her door had been fixed. She went across the hall and thanked the Purvises for taking care of it.

"I need to ask you another favor. I'm flying to Minnesota in the morning, and I wonder if you'd water my plants."

Mrs. Purvis nodded. "Of course. But I'll probably kill them. Mine always die."

"They won't need it till Thursday and I may be—I hope I'm back by then. But if you don't see me—"

Except for an overnight case, her luggage was stored in the basement. So after she picked at a serving of microwave chicken tetrazzini, she went down the stairs, around past Ray's door, and down another flight into the dimly lit basement. It had been divided into sections. On the west side of the building a laundry area with three washers and three dryers was partitioned off. She could hear the sound of one of the dryers.

The center area housed the mechanical plant for the building—furnace, water heater, maintenance equipment. A maze of pipes ran overhead, lowering the clearance to seven feet, six in some spots. The remaining part of the basement had two rows of wire cubicles which functioned as storage for the residents.

Sandy ducked under a pipe and went down the aisle between the cubicles. A moldy smell hung in the air and she worried briefly about the things she had stored, wondering how they were holding up in this less-than-perfect environment.

There were her things. Stick-on mailbox numbers were affixed to a flat plate on the gate. With only the light from the furnace area to see by, she had trouble getting her key into the padlock. Finally the wire gate swung open.

This storage area was one reason she'd chosen this particular building; the apartment itself wasn't any great shakes. She'd come down from a three-bedroom house with a living room and a den in Minneapolis to this one-bedroom. Even after her ex-husband had furnished an apartment and she'd sold quite a bit, she still had too much stuff. Yet she couldn't bear to part with some items. For instance, the wicker settee which was now pushed against one side of the cubicle, covered by a king-sized sheet. It had belonged to her grandmother.

She pulled a string, and a single light bulb dangling overhead dimly lit up the small space. She peeked under the sheet. The wicker didn't seem to be sprouting any mold, but the smell down here wasn't promising.

Maybe she should take the settee upstairs, even if it would be crowded. It belonged on a sun porch, but there was no sun porch in sight in her near future.

With a sigh, she dropped the sheet back over the settee and turned to the task at hand—locating a suitcase.

She moved several boxes and pulled out an old brown Samsonite bag, a two-suiter, part of a set her mother and Willis had given her when she graduated from high school.

As a hint that she should move out, it had failed. She lived at home while attending college. Marriage finally drew her from the nest. It had come two weeks after graduation, meaning she'd never really lived alone—till now. It took some getting used to, but it was easier here than it would have been in Minneapolis. When she and Charlie first separated she kept expecting to hear his car or his key in the lock, his voice, little things. Here, she had no expectations.

She ran her finger across the suitcase. Dusty. This was the

only bag she needed. It would hold plenty for a short trip. She was tempted to take the time to peek in some of the other boxes, to see some of her old treasures and maybe haul a few things upstairs, but no—

There was a noise at the other end of the basement. She looked around. Had someone come down to check the now silent dryer? No. The other end of the basement was dark. The only lights were those she'd turned on.

Reason told her that it was nothing, that she was hypersensitive because of the break-in, but her nervous system didn't respond to logic. Her neck stiffened with tension, and prickles shot up her arms.

She pulled the string on the light, switching it off so she wasn't spotlighted, then moved slowly out of the cubicle and closed the wire door behind her. She wasn't going to get trapped in here. She quickly pushed the lock together, flinching at the click it made as it settled into place. She eased forward between the wire cells, holding her suitcase with both hands in front of her like a shield. Up ahead lay the furnace. She creeped behind it, silently, her eyes and ears alert to any movement.

With no warning, the furnace jerked to life. She jumped back and the suitcase went sliding to the floor with a clatter. So much for stealth. She grabbed it up and leaned against the wall for a moment, trying to get a grip on herself. She was down here all the time doing laundry and it had never bothered her before.

She peered along the wall to the other side of the room. There was a long shadow by the stairs. Someone was there. A line of sweat beaded her forehead and her breathing became shallow. She pressed hard against the cold concrete, trying to get a better look. The shadow was moving; she could see part of a figure through the welter of pipes.

A whispery voice floated down the stairs. "William? Is everything okay?"

The shadow straightened and Sandy relaxed. She ran around the furnace.

"It's you!" William Purvis said to Sandy. "I thought I'd caught your intruder."

"You almost scared me to death! What were you doing?"

"Esther and I went out for coffee and of course the front door was open when we got back. Then I noticed the door to the basement ajar, and I didn't hear anyone down here. I thought I'd better investigate."

Esther Purvis now came down the stairs rather tentatively.

"It was just me," Sandy said. "I was getting a suitcase. And if it was the intruder, you shouldn't be investigating on your own anyway. What if it had been him? What would you have done?" She started up the steps. This man may be dangerous, she thought. Dangerous to himself.

"I told him the same thing," Mrs. Purvis said, following Sandy. "He's a crazy old man."

"I'd have taken care of him," the old man said stiffly. "You don't need to worry about that."

Another rescuer, she thought, as she trudged up the stairs. At least it wasn't Ray Champion. She'd hate to get caught in the basement alone with him.

6

HER stepfather was hunched over a flower bed when she pulled into the driveway of the Cochran's three-bedroom home in suburban Minneapolis. He stood up, raised his hand in greeting, and approached the car as she climbed out.

Sandy gave him a warm hug. He was a good man, a robust contrast to Sandy's rather withdrawn father. Willis Cochran was a hail-fellow-well-met, absolutely essential for piecing her mother back together all those years ago. He had just ramrodded his way into their lives.

"Let me get your bag," he offered.

"Thanks," she said, releasing the front seat so it moved forward and he could drag the bag out. "How have you been, Willis?"

"Fine. Just fine. How was your flight?"

"Smooth. Not an air pocket all the way." She had thoroughly enjoyed the trip, catnapping to make up for lost sleep.

"This is a nice little car. A rental?" He patted the door after she closed it. "Your mom said you were going to rent one at the airport. I hear they sell some of these off from time to time. Fella can get a good deal.''

Her mother ran out on the porch and down the front steps to meet Sandy.

''Oh, I'm so glad you're here.'' She hugged her daughter tightly, then held her at arm's length for a good look, then hugged her again. ''You're looking real good, honey.''

Sandy laughed. ''What did you expect?''

''I just worry that you aren't eating right or taking care of yourself.'' They went arm in arm up the steps. A bunch of cornstalks and three pumpkins were set out on the porch, and an old stuffed witch rode a broomstick across the door, just as it had ever since they'd lived in this house.

''You don't need to worry about me. I'm a big girl,'' Sandy assured Pauline.

''I know. But I'm a mother. I miss having you here, close by.''

Sandy's stepfather followed behind with the bag.

Catching sight of the cluttered kitchen table, Sandy started to ask facetiously if the burglars made the mess, but she suppressed the urge and instead asked, ''What are you up to?''

Red and green ribbons, packages of gold and silver glitter, construction paper, and an array of craft items covered the top of the table. Life seemed to be telescoping, with Halloween being celebrated on the porch, Christmas in the kitchen. One season bled into another nowadays.

''You've caught me in a mess, but we're having a church bazaar—I think I mentioned it to you on the phone—and the girls have been coming over here to work on ornaments. It's just easier to leave the stuff out on the table, and Dad and I eat on TV trays.''

''Oh, yes, I remember you told me you were working on the bazaar. Tell me about the burglary.''

Pauline repeated what she had told Sandy on the phone.

"I see you've already gotten the panel by the door fixed," Sandy said.

"You bet," Willis said. He'd taken her suitcase to the bedroom and was now standing at the entry to the kitchen. "We got a man out right away. I think we're going to install a burglar alarm."

A day late and a dollar short, Sandy thought. Should she tell them it probably wasn't a random break-in? Or let them go ahead and spend the money on a security system? She opted for the latter; otherwise she would have to spell out why she was going north. Besides, a security system wouldn't hurt.

"Honey," Willis said to Pauline, "I'm going back out and drain the hoses and put them up. Unless there's something you want me to do."

"No, that's fine. Sandy and I will just visit."

But her mother couldn't just sit down and talk, so Sandy settled herself in a kitchen chair while her mother fussed with a casserole, chattering while she worked. "Gladine Knightly's husband died—do you know her?" At Sandy's nod, she continued. "I'm making this chicken dish for the family. Mildred Hale—that's the one whose son you met— she's going to pick it up and take it over when she goes. After I get this out of the way, we can just relax."

I bet, Sandy thought. "Do you need to go to Gladine's?"

"No. I'll go tomorrow afternoon after you leave."

Mildred Hale showed up right on schedule and Pauline introduced the two women. Dave's mother was as short as he was tall. Her polyester slacks and overblouse stretched over a rotund middle, but her weight didn't keep her from being bouncy. Snow-white running shoes seemed to put even more spring in her step.

"I'm so glad to meet you," Mildred said. "Dave said he

really enjoyed going out with you when he was in Washington. Your mother and I''—her eyes twinkled and she wrinkled up her nose—''we had big plans for you two, didn't we, Pauline?'' She reached over and patted her friend's shoulder. ''We wanted to be related.''

Pauline nodded. ''We sure did. But you can't predict these kids.''

''How is Dave?'' Sandy asked.

His mother waved her hand. ''I wish I knew. He's off in Arizona on some research project.''

Sandy briefly wondered what had happened to his study of the Great Lakes mussel problem, but turned her attention back to Mildred Hale. The woman was much more likable than her son.

''I certainly haven't been hearing from that boy much,'' his mother continued.

''That's a son for you,'' Pauline said, shaking her head. ''They're not like daughters.'' She smiled at Sandy.

''Now, Mother, Jerry usually calls you every week and you know it.''

Her mother brushed off her comment. ''It's not the same. Just wait till you have some children of your own.''

''Well, I don't mean to complain,'' Mildred said. ''Dave's a good boy, but I wish I could get him married off—you know, he's never been married. He was a late bloomer. But I think now's the time. I'd like some grandchildren before I'm too old to enjoy them, and my other son and his wife have decided not to have any children.''

Pauline kept silent, but she gave her daughter a quick, wistful look that made Sandy feel a twinge of guilt. During the first few years of Sandy's marriage to Charlie, her mother'd kept asking when they were going to start a family. Sandy had told her to hold her horses, that she wanted to teach for a few years before having children. And it really had been her intention. But when being married hadn't cured Charlie's drinking problem, when it became more and more of an issue, she'd postponed a family indefinitely.

Sometimes Sandy thought it was for the best. Maybe she wouldn't be mother material. Look how her brother had turned out, and it was she who had mothered him during those first few years the experts said were critical.

The women visited a few more minutes, then Mildred took the casserole and left for Gladine's They followed her to the car.

"Will you be able to stop back through here on your way home?" Pauline asked as they watched Mildred back out of the driveway.

"No, I'll fly out of Duluth on the way back. But I wanted to see you, so I thought this was a good way to do it." Actually she hadn't even made her return reservation yet. But what lay ahead was so uncertain she didn't want to make promises.

"I'm so glad you're going to look up your brother," Pauline said, locking elbows with Sandy as they walked to the porch. "I'll feel a whole lot better."

The casserole was out of the way, but still Pauline couldn't seem to settle down. She got lunch going, they ate, and she suggested they take Sandy to show her the new mall.

Usually they would find time for a mother-daughter tête-à-tête, but that didn't happen. By evening, as they sat watching television with Willis, Sandy was convinced that something was bothering Pauline, something she didn't want to talk about. Either that, or they'd completely lost touch with each other. Whatever it was, it left Sandy feeling despondent and wondering whether she should force it.

"Tell me about your trip to Brainerd," she said to Willis. "Mom said you got a new camera."

Willis beamed, almost vaulting out of his recliner. "I got some great pictures." He fished them out of an end table and began showing them to her.

Pauline laid down the potholder she was crocheting to join them.

"Had another roll to take in to get developed," Willis said, "but I can't figure out what I did with it. Maybe it will turn up," he muttered. "Some of my best pictures, no doubt." He grinned.

Sandy had a good idea what had happened to the film, but she kept quiet.

"We're getting awfully forgetful, Sandy," Pauline said with a laugh, going back to her crocheting. "I think we're getting Alzheimer's."

Weariness from the trip and accumulated emotional tension finally caught up with Sandy, so when the eleven o'clock news came on, she excused herself and headed down the hall.

She cleaned her contact lenses, brushed her teeth, then went into her old bedroom, now the guest room. The personal touches were gone, just the furniture was the same. She took out her nightshirt and slipped it on, then pulled back the covers, climbed under them, and turned off the electrified hurricane lamp on the bedside table. The faint glow of a street light filtered through the venetian blinds, bathing the room in familiarity. For a moment, the years fell away. A bittersweet feeling began to steal over her, and she closed her eyes to block it. She couldn't handle it right now.

She began thinking about Pauline's agitation. When she'd referred to it during the afternoon, Pauline had become defensive.

"The house was burglarized, Sandy. I just don't know

how long it will take me to get over that. You just don't know what it's like, having someone break into your home. It makes me afraid to go out for fear they'll be here when I come back. But I'm afraid to be home, too."

And perhaps that's all it was. Maybe Sandy was transferring her own fears about Jerry to her mother. Probably.

There was a light knock on the door. "Are you still awake?" It was Pauline.

"Yes. Come in."

Her mother walked in, leaving the door ajar. A sliver of light shone from the hall. "I'm glad you're here," she said as she sat down on the edge of the bed in the dark.

"I'm glad to be here."

There was a short silence and Sandy noticed that her mother was twisting her hands.

"Sandy, there's something I need to tell you."

A knot of dread formed in Sandy's stomach, although she couldn't imagine what kind of a secret her mother was harboring. Surely it couldn't be as ominous as her voice suggested. So often the word "need" foretold a confession that a person didn't *need* to hear at all.

"What is it, Mom?"

"I hope you find Jerry."

"I said I'd try. Without an address—"

Her mother interrupted. "I'm afraid he may not be in Duluth."

"Really?" Sandy said, interested. "Why not?"

"I'm afraid he's looking for your father. He was asking about him the last time he was here."

"What did you tell him?"

"Not much. I don't want him to find him."

Sandy hesitated and propped herself up on one elbow. "Do you know where my father lives?"

"Well, I know where he went after the divorce, but I haven't kept track, if that's what you mean."

"Did he go to Northlake?"

Her mother caught her breath. "How did you know that? Does Jerry know?"

Sandy explained how Jerry had asked the Senator for his help.

"Why didn't you tell me this before?"

"I just found out yesterday. Jerry asked the Senator to keep it confidential, but under the circumstances—"

"What circumstances?"

Uh-oh. Sandy searched for a logical explanation for her slip of the tongue. She didn't want to tell her mother about the film and the note. "I happened to mention you were worried about Jerry and since I was going to be in Duluth—"

She seemed to accept this. "Maybe you can stop Jerry, keep him from finding your father."

"I doubt if I can do that, Mom. It's possible he's been there quite a few months now. If there's anything to learn, he's probably learned it. But I can at least find out why he hasn't called." *I hope,* she added to herself.

Sandy reached out and took Pauline's hand. It was cold to the touch as if the blood had drained out of the woman's body. "Mother, what is it? What if he finds Dad?"

"It's—it's just that your father—it's the reason he left. I—I sent him—I made him leave. He—I—" She was shaking now, light little convulsions of her body.

Sandy sat up and put her arms around her mother. "It's going to be okay, Mom."

Pauline was on the verge of tears.

My Lord, what is it? Sandy thought.

"It will never be okay. I don't know how to tell you this, but your father—he was—is a homosexual."

Sandy's first thought was that this was some outrageous ploy to keep her from wanting to find her father. It wasn't something she'd ever expected. But, could it be true? If so, how could it have been a secret all these years? "How come you've never told me this, Mom?"

"Because I didn't want you to know. It was so embarrassing. To be married . . . He had me fooled for years—years! I felt so cheated on. We were married for twelve years—happily, I thought. I had no idea he had a secret life, not an inkling until your Uncle Bill got wind of it from someone. Then I confronted your father. And he admitted it!"

"Did he—was he—the whole time you were married?"

"I don't know. He claimed he was straight for the first few years. He kept pushing those other feelings back, he said, 'wouldn't admit them,' but finally—well, he acted on them. Oh, Sandy, it was awful." Her voice held an edge of disgust. "I felt like something was really wrong with me, that I'd done something to turn him away from women."

Sandy clicked something off in her mind. She wouldn't think about her father now; he was a stranger. Pauline needed her support. "Mother, there's nothing wrong with you. What happened was not your fault."

"I know that now, but sometimes even when you know something in your head, you feel it differently."

Sandy knew very well. The end of her marriage had left her feeling like a failure, even though she'd tried her best to hold it together.

"I had to ask myself how could I have been happy married to someone who was—was like that."

"So, then, did he ask for a divorce?"

There was a short pause. "No. He wanted to go on the way we were. But I couldn't have. He was staying out late, sometimes all night, and I worried about him getting into trouble. Terrible things happen to homosexuals; people beat them up, even kill them. I couldn't live with that or with him like that. And I didn't want him and his friends around you kids. He had this—this one friend. He always competed for your father and I was too stupid to see it."

Sandy remembered a big bear of a man who'd spent time at their house. She hadn't thought of him for years. He'd always taken time with her, throwing her up in the air and catching her, swinging her by the arms on the lawn. She'd been very fond of him. Her father's friend. "Gus."

"Yes. Gus. I didn't know it was more than just friendship—I mean a lot of women's husbands have hunting buddies. But I was always jealous of their friendship. It turned out I had good reason," she added darkly.

Sandy let go of her mother and dropped down on her elbow again. "Was it Daddy's idea not to visit us?"

The bed creaked as Pauline shifted her weight.

"Tell me, Mother. I want to know. This has been a secret long enough."

Her voice was defensive. "No. He wanted to have visitation rights. I refused to let him."

Anger rose within Sandy. She'd been denied her own flesh and blood father all these years. *And he had loved them, wanted to see them.* She lay back on the pillow, gripping the covers tightly. Emotions surged up in her, threatening to choke her. Here she was in her mid-thirties, feeling like a ten-year-old child who'd just been abandoned.

Her mother's voice seemed distant. She was saying something. "—and the judge saw it my way, considering the circumstances."

"But," Sandy said, trying to keep her voice even, "he was still *my father.*"

"It was a long time ago, Sandy. I don't know if what I did was right. It seemed right for you children at the time. I didn't want him to have an influence on you, especially Jerry.''

She wanted to say, *He had an influence, whether he was around or not. Walking out, what I thought was his walking out, had an effect.* But she held her tongue. It was a long time ago, and it couldn't be rectified through recriminations.

''I'm afraid Jerry will find your father. Maybe he already has and that's why he hasn't called me. He may have turned Jerry against me.''

''Mother, he couldn't do that. Jerry may be a little irresponsible, but he's not stupid.''

Pauline patted Sandy on the shoulder. ''We'd better get some sleep.'' She stood up and Sandy watched her leave the room, her shoulders sagging. Obviously letting go of her secret hadn't helped Pauline. Maybe it took time, Sandy thought, to feel free of such a long-kept burden.

She stared at the ceiling, wondering how such a profound revelation would affect her. All these years she'd thought her father didn't love her enough to stick around or to contact her. And it wasn't that at all.

It was something to get used to, but the most amazing thing about it was how her mother had kept it a secret all these years.

She knew that a lot had happened to change attitudes toward homosexuals in the more than twenty years since Forrest Ahlgren had left them. But for all the increased awareness and acceptance, Sandy was sure that many a woman who discovered her husband was gay would still react just as Pauline had. For one thing, infidelity was infidelity. It would be hard to distill its effect from the added confession of his bisexuality. The women she knew whose husbands had been unfaithful had the same question Pauline did: Is there something wrong with me that my husband is interested in someone else? It was typical of women to turn the blame inward.

PAULINE Cochran was in the kitchen when Sandy got up the next morning. She looked as if she'd had a sleepless night. Her hair, touched with gray, was disheveled and her eyes were puffy. Looking at her mother's eyes was for Sandy like looking in a mirror.

"Good morning," Sandy said as she came through the door.

Pauline was cutting biscuits and putting them in a round cake pan. She glanced over her shoulder and gave her daughter a quick, self-conscious smile.

Sandy put her hand out and touched her mother's back. It's all right, Mother." There was no point in harboring anger at Pauline.

Her mother turned, floury hands and all, and held her arms out to Sandy. Sandy stepped into a hug.

"I'm sorry, Sandy," her mother said. "I'm so sorry."

"You did what you thought was best, Mom. That's the most a child can hope for from a parent."

"Yes, but—"

"No yes, but's."

Willis came into the kitchen. "What's going on?"

Pauline pulled away from Sandy. "Nothing. We're just hugging. And I'm getting some biscuits ready to put in the oven."

Sandy wondered if Willis knew about Forrest Ahlgren. From her mother's strained reaction, she doubted it. Pauline Cochran had probably kept her first husband's bisexuality a deep dark secret from everyone. Except Uncle Bill had known. Uncle Bill, who was so bigoted about everything. How many times had she heard him make tasteless jokes?

And now Pauline's son was threatening to put a wrinkle in the world she'd carefully smoothed.

After breakfast, Willis carried her bag to the car. He and Pauline planned to leave for church as soon as Sandy hit the road, so she didn't linger.

"Well, it was short but sweet," Willis said as the three of them stood in the driveway.

Pauline hugged her, whispering in her ear, "Find your brother, honey."

Sandy barely nodded. "I'll be home for Thanksgiving," she said. "And Mother, I'll call you."

With a final wave and a smile, she backed the car out of the driveway.

Pauline believed it was bad luck to watch someone drive over the horizon, so she and Willis had already disappeared into the garage when Sandy looked back at the house in her rearview mirror. Leaving always felt so permanent. She was glad her mother had plans this morning, something to occupy her mind. Sandy wasn't so lucky. She had about a six-hour drive ahead of her, time to think, whether she wanted to or not.

7

AUTUMN at its finest began somewhere around Hinckley. The trees were stunningly colorful in the afternoon sun, afire with enough promise to keep a person going till spring. Gradually the maples yielded to a preponderance of aspens and birches, bright yellow mixed with evergreens; then the autumn flame died to a flicker as Sandy drove toward winter.

She hadn't stopped for lunch and by the time she reached Northlake in late afternoon her stomach was grumbling for food. The car's tank was also empty, so she pulled up to a convenience-store gasoline pump.

It felt good to stretch. She rolled her head back and rubbed her neck to get the driving kinks out, then started filling the tank. There was a slight wind and the day had cooled considerably. While the tank filled, she opened her suitcase and pulled out an oversized gray cardigan and put it on.

When she went in to pay, she asked the blonde-haired girl behind the counter if she knew a Jerry Cochran. Might as well get right to it.

The teenager shook her head. "Unless someone uses a credit card, I don't know their names."

As Sandy pulled her own plastic from her billfold, she realized she might have a photograph. She fumbled to get the accordion of photos out and extended it toward the clerk. "This is a picture of him. It's a few years ago, but he hasn't changed much. Longer hair maybe." It was Jerry's graduation photo.

The blonde studied it. "Oh, *him*." Her voice had a warmer quality to it. "He buys gas in here."

"Have you seen him lately?"

The girl shrugged. "Not in a few days, maybe a week. But I only work part-time."

"You don't happen to know where he lives?"

The clerk shoved a credit card receipt over for Sandy to sign. "No, I don't know that." She giggled. "Wish I did. Sorry. Why you lookin' for him?"

"He's my brother and I came to see him."

"And you don't even know his address?" She tore the receipt off. "Want your carbons?"

Sandy shook her head. "I just have a post office box number and he doesn't have a phone. Do you know what kind of car he drives?"

"A Ford pickup. White."

Same rattletrap he was driving when he'd come to Washington to visit her. She'd wondered how the truck had made it that far.

Another customer came inside and the clerk turned her attention to him. Then, as if remembering Sandy's dilemma, she said, "Show that picture to J.J. here. Maybe he knows where your brother lives."

Sandy showed the picture to the man, and the girl explained the situation.

"Nope. Never saw him. Give me a pack of Camels, hon."

"Is there anyone else here who might know him well enough to know where he lives?" Sandy asked.

The clerk shook her head and took the man's money.

After he left she said, "No, I'm working alone tonight. You might ask Harmon. He's the owner and he'll be here tomorrow morning at seven to open up."

"Another thing. Do you know a Forrest Ahlgren?"

The clerk thought a moment. "Well, it kinda sounds familiar, but I don't think so. Do you have another picture?"

"No, not of him."

"It rings a bell, but"—the girl shrugged—"you know."

"May I borrow a phone book?"

"Sure."

Sandy thumbed to the A's. There were no Ahlgrens listed. She felt a twinge of regret, but finding him just by looking in the phone book or asking the first person she met would have been too easy.

So had Jerry's trail met a dead-end here? Or did their father live here with his friend? *How stupid of me,* she thought. *I didn't get the friend's last name from Mother.* All she knew was Gus. But a phone call to her mother could remedy that.

She closed the book, handed it back to the girl, and thanked her.

"Any luck?"

Sandy shook her head and asked where the restroom was.

The girl hailed her as Sandy started to leave the store a few minutes later. "Where can I find you—if I see him?"

"I'm staying at Senator Mattingly's place. Do you know where it is?"

"Oh, yeah, sure."

"Thanks," Sandy said and went back to her car.

This wasn't going to be easy. Jerry was relatively new in

town, with no phone. It was like finding a needle in a haystack. Her only option seemed to be to ask around—the way television detectives did it: show a picture, drop his name, drive around and look for his truck. At least the girl had seen him. But why not? Jerry stood almost six feet tall, wore his thick dark brown hair almost shoulder length, and he had a face fit for a movie star. Even if he was her brother and she was biased he was every bit as good looking as Mel Gibson.

Northlake looked much as she remembered, only it was spread out a little farther now. It still had an outpost feel about it. Shops were interspersed with residences, some of them operating out of remodeled houses. She passed three outfitters, one sporting goods shop, a bait shop, and a motel, in addition to a grocery store, a laundromat, and a country-crafts store. All except the laundromat had racked canoes in front for rent. The convenience store where she'd stopped also rented canoes as a sideline. The sheer numbers made her realize what a busy place this must be during the summer season.

Now though, on a Sunday evening, there was little traffic. Occasionally she met a car, but the place was essentially dead.

The houses were primarily two-story frame structures with double-hung windows. Most had covered porches boxed in at least halfway up, sometimes completely. The front yards were tiny. People had minimized the amount of sidewalk they would have to shovel come wintertime.

Sandy drove slowly down the street, looking for a place to eat. She had already seen a Dairy Queen at the edge of town, then a Pizza Hut, which had at least a dozen cars parked outside it, but she settled on a place called Hurd's, which was located in the main business district, next to the Sears catalog store.

Probably a place where she would be overcharged for bad food, with poor service thrown in free. She'd had the experience before. But maybe the people working here would be older and would keep up with who was new in town. It might be the perfect place to find out about Jerry.

There were several cars parallel-parked in front. She pulled into an empty space, but was too far from the curb. It took several tries before she got the car positioned adequately to satisfy herself and any policeman who might happen by. She'd flunked the parallel-parking part of her driving test years ago, and she still hadn't perfected the skill. She picked up her purse, got out, then pressed the automatic door lock and headed toward the café.

Hurd's was a substantial-looking place that probably hadn't changed much since the day it opened. It was built of gray granite blocks, with a deep overhang that jutted out over the sidewalk, to protect customers from the elements.

Inside, two rectangular rooms comprised the café. As Sandy entered the café, she was facing a barstool-lined counter. Behind it, through double doors, lay the kitchen. The place smelled of old grease and stale cigarettes. Not very appetizing.

To her right there was a larger room with red cracked booths along the front and sides. Tables that could be shoved together to accommodate either large or small groups filled the area between the booths. They were all empty, although several still had dirty dishes on them.

A lone man lounged in the nearest booth, one knee bent, his foot in the seat. He was drinking a cup of coffee and smoking a cigarette. He acknowledged her with a nod.

Sandy sat down in the second booth, facing the door, and pulled off her sweater.

"Brigitte!" the man hollered. His voice sounded like gravel being crunched. "You got a customer."

The doors to the kitchen swung open a moment later and a girl came out, picked up a glass, filled it at a spigot, grabbed a plastic-covered menu, then came over to Sandy. She was wearing a yellow North Stars hockey team T-shirt, tucked into blue jeans. Not everyone could wear that shade of yellow, but she did it nicely, Sandy thought.

"Hi. Do you want coffee?" Brigitte pushed her long blond hair behind her ears with fingers whose nails were bitten almost to the quick.

"Yes, please," Sandy said as she opened the menu.

"Cream?"

"No thanks. Just black."

"I'll be right back."

Sandy looked the menu over but nothing appealed to her, even though she'd felt hungry.

Her eyes strayed around the café. The booths were patched with plastic tape, now dark around the edges, where it had given slightly and trapped soil. The tables were beige laminate, the kind that had been around since plastics made their way onto countertops, complete with metal rims. It looked like a hamburger joint, so that's what she would have. It would be hard to go wrong with a hamburger fried on a grill.

She looked over at the man in the front booth. He was about fifty and had a weathered look, as if he spent a lot of time outdoors. Well, this was the country for it: canoeing, hiking, and fishing in the summer, cross-country skiing, dog-sledding, and snowmobiling in the winter. And then there was the hunting. She thought maybe hunting season was year round.

The man's eyes met hers as he inhaled, then removed his cigarette from his mouth, jutted out his lower lip and let the smoke slowly escape. It formed a cloud over him. He lowered his eyelids and smiled slightly at her. "You new to Northlake?"

"Yes," Sandy said, grateful that Brigitte came slouching back with the coffee just then. There was something she didn't like about the way the man looked at her and she had no desire to start up a conversation.

"Have you decided?" the girl asked.

Sandy nodded, closing the menu. "I'll just have a hamburger."

"You want fries with that?"

A foursome came in the door and came over to one of the booths.

"No thanks."

Brigitte was about Jerry's age, and he never let any grass grow under his feet when it came to pretty women. She could almost bet that her brother knew the waitress.

Brigitte had turned away, heading down to bus one of the tables with dirty dishes, but Sandy called after her. "May I ask you something?"

The waitress turned. "Me?" Her eyes darted to the man, then back to Sandy.

"Yes."

The girl came back Sandy's way.

"Do you happen to know Jerry Cochran?"

The girl's eyelids flicked closed several times in rapid succession, and she darted another glance sideways at the man in the first booth.

The man put his cigarette back in his mouth and straightened up, pulling his arm off the back of the booth. "Brigitte, you got things to do," he said.

"No, I don't know him," Brigitte said quickly. She turned away and tossed a "sorry" over her shoulder. From the girl's reaction, Sandy was certain she was lying.

"Who's that you're looking for?" the gravelly voiced man asked.

Something was going on here. "Jerry Cochran," she answered warily.

"What's he to you?"

"He's my brother. Do you know him?"

The man shook his head. "No." He took a slow drag on his cigarette. Now he was leaning on the table. "And I know about everyone around. That's why I knew you were a newcomer. Is he—your brother—is he supposed to be living here?"

Sandy nodded. "At least this is where his post office box is."

The man nodded. "That explains why I don't know him. He probably lives out in the woods somewhere. That's what most newcomers up here do. They come up and get a place on a lake." The man slid from the booth and came over by her table. He was built like a bull, strong, big neck and chest, narrow hips. He was carrying his coffee cup, and the cigarette dangled from his lips. She thought for a moment he was going to sit down, uninvited.

"Where are you from?" he asked her.

"I live in Washington."

"D.C.?"

She nodded.

"What do you do there?"

"I work for Jim Mattingly."

The man squinted his eyes at her. "Is that right?"

She nodded.

"Well, I guess that makes you almost a celebrity."

She felt the color rise in her face. He was making fun of her.

"I know ol' Jim. We're good buddies. You know, he has a place out north of here."

She nodded.

"So you're looking for your brother. Now, how come you're doing that?"

She looked at him coolly and didn't answer. It really was none of his business.

The man took the cigarette from his mouth and dropped it in his coffee cup, where it sizzled, then he turned away, saying, "Well, you enjoy your dinner." He followed Brigitte, who'd gathered up an armload of dirty dishes and was heading for the kitchen. Sandy wondered if he was just familiar with the place or if perhaps he was the owner, Mr. Hurd.

Reflecting on the last few moments, Sandy was sure the girl knew Jerry, even though she denied it. The man had been awfully interested, too. Nosy, actually.

Shortly, Brigitte brought Sandy's order, but the girl didn't linger. In fact, she almost slung the hamburger basket in front of Sandy, she was in such a hurry to get back to the kitchen.

More people came in and Brigitte was kept busy, so there was no chance to question her further until Sandy was paying her check.

"Are you sure you don't know Jerry?" Sandy asked her again, pursuing her feeling. "Let me show you his picture." She pulled the pictures from her billfold again and showed the girl.

"That was seven years ago," she said. "His hair is longer."

Brigitte looked, and Sandy, watching her closely, thought she detected a smile, but then the girl's eyes narrowed. "No. I told you I don't know him."

The man had come out of the kitchen, and was standing behind Brigitte. He looked on as the girl put Sandy's money in the cash register.

"If you recall ever seeing him, you might call me. I'm staying at Senator Mattingly's place."

"So you're staying out there," the man said.

Sandy nodded.

"That's a nice place," he said, "if you like wilderness. Dangerous for a city girl alone, if you ask me."

I didn't, she thought.

"Lots of wolves and bears out there. You better be careful. There's no one out that way this time of year if you need help."

"I think there's a caretaker."

One corner of the man's mouth curled. "Niles Benson. Yeah, he'll take care of you all right. Only maybe not how you think." He snorted at his joke. "Besides, lady, his place is a mile, mile and a half away. A bear or wolf could have your innards tore to bits before he could get there—if he even knew you needed help." He thrust his hands in his pockets. "You just better be careful out there alone."

"I'm sure I'll be fine." She stared at him coldly. "By the way," she asked, "where is Skaar's Taxidermy Shop?"

At her question she saw his heavy jaw tighten slightly.

The girl glanced toward him very briefly, as if wondering if he were going to answer. When he didn't, Brigitte focused back on the cash register and mumbled, "It's across the street and down the block, west."

8

SKAAR'S Taxidermy Shop looked misplaced, a log building wedged between two brick ones. A sign dangled from a suction cup attached to the inside of the door. It read "Gone Fishing." A ruffed grouse and several other stuffed birds peered at her through glass eyes from the narrow display shelf below the window. What lay beyond them was hard to distinguish because of the reflection of the streetlights which had come on while she was in the café. Hadn't the owner heard of security lighting?

Sandy framed her eyes and pressed her hands against the window to get a better look at the dim interior. A glass display counter stood about fifteen feet back in the room. A moose head stared at her from the back wall. Below it were mounted fish and antlers of all kinds and sizes. Several deer heads hung on the side walls. Were they the owner's personal trophies or prizes for customers to take home without even casting a line or shooting a gun?

"What are you doing?" a gravelly voice behind her asked.

Adrenaline shot through her. She turned to see the man from the café. He was wearing a baseball cap and a dark windbreaker with the collar turned up. In the pasty light cast from the streetlamps he looked even more bull-like and sinister.

He had startled her, but there was no way she was going to show it. "Is there a law against looking in a window?" she asked coldly.

The man met her gaze evenly. "Depends on why you're looking. You're a stranger in town. The police might think you're up to no good."

"I just want to see the taxidermist."

He snickered. "You have something you want mounted?" She started to walk away.

"You want to know about Skaar?" he called after her.

Reluctantly she turned back toward him, pulling her sweater more tightly around herself. He knew what bait to throw out. Prolonging their conversation was not high on her list of things she wanted to do, but she did need information.

He came up to her. "Like his sign says, he's on a fishing trip. Sometimes they're extended." He snickered again and tipped his cupped hand up to his mouth to represent drinking.

"Do you know where he lives?"

He jerked his thumb upward toward the windows above the shop. They were dark.

"Oh. Well, thanks," she said drily.

"You betcha." He stood there in front of the shop while she hurried across to her car, quickly unlocked it and climbed in, eager to be away from there. He came sauntering across the street as she pulled away from the curb, and she had to wait for him to pass. He gave her a little salute.

Was it simple nosiness that made him follow her to the shop? Or something else? Whatever it was, he certainly didn't exude small-town charm. She felt threatened.

She pushed her feelings aside and thought about the shop. Its stationery was her only link to Jerry. If he knew the taxidermist well enough to borrow his stationery, maybe the owner would have Jerry's address or a phone number where he could be reached. Of course, there was still the possibility that Jerry had simply taken the letterhead. She definitely needed to come back here tomorrow to find out.

Meanwhile, she might as well pick up a few groceries so she wouldn't have to eat every meal out. She remembered passing an IGA store as she'd come into town, and she drove back there and bought a box of cereal, a microwave entree (surely there was a microwave at the Senator's), a carton of milk, frozen orange juice, instant coffee, a two-liter bottle of soda, and a few other things. It was hard to know what to buy since she had no idea how long she would be here. Only a day or two, she hoped.

Back at the car, she studied the map Jim Mattingly had given her. It seemed easy enough. Follow the highway to a sign for Summer's Inn, turn left and go north 7.3 miles. Very specific. She put the car in gear and headed east out of town.

When she'd gone into the IGA, the moon had just risen over the horizon as orange as a basketball. Now it was getting higher and was casting a silver aura on the ragged horizon. It was so unlike Washington, Sandy felt as if she were driving into some alien world. Very few people lived beyond the edge of town year round.

She almost missed her turnoff. The Summer's Inn sign had been targeted by vandals and was lopped over at a strange angle, pocked by bullet holes. It would probably be repaired before the next season began, but why fix it before the hard winter to come?

The brakes on the car squealed as she made a sharp turn onto the gravel road. A welter of rocks spewed up from behind the tires and she felt for a moment as if she were losing control, but the car straightened and everything was okay again.

On either side of the road pine and balsam trees grew in lock step, a dense, foreboding presence by night. Her headlamps led her deeper into the wilderness and by the time she passed the turnoff to the Inn at the three-and-a-half-mile mark, she hadn't encountered a single car.

Her headlights caught two deer grazing beside the road. They looked up, momentarily mesmerized. She sucked in her breath abruptly, slowing, realizing she'd been driving too fast. If she accidentally hit a deer, she might be stranded, and she didn't want that. The night seemed hostile.

An instant later she was glad she'd slowed down as one of the deer bolted across the road and into the woods.

Around a curve the landscape became desolate. Loggers had been there. She knew from the newspapers that clear cutting was a big concern between commercial interests and environmentalists. Would the logging eventually help or hurt the forest? That was the big environmental issue. The economic bottom line was dollars and jobs. Some people thought that as long as no more was logged off than could grow in a year everything was hunky-dory, but that ignored the fact that old-growth forest would become increasingly rare, and with it, certain kinds of wildlife might disappear.

It was a complex issue, but one thing was indisputable: the aesthetics of clear cutting were awful. The area spotlighted by her headlamps looked as if it had been bombed. She continued along and the scene once again became pristine forest.

After several more miles she saw her second landmark, a wooden sign shaped like a wolf howling at the moon. It was attached to the mailbox post, next to a narrow lane that disappeared into the trees. This was the Senator's place.

The woods were too dense, even in the moonlight, to catch a glimpse of the house. And of course, no lights would be on. She wondered how far down the lane it was.

She continued along the main road for another half mile,

then began looking for the turn to Niles Benson's. When she'd gone over a mile, she knew she'd missed it and started back. On this trip she spotted two ruts into the woods at about the right mileage.

So this must be the place, hidden away in the shadows. She wondered why he had no sign.

Rather reluctantly, she left the highway and jounced slowly along the deeply etched lane, remembering the gravelly-voiced man's comment about Niles Benson. *He'll take care of you, all right. Only maybe not how you think.* And then the crude laugh.

Tree branches hung over the road like arms reaching out to envelope her, scraping against the car as she inched along the ruts. An unreasonable fear prickled at the back of her neck. Could this possibly be the right road? Could it possibly harbor anything civilized? If so, this Niles Benson person was making as little mark on the land as was humanly possible. She glanced to her left, but her lights barely bled to the side, and the wall of trees looked impenetrable and foreboding.

It seemed a long way in and there was absolutely nowhere to turn around. If this was a dead-end, she would have to back out, something she handled about as well as parallel parking.

But it wasn't a dead-end. The house came up suddenly as the car heaved around a stand of dense evergreens. It fit into its surroundings so well that she'd had no idea she was almost there.

Cabin more aptly described the tiny place. It was not over twenty-four feet across the front. Tall pines shot skyward so close beside the door that they visually formed an integral part of it. Welcoming yellow light shone at the two front windows like eyes, she noted with relief.

She pulled up next to a dark pickup truck which had a

crumpled and neglected left back fender. There was an empty gun rack in the rear window. She stepped out onto a soft mat of pine needles, closed the door gently, and walked to the small porch.

She thought that perhaps Niles Benson would notice her car lights or the sound of the engine, but no one looked out or turned on the outside light.

She rapped on the door and waited, looking around uneasily. This was too eerie. She wished this Niles person would hurry up and answer the door. What was he doing in there? Sleeping? Rather early for that. After a moment she tried again. Surely he was here—the truck was, and the inside lights were on. She knocked again. Still no answer.

She stepped off the porch and started for her car, uncertain about what to do next. Sit in the car and wait? Go back to town and try again later? Suddenly a sound stopped her dead.

It started low, almost a moan, then crescendoed, gaining strength as it rose. The howl sent a shudder along Sandy's spine, dredging up a primal chill from some deep genetic memory. The sound lingered on the night air. Then, from another direction, came an answer.

Silence fell over the woods again, the more complete now that the howling had stopped. It seemed almost as if she'd imagined it. A light breeze touched the pines and they sighed high above her. It took a moment before the breeze kissed her cheek. And then there was another howl.

Sandy moved into action, covering the remaining few yards to the car at a gallop.

Though she was reproaching herself for being a scaredy cat—and was glad that no one was observing her flight—she couldn't get to the car too soon. She was just reaching for the door handle when she heard something crashing out of the woods toward her.

9

WITH her peripheral vision, Sandy glimpsed a shadowy creature running toward her. She grabbed the door handle of the car, but damn! She'd automatically locked it when she'd gotten out. She ripped at her purse to find the keys, glancing toward the woods. The animal was heading right for her.

But her fear began to dissolve as soon as she looked directly at it. It wasn't a wolf, that was for sure. Much too small and fat, and it was making gruff little woofs. The threat completely dissipated at the comical sound.

It reached her and started snuffling around her ankles. It was a basset hound, or at least part basset judging by its long, low-slung bulky shape, short legs, and drooping ears.

"Nice doggie," she said, reaching down to let it sniff her hand.

"Clyde!" a male voice commanded, coming from the direction of the woods. The dog lost interest in her immediately and scampered away.

Sandy looked toward the sound and saw someone coming out of the woods.

Niles Benson? She'd been expecting someone old; "caretaker'' implied ancient. The old family retainer. But the well-built figure coming her way dispelled that presumption. The light coming from inside the cabin shone on his face and dark curly hair. He was obviously not old, with broad shoulders on a trim but not thin body. Could this dark-haired man be a Niles Benson? He looked anything but Scandinavian. More like an Apollo or a Zeus.

"Niles Benson?" she said tentatively.

"Yes."

So much for stereotypes, she thought.

"You must be, uh, Mrs.—"

"Wilson. Sandy Wilson."

"Yeah. Okay. Come on in." He strode by her and opened the door to the cabin. Clyde almost broke his neck to be first inside. After the dog had passed, Benson stood back and let Sandy in. She caught a whiff of balsam or pine or some equally woodsy smell as she brushed past him. Very masculine.

Her breathing had gotten shallow and she realized she was having a physical reaction to this complete stranger.

Get hold of yourself. She took a deep breath and looked around the room.

The pine logs that formed the interior as well as the exterior of the cabin were varnished to a golden hue inside. A time-worn Early American couch with a high back sat along the wall facing the door. It took almost the entire space. A fur robe was thrown over it.

Clyde had made a beeline for the kitchen which was in an ell off the right-hand side of the main room. Now he reappeared, labored up onto the couch, scratched the upholstery a few times, walked in a circle to find the very best spot, disregarding a *Field and Stream* and the telltale yellow of a *National Geographic* beneath it. He just plopped down on top of them. His chin rested on his paws, but he kept his sorrowful eyes on Niles, following his movements.

Across from the couch was an old beige nylon frieze easy chair. The center of the cushion had a permanent depression from long use. It looked ancient but comfortable.

A deer on the far wall gazed down at Sandy, its eyes questioning, and she quickly looked away, thinking of the two deer on the road. It made her sad to think they might end up like this.

A tubby black woodstove squatted in one corner of the room, generating enough heat to make the room uncomfortably warm.

"Sorry I wasn't here when you drove up," Benson said. "Have you been here long?"

"No. I just got here." Her excitement came through in her voice, making her sound nervous.

"Good. Clyde and I just went out for a walk. I get a little stir crazy. Did you have a good trip?" he asked.

"Yes. It was fine," she answered perfunctorily. "Senator Mattingly said you would have a key to his cabin."

He nodded, a slight smile catching one corner of his mouth. "Cabin," he said.

"Yes."

His khaki-colored eyes looked almost wolflike as they captured hers and held them a moment longer than was polite. A wicked pulse in her started sending out tantalizing beats.

No, Sandy, she lectured herself, you are not going to do this to yourself. Charlie was the cure, right? Forget it. You're just under a lot of stress.

"You must be tired," he said, his voice sounding like velvet. "It's a long haul from the Cities. How about a drink?"

Yes, yes, the pulse hammered. *Take care of me.* She nodded.

"I have some Scotch, or a beer."

"Beer," she said, her voice breathless.

She was glad he disappeared into the kitchen so she could breath normally again. She heaved a deep sigh, then moved slowly around the room, looking at things without seeing them, constantly reassuring herself that she was in control.

She was standing in front of a door leading out of the living room, unconscious of what was beyond, and wasn't aware when he came up behind her until he spoke.

"Interested in seeing the rest of my place?"

She felt color come up in her face. She'd been staring into his bedroom. If he only knew—or maybe he did; maybe her autonomic reaction was as obvious to him as it seemed to her. She remembered the comment the man from the café had made and she felt uneasy. "I'm sorry. I was daydreaming," she said, turning toward him. Again his eyes locked on hers and held a moment too long, and his hand brushed her fingertips as she took the beer he offered, sending an electric charge through her. She couldn't breathe.

He looked down, half smiling, then spoke. "Have a seat." He gestured at the couch. "Just push him over," Niles said, indicating Clyde. "I'm going to open a window; it's gotten too hot in here."

No kidding, she thought, fanning herself and rolling her eyes at her own discomfiture.

Clyde appeared loath to move. When she gently prodded him to make room for her, the dog looked up dolefully and, after a moment, clambered heavily to the floor. "You didn't have to get down, boy. You just need to share," she told him. "You can't hog it all." Sandy pulled her sweater off before she sat down. "That little stove really puts out a lot of heat."

He had opened a window at the far end of the room where a kitchen table sat; now he dropped into the easy chair. "Yes. It's a workhorse. Tell me if it gets too cold in here now that I've opened the window."

Clyde sat at her feet with a look of longing and she patted the couch beside her. "You can come up." Once again he laboriously got on the couch, and stretched out. She pulled the magazines out of his way, then scratched him behind the ears.

"You don't have to let him up there," Niles said. "He's spoiled."

"It's okay. I haven't had a dog in years, so it's kind of nice."

Niles took a long pull on his beer, then put it down on a TV tray alongside his chair and picked up a whetstone—she noticed he wasn't wearing a wedding band—and began sharpening a hunting knife. He moved the blade in tight circles, over and over again. To Sandy, the movements seemed rather provocative. Or maybe it was just him. Maybe anything he did would have been provocative to her at the moment. She hugged herself protectively.

"Cold?" he asked, glancing at her.

"No."

He was wearing a navy and forest-green checked flannel shirt. The sleeves were rolled up to just below his elbows, and as he moved the knife, the muscle in his lower arm flexed. Some women were suckers for a good set of buns, but for her it was a well-turned brachioradialis. The name of that particular muscle had stuck with her long after a college physiology class, because it seemed to be her own personal Waterloo. She watched him in rapt silence for a few moments.

He made no effort at conversation and she found herself wishing she hadn't said she'd stay for a beer. It was foolish to be alone with someone she found so attractive. The silence made her uncomfortable and she knew it would take an effort not to begin blathering. It was so tempting to fill the emptiness with mindless chatter. Maybe she could get him talking. "So you're a trapper," she tried.

He nodded. There was another long silence as he chugged down some more beer. She tipped her glass and took a long drink. If she drank, she couldn't talk, that was for sure. Besides, the sooner she got rid of the beer, the sooner she could end this torture.

She felt a little twinge of hostility toward him for making her feel as if she was the one who needed to be sociable. After all, he was the host. It was his obligation to entertain her with conversation, not the other way around. But she always felt like this with these macho types. It had something to do with the sexual imperative that seemed to hang between them.

She took another drink and looked around the cluttered room.

"What kind of things"—she waved her hand nervously—"do you trap?"

The hunting knife he was sharpening made even circles on the whetstone. "People," he replied. "The ultimate hunt." His eyes darted up to meet hers momentarily and a slight smile turned up one corner of his mouth again.

He was trying to startle her. Well, she wouldn't give him that satisfaction. "What is the market for that?" she said impatiently.

"You don't believe me?" Again the smile. His hand stopped moving and he eyed her lazily.

"No."

He shrugged, took a drink; then the incessant sharpening began again, small circles with the tip of the knife blade. "Ah, well. Would you believe otter, fox, beaver? Whatever

I can get that'll sell." He held up the knife and touched the blade with his thumb.

"I can believe that," she said, "but I didn't know a person could make a living as a trapper these days. It seems rather—oh—" She drew a word and drove it in. "Outdated."

He snorted. "I have a modest lifestyle." He gestured to the cabin with the point of his knife. "I take care of the Senator's place and in the summer I do some yards."

Another Jerry. Another Charlie. An underachiever. They could really pull her strings. She'd be interested in knowing more about making a living out here, but an alarm was going off in her head and she knew she should heed it. *Don't find out any more about him. You don't need to know.*

"How about another beer?" he asked.

"No, I'd better be going." She stood up and felt slightly dizzy from swilling down the beer so fast. "I've interrupted your evening."

"It's no big deal. There's not much doing out here in the woods."

She slipped her cardigan back on. She wondered how much the Senator had told him about her visit here. Did Niles know Jerry? Would it be worth the risk of asking him? She didn't know what kind of trouble Jerry was in or who it involved, so maybe she should wait to talk to the taxidermist before she asked any more questions of anyone.

But her curiosity about Niles himself got the better of her. "Have you lived up here a long time?"

Her question seemed to spur him into action. He stood up and strode toward the door. Clyde opened an eye, saw his master, and lumbered off the couch. Niles wasn't going to get away from him.

"No. Just about a year." He removed a denim jacket from a wall peg and slid his arms into it. "I'll see you over to the Senator's, see if everything's okay." Question and answer period ended.

"You don't have to do that," she said.

"I want to." He looked up from buttoning his jacket. His eyes met hers squarely and she felt that strong pulse start up in her again.

They stepped outside and she wrapped her arms around herself against a sudden chill. "Brrrr. It's getting colder."

"You been up here before?"

"Only once, when I was a child."

"The Senator says you're on vacation."

So that was the story. "Uh-huh."

"All alone?"

He must know that, too. "That seems obvious."

"I meant is anyone joining you?"

She suddenly felt vulnerable. What did she know about this man? "No."

"Seems like you'd get kind of lonely."

"Well, you live alone, don't you?" There'd been no sign of a "significant other" in his cabin.

"Yeah, but not by choice."

Of course it's a choice, she thought. Living in the woods, being a trapper. Women wouldn't wander into his life. That was a kind of choice.

"Well, I just needed to get away," she said.

"A man?"

It seemed like a good excuse for being out there alone. "Yes," she lied.

"Break-up?"

"Uh-huh."

"Sorry."

She shrugged, and opened her car door, then stood behind it as if it were a shield, one hand on top of it. "You really don't have to go over there. I'm perfectly capable—'' Her voice sounded stilted.

She heard Clyde struggling up into the car behind her.

"I'm sure you are. Damn capable. But I'm going anyway. Did you see the turnoff to the Senator's place as you came by?" he asked, putting his hand on the door next to hers, barely brushing it. "The howling wolf sign?"

"Yes," she said, moving her hand slightly to avoid another accidental touch.

"Good. I'll follow you over there. C'mon, Clyde. Get out of there."

"It's okay. He can ride with me."

Clyde rode shotgun to the Senator's place, peering out the side window. Niles's headlamps dogged them in the rearview mirror until she pulled to a stop on the asphalt circle drive in front of the house.

It was larger than any house she'd ever lived in. No wonder Niles had smiled when she'd called it a cabin. She got out, let Clyde out, then removed her suitcase and her groceries from the back seat.

"Let me get those," Niles said as he reached her side.

"If you'll take the suitcase, I'll carry my groceries," she replied.

A low but intense moan intruded like a foghorn through the night.

Once again the sound connected with some hollow place inside her, filling her with an intense longing. She glanced toward the woods, wondering for a moment if she hadn't always been here, hearing the creatures of the night.

"Wolves," he said.

"I heard them earlier, at your place."

"It's the same pack. Don't worry about them," he said, putting his free arm casually around her, ushering her toward the house. "They'll avoid you."

The howl crescendoed in the distance.

Suddenly she wasn't worried. Her mind was too preoccupied with the physical effect his touch was having on her. Clyde broke the mood by throwing back his head and baying into the night. His loud bellow came in comical waves, its intensity almost bowling the animal over.

Niles and Sandy both laughed. Niles gave her shoulder a little squeeze, then dropped his hand and hushed the dog. "Enough, boy. It's okay."

Clyde had a hard time turning it off, but by the time Niles had the key in the lock, the dog was silent and snuffling to get in the door.

"Oh, no, you don't. You can stay outside and bay at your wolf compadres for a minute," Niles told the dog, moving him aside, while Sandy slipped into the house.

A wide terrazzo entryway welcomed them. Niles turned on an overhead light. Straight ahead there were two steps down into a huge living room that seemed created for parties. There were three separate conversation areas, the largest centered around a massive stone fireplace which extended upward into a cathedral ceiling. A balcony overlooked the area from behind the fireplace and tucked underneath was a bar. Beyond that was a wall with heavy drapes.

"This is some place," she said. "I think if I were you, I would sneak over and live here when the Senator's not around."

He smiled. "Who's to say I don't?"

She didn't know how to respond, so she turned her back to him.

"I'll take your bag to the master bedroom," he said. He started off toward the right wing. "You sure are traveling light. They say we're in for a cold snap. Hope you brought some warm clothes."

"You sound like my mother."

"I just know you city types," he called back.

"You do, huh? Well, don't be so sure. I brought plenty of things; I'm just an efficient traveler." She probably *didn't* have warm enough clothes, but she wasn't going to admit it to him. She'd forgotten how much colder it was up here, but she could always buy something if she needed it.

While he deposited her bag, she wandered along the left side of the entryway, which led to the kitchen. She put her grocery bag on the counter and took out the milk and frozen juice. The freezer compartment of the side-by-side refrigerator was completely packed with plastic bags of—she took a close look—some kind of specialty meat. She made a face and shut the door, then stuck the milk and the juice in the refrigerator section. The orange juice could defrost there and be ready to stir up in the morning.

To the back, along the same window wall she had seen from the entryway, there was a dining area which led back around to the living room. To the left of the dining area, there was a door. Something was scratching at it. She undid the bolt, pulled the door open, and Clyde darted in, moving pretty fast for Clyde.

"Cly-de!" She looked out. It was a screened porch, stacked with wood; the outside door stood ajar. She went out and pushed it shut.

When she got back to the living room, Clyde was ensconced on one of the couches. "Well, make yourself comfortable, mister."

Niles was coming down the hall. "What?" he asked.

"I was talking to Clyde."

"How did you get in?" Niles asked the dog. "Get down from there."

"I let him in; he was scratching at the back door."

"He doesn't need to be in here. C'mon, boy." Clyde

reluctantly moved as Niles kept after him and shooed him out the front.

"I assumed you wanted the room with the sauna and the whirlpool," he said as he closed the door after the dog.

"A sauna and whirlpool? I'll feel like I'm on vacation."

He gave her a sharp look. "You are, aren't you?"

"Well, yes, of course, but I didn't expect—" She didn't finish.

"Well, if you don't want such posh accommodations, you could have one of the more modest bedrooms upstairs."

"May as well take the best," she said. Right now the luxury of her surroundings was diminished by the fact that the house was bone-cold. She wrapped her arms around herself.

Niles noticed. "Want me to lay a fire?" he asked as he went to the wall and fiddled with a thermostat. A furnace kicked on.

"It would be nice, but I don't want you to go to any trouble," she said, looking for a heating vent to stand near.

"No trouble."

"No. I'll probably forget and let it die."

"Okay. Whatever's your pleasure." His eyes lingered on hers. "It would just suck most the heat out of the house anyway—make the bedroom colder."

She felt color rise in her face again, responding not to his words but to her own thoughts at his words. Her pleasure would be to be swept off her feet by this stranger, to be enfolded in his strong-looking arms under a comforter somewhere. She wanted him to take her into the master bedroom and make love to her so she could drown in egocentric passion.

Inwardly she scoffed at herself. *Lady Chatterly and the Gamekeeper.* Aloud she said, "You'd better go." Her tone, responding to her thoughts, was more abrupt than it needed to be.

"Yes," he said, "I'm sure I'd better go." Clyde was scratching at the front door now. "I'd better appease the dog."

Suddenly she was tired of her life, tired of worrying about Jerry, tired of being on her own, tired of *should's* and *should not's*, everything she could think of and some things she couldn't. She wanted to be back in her own apartment before the film had arrived, before someone had broken in and had deprived her of her security in her own space, before she knew the truth about her father. She barely got the door shut behind Niles before she lapsed into tears.

10

SANDY'S tears lasted only a few minutes, and she immediately felt better. Crying released a lot of tension. Cheap therapy. But her tears had always infuriated Charlie.

"You use your tears like a weapon!" he'd shouted at her one night when she'd started crying after a stressful day of teaching. It was early in their marriage.

His lack of sympathy was one of the first wedges between them, a side of her she no longer shared with him. From then on, she kept her tears private. She wondered if that had been the beginning of the end.

But no. She could have managed hiding her tears, if he had gotten hold of his drinking. She'd known he had a problem shortly after they met, but with the hubris of youth she was certain that *she* was the solution, that once they were married, he would quit; that she could help him. The truth was she'd compounded the problem. Charlie was a child wanting a mommy.

As she reached the master suite, the phone beside the bed rang. It was Senator Mattingly.

"Did you get there okay?"

"Yes. And your place is wonderful. I really appreciate your letting me use it."

"That's okay. Did Niles get the heat turned on for you?"

"Yes, he did."

"Feel free to enjoy the place any way you can. There may be some food there. Use it up. I don't know when I'll be up there again."

"You can rest assured that the stuff in the freezer is safe from me."

"What do you mean?"

"That liver—or whatever it is. I've never been a connoisseur of specialty meats."

He hesitated a moment. "Did I leave some bait in there?" Then he laughed. "You can use it if you decide to go fishing."

"I doubt I'll be tempted. It's colder here than I thought."

"Have you made any progress in finding your brother?"

"Not really. But I just barely got here. I spent last night with my parents. I did ask about Jerry at the convenience store where I stopped for gas. The girl there recognized his picture, but doesn't know where he lives. I ate dinner at Hurd's café and I'm sure the waitress there knows him, but she clammed up and wouldn't talk about it. I have one lead and I'll follow up on it tomorrow."

"What's that?"

"That letter I got from Jerry. It was on stationery from the taxidermy shop here in town. I went there, but being Sunday evening, it was closed. I'll check it out tomorrow."

"Well, good luck. And I'm glad you got there safely."

Sandy thanked him for calling, then hung up. It was nice of him to check on her.

It had been a long day, so she cleaned her contact lenses, washed her face and brushed her teeth, then peeled off her clothes and climbed into bed, thinking she would fall asleep immediately. But the cold sheets acted like a good dose of caffeine. No sooner did she hit them than all thoughts of sleep fled, and she began sorting through the file cabinets of her mind, analyzing what had happened in Northlake.

She was certain the waitress knew Jerry, and so did the gravelly voiced man. Why had he followed her to the taxidermy shop? What role did the place play? Her best hope at this point seemed to be the taxidermist. Next, the waitress. Maybe the girl would reconsider and call Sandy.

Jerry, damn it, where are you? she thought. *And Forrest Ahlgren. What about you? Are you alive and living in Northlake? Has Jerry stumbled onto something about you?*

She squeezed her eyes shut and tried to relax, stretching her toes out and releasing them. Tensing her ankles. Releasing. Slowly she flexed her muscles one at a time, then relaxed, moving up her body. She turned on her side and punched the pillow into shape and nestled it against her breasts.

Her thoughts wandered to Niles Benson and her less than adequate love life. *Why was she so attracted to a person who was so totally inappropriate?* Her life was so caught up in the fast pace of the nation's capital. This guy trapped and mowed lawns, for God's sake. She went to concerts and movies for entertainment. He sharpened his knife. She remembered his arm as he made those slow circles on the sharpening stone.

She buried her face in the pillow. *I am a complete idiot!*

The fire in her body needed dousing, so she padded to the kitchen in the still cool house; the tile was like ice on her feet. Earlier she had only put away the perishables, and somewhere down in the bottom of the grocery bag there was a Reese's Peanut Butter Cup. Chocolate equaled comfort and indulgence, and she needed it right now. She dug around, found the package, and took it out, then went into the living room and walked over to the draped wall and pulled the cord.

The heavy, insulated drapes moved sideways with little resistance, dropping a wall of cold air into the room. Only the hall light was on, so she could see the view outside. There was a deck that ran along the back of the house and, about a hundred yards of sloping lawn beyond it, a lake. To the left, down near the water, was a shed, probably a boathouse.

She rolled a bite of the candy around in her mouth, savoring it, reveling in the sensation of melting peanut butter as she viewed the panorama before her. The moon had positioned itself over the lake, and reflected like a large pearl in the onyx of the water. She stood and stared a long time, finishing the candy. Finally, the last morsel savored, she started to turn away, when something moved onto the lawn.

While she watched, a wolf trotted halfway across the yard where the land sloped down to the lake. The creature stopped and looked toward the house, then back the way it had come. Another animal came from the same direction, and the two of them sniffed the ground, checked things out, then moved closer to the house. Maybe they smelled Clyde. They disappeared around the screened porch on the south side of the house.

She had been holding her breath. Now she let it out, feeling blessed to have seen such a thing. A shiver ran up her spine, and the longing she'd felt earlier came back. What a strange effect these wild creatures had on her. She pulled the drapes shut against the cold and hurried down the hall to the bedroom.

She brushed her teeth again, then climbed back into bed, rubbing her feet together to warm them up, feeling sorry for herself, remembering how nice it had been to cuddle up to

Charlie, who had always radiated heat like an oven. Finally, she must have drifted off to sleep, because the next thing she heard was a doorbell.

She struggled into a half-sitting position, clutching the covers, and looked around, wondering where she was. After a moment she remembered. Senator Mattingly's. Northlake. Jerry.

Sunlight leaked around the heavy drapes. She picked up her watch from the night stand. Nine o'clock. Late for her. Of course it was only eight back home. *Excuses, excuses.*

The doorbell sounded again and she jerked the covers back. She slipped her feet into the toes of her Avias and slogged down the hall squashing the backs of them down into crescents, wiping the sleep from her eyes and smoothing her hair down. She was glad she had on a flannel nightgown and not some flimsy thing since she hadn't packed a robe.

Standing behind the door, she cracked it open. It was Niles.

"Hi. Uh—did I wake you?" he asked. Clyde pushed his nose through the opening, but his large, sausagelike body wouldn't fit.

"It was time to be up," she said. "Good morning, Clyde."

There was a brief silence. Then Niles said, "I just thought I'd come over and see if you had any problems with anything last night."

She gave him a puzzled look, still holding the door open only a little way.

He waved his gloved hand. "You know. Maybe the sauna didn't work or something."

"I was too tired to try it."

He stomped his feet and patted at both his arms. "Well, you didn't have any problems, then." It was obvious he wanted to be asked in. It wasn't all that cold out, and he was dressed for it, but he was acting as if it were 40 degrees below.

"Do you want to come in? I can fix some coffee."

"Sure."

She pulled the door open, while Niles pushed Clyde back and darted inside. "You'll have to forgive my appearance. I didn't bring a robe."

He smiled. "My mother always wore flannel nightgowns."

Great. I remind him of his mother. That does a lot for my ego. This impromptu visit should keep him from any amorous feelings toward her. She was at her least appealing, burdened with morning-mouth and probably looking frightful.

He, on the other hand, still looked great. But her own insecurity about her appearance had dampened her reaction to him—or maybe it was just the cold reality of daylight.

She padded toward the kitchen and he followed.

"I like the shoes," he said. "With the nightgown, I mean."

"Thanks. I have to have some orange juice before I can do anything," she said, taking the can out of the refrigerator, then opening several cabinets till she found a pitcher.

"I thought it was coffee."

"What?"

"People usually need caffeine."

"That, too."

"How about I make it?"

"Okay. It's in the bag." She poured the orange juice concentrate and three cans of water into the pitcher and stirred, then poured herself a glass. "You want some?"

"No, I've already eaten."

"I'll go get dressed." Clyde was scratching as she padded down the hall carrying her orange juice. Ten minutes later she heard Niles's voice at the bedroom door. "You decent?"

"Yes," she said. "Come on in." Presumptuous of him, she thought, coming to her bedroom.

He handed her a cup of coffee. "I didn't put anything in it."

"That's how I like it. Thanks." She took a sip, then set it down while she worked with her hair, trying to get it tamed. Her eyes drifted over to his in the mirror. He was taking a sip of his coffee, watching her.

"You must be a morning person," she said.

He shrugged. "Anytime person. As long as there's something to look forward to."

"Hmmm," she said and went back to her hair, pulling it behind her ears with tortoise-shell combs. There, she was finished. She stood up and turned toward him, more presentable now. "You really are a trapper?"

He wrinkled his forehead, puzzled at her question.

"What did you do before that?" Maybe he was really a professional who had gotten fed up with the fast track and had opted for this cold paradise.

His eyes left hers. "I—uh—worked at this and that, bummed around."

Yup, she could pick them. She picked up her cup and went down the hall. I am definitely a snob, she told herself.

"What are your plans for the day?" he asked when they were sitting at the dinette table. Sandy had pulled back the curtains and they had a spectacular view of the lake outside.

"Well, I need to go into town—" There was Clyde on the back lawn. He'd given up his door-scratching and was sniffing the trail of the wolves in reverse, marking first one tree then another as he tracked.

"Need? Are you here to relax or what?"

"Yes, but—"

"Take a walk with me. The leaves are spectacular. I'll show you a beautiful spot south of here."

She hesitated a moment. The taxidermist would still be open this afternoon, if he was there at all. "Okay," she said as she finished off her coffee. "Let me get something warmer." She went to the bedroom and pulled a red sweatshirt over her blouse, then put on the cardigan. The layers would probably keep her warm enough.

"Don't you have a coat?"

"No. I'll be fine." She wasn't so sure. Cold wasn't something she appreciated unless it came in the form of ice cream.

Niles stopped at his truck and pulled a backpack out of the cab.

"Sandwiches and drinks," he said, slinging it over one shoulder. They crossed the yard and went by the shed she'd seen last night.

"Is that a boathouse?"

"That, and a catchall," he answered. "Every place needs one." Clyde had joined them and was frisking along in dog heaven, smelling everything. About three hundred yards beyond the Senator's property line, Niles led her on a path into the woods.

At first she was uncomfortably chilly, but as soon as they started uphill, she began to perspire and had to take off her cardigan. She tied the sleeves around her waist. The unaccustomed physical exertion was a strain on her and she was soon out of breath, but she pushed herself to keep up with Niles. She didn't want him to think she was a wimp.

They paused at the crest for a drink of water; Sandy leaned back against a granite boulder. The lake sparkled below them, clear blue, circled with a border of green and yellow. A loon laughed in the distance as Sandy tipped the canteen to her lips. A fine trickle of water ran down beside her mouth and she wiped it away. Nearby a bird gave a low little call.

"What kind of bird is that?" she asked, passing the canteen to Niles.

"A loon?" Niles asked skeptically.

A Minnesotan would have to be unconscious to not know a loon when he heard one. "No, not that," she said with a laugh. "Listen." The other bird cooperated and whistled again. "There, that one."

"Oh. Sounds like a nuthatch." He mimicked the sound accurately. "There it is." He pointed.

A tiny bird went from one tree to another where it paused to climb down the trunk, head first.

"They're little acrobats," Niles said, screwing the lid on the canteen when Sandy refused another drink.

"I don't know much about the outdoors," she said.

"Didn't you ever camp out when you were a child?"

"Once. It rained and it was awful."

"Where did you go?"

"Up here somewhere. I don't remember exactly. I do remember driving through Northlake; it hasn't changed much." She hesitated; a flashback pricked her memory, then was gone. "Is this the place you were telling me about?" she asked.

"No. It's a bit farther. C'mon." He nudged Clyde, who was resting. "You, too, boy. Up."

They followed a deer trail—Niles pointed out sign along the way—down to a creek. Clyde plunged right in and ran across. It was only knee-deep on the dog. "He knows where I'm going," Niles said.

"Don't expect me to follow him," she answered.

As she said it, Niles took a giant step onto a rock that jutted out of the water, then hopped from rock to rock on across.

"I can't do that."

"Sure you can. C'mon."

Where he'd taken a giant step, she had to leap. She landed on the first rock rather precariously and started to slip. No. She was determined not to make a fool of herself by falling in. Milliseconds before her foot hit the water she propelled herself toward the next rock, and the next. It was all over in seconds and she was on the other side.

"See? You did it."

She gave him a dirty look, but secretly felt rather proud of herself.

"This is a portage along here," he said, pointing out a well-worn trail. "Canoes can't get through this creek, so they have to be carried to the next lake in the chain."

They followed the portage trail downstream, with Niles entertaining her by pointing out various plants and telling her what they were used for. He knew a lot about the woods, but she supposed a trapper would.

"Did you camp out a lot when you were little?" she asked.

He nodded. "Our family did. We had a favorite place in the Catskills."

"You're from back East?"

He was walking slightly ahead of her. At her question, he glanced back and said, "Uh—no, I'm a Minnesotan. We only went there a couple of times. My—grandparents lived back there. C'mon, we'll head this way." He angled off the trail into the deep woods.

Everything was dressed in repetitious greens and yellows till they entered a small grove where maple trees mingled with the birches. In a burst of autumn bravado, these mavericks turned the atmosphere vibrant with the cast of their red and orange leaves. Here and there leaves floated to the ground, singly, then in drifts when a slight breeze shook them. Sandy and Niles walked on a patchwork quilt of color with Clyde waddling ahead of them.

"This is the place, isn't it?" she asked quietly, marveling at the beauty. It seemed a sacrilege to speak above a whisper.

"Yes," he answered.

"I'm glad you brought me."

Niles suggested they stop for a few moments.

"Can we eat?" she asked. "I'm starving."

"Why not?"

Sandy dropped down on a fallen birch log. "It's easy to forget there's anyplace this peaceful when you live in the city." She began pulling at a papery piece of the bark, trying to peel one unbroken strip for a souvenir, while Niles knelt down and opened his pack. A breeze lightly touched her cheeks. It was cool here in the shade. As she untied her sweater and put it around her shoulders, she looked up at the trees. "Those leaves are incredible."

Niles handed her a sandwich. "PB and J," he said.

"My favorite."

He swiveled around to sit on the ground, leaning on the log, his knees propped up, also looking at the leaves. He nodded as he unwrapped his sandwich. "You know why they're that color, don't you?" As he took a bite, he pulled a dog biscuit out of the pack with his free hand and gave it to Clyde, who carried it to a shaft of sunlight that penetrated the leaves, and lay down to munch on it.

Sandy laughed. "Biology class is a long time behind me, but doesn't it have something to do with the leaves choking off the flow of—"

"No, I mean the *real* reason."

She frowned at him and tipped her head to one side in puzzlement, using her tongue to dislodge a wad of peanut butter stuck to the roof of her mouth. He'd made really thick sandwiches.

He'd just bitten off another piece of sandwich, and paused before replying. "Well, every night in the north sky there are these four hunters"—he waved his arm toward the north—"and they're pursuing the Great Bear. In mid-autumn they catch it and try to kill it. But so far they've only succeeded in wounding it, and it's the bear's blood that spills down on the leaves and stains them red." He took another bite of his sandwich.

She made a face. "Gruesome."

"It's an Indian legend. I like it."

"How can you like it? It's gory."

He squinted his eyes and looked off into the distance. "I like the way ancient peoples interpreted nature. They made up stories to explain things. It seems a simple approach to life. Do you want a can of soda?"

She nodded. "But killing a bear—"

"The bear was an important animal to them, not only as a symbol of renewal when it seemed to come back from death in the spring, like the trees, but also for survival." He handed her a can. "Imagine, when food was scarce during the winter, the satisfaction of finding a hibernating bear. It would have been a godsend."

Tree bears. She remembered Jerry's fear of the "tree bears." An eerie feeling that he was out here in the woods somewhere stole over her. A drift of cool air touched her again.

"Do you see bears out here much?" she asked, suppressing a shudder.

He nodded, then swigged down some soda. "Lots of them. I hope you get to see one while you're here. They are truly magnificent creatures." Clyde was back and begging.

Niles took another dog biscuit out and handed it to him. The dog retreated.

Sandy glanced around uneasily. "No, thanks," she said. "You can have the bears. I'd be scared to death. I read about this woman who was camping and the bear came up in the night and—"

He brushed off her fear. "That was a grizzly. These are black bears. We don't have any grizzlies in Minnesota."

"I know that. But a bear is a bear to me."

"Well, it's not true. A black bear and a grizzly are very different. For the most part, if you happen on a black bear you can bluff it into running away. However—" he raised a finger to make his point, "don't try that with a grizzly. In fact, the best thing to do around a grizzly is not to have an encounter at all."

"I don't plan to. Not with a black bear either, I hope."

"Well, black bears aren't as aggressive, although—" He stopped and took a drink.

"Although what?"

"Black bears do sometimes kill people. Not often. A couple of dozen people during the past century."

"What turns them into killers?"

"No one really knows. Maybe just an aberrant mind—"

Aberrant mind? she thought, surprised by his choice of words. This guy was no intellectual slouch.

He was continuing, "—like mental illness in humans. They seem to be underweight, undernourished. So maybe their body chemistry is out of whack. When bears are really hungry, they might be more aggressive, but normally even then they aren't predacious. But every once in a while they turn."

"What do you mean?"

"I mean, they stalk their prey, sneak up—no warning—

and go for the kill. It's not like they're defending themselves or something. It's as if it's—'' he paused.

''As if it's what?'' She leaned toward him.

''Premeditated.''

Her face must have shown her dismay. He smiled and said, ''You don't need to worry about predacious bears. You probably won't even be lucky enough to see a bear at all. It's about time for them to den up for the winter.''

They sat silently and ate for a few moments. He was certainly more talkative than he had been the night before and it was a pleasant interlude. She could almost forget her real purpose for making this trip to Minnesota.

She finished her sandwich, and slid down off the log so she'd have something to lean against. Then she closed her eyes for a moment to better experience the smells and the sounds.

Far off in the distance she heard a high whine start up. ''What's that noise?''

''Loggers. They're clear-cutting a couple of miles south of here.''

She smiled. ''I always think of lumberjacks as bigger than life.''

''Why's that?'' he said around a bite of sandwich.

''Paul Bunyan, of course. Didn't you hear all those stories when you were a child?'' A beam of sunlight filtered through the leaves and she lifted her chin toward it. ''I thought everyone in Minnesota did.''

''Oh, yeah. Paul Bunyan.''

They were quiet for a moment, then she asked, ''What do you think about it?''

''About the stories?''

''No, I mean clear-cutting.''

''I believe in managed forests, if that's what you mean, otherwise we're going to destroy the biological diversity.

Some of the stands have to be allowed to mature and die naturally if—'' He paused.

She had her eyes open slightly and she studied him through her lashes. Funny, she'd had him figured for someone who wouldn't want any government restrictions. It seemed to fit his lifestyle.

Unaware that he was being observed, she saw him wince, then recover his composure and start talking again, his voice taking on a more belligerent sound. ''But I don't want a damn bunch of regulations, telling me what I can and can't do.''

She closed her eyes. That sounded more like what she expected from him. But why had he cringed after his first statement? Strange guy.

They were quiet for a few moments, then he said, ''How long have you been divorced?''

She opened her eyes. ''How do you know I'm divorced?''

''You're Mrs. Wilson. And you're here on an R and R.''

The web tangles.

''I've been divorced for a year and a half. But that wasn't why I came here.''

''Oh.''

''How about you? Have you ever—''

He interrupted her by standing up. ''You know, we'd better be going if you want to get into town.'' He began packing their trash into the pack.

He'd effectively evaded her question. She glanced at her watch. It was past noon already.

As they retraced their path to the trail, she told him about seeing the wolves on the lawn the night before.

''You were lucky to see them.''

''Do you trap wolves?''

''No. They're a protected species. It's against the law.''

"But you would if it wasn't against the law?"

He picked up his pace, moved ahead of her, and began to scan the woods as if looking for something. Maybe he hadn't heard the question.

"Would you trap wolves if it wasn't against the law?" she called after him. "And how about bears? Do you hunt them?"

He stopped abruptly and turned back to her. "I kill to survive. It's my livelihood." His voice was chilly. He turned and set off again, his stride determined. Clyde scampered to keep up.

The wind whispered through the pines overhead, and the sky darkened slightly. Sandy looked up. A drift of afternoon clouds had appeared and blotted out the sun. She stuck her arms in the sleeves of her sweater, buttoned it around her, and followed Niles, hoping the clouds would pass and she would come out into the sunshine again.

11

I T was late afternoon before Sandy made it to town. She drove directly to the taxidermy shop and parked across the street. The ''Gone Fishing'' sign was still hanging there, but she ignored it. She went over and tried the door, then rapped loudly on it several times, but no one responded. Perhaps the man from the café had been right about the taxidermist's fishing trip being an extended one.

She sighed. A dead-end. She turned and looked up the street toward Hurd's. Maybe she could salvage something from her trip into town by seeing Brigitte again and questioning her a little more directly—if the gravel-voiced man wasn't in attendance. She was sure the girl knew Jerry, and it seemed to be the only lead she could follow at present.

The café was busy, but Brigitte was nowhere to be seen. Neither was the man whom she'd begun to think of as Hurd.

Sandy ordered a ham steak with mashed potatoes and a salad. While she waited, she went up by the door and bought a Minneapolis newspaper from a dispenser.

When the waitress returned with the food, Sandy asked if she happened to know Jerry Cochran.

The waitress brightened. ''Sure, I do. Good ol' Jerry.''

''Do you know where he lives?''

The girl threw her weight onto one hip, frowned and stretched her mouth to one side, and bit her bottom lip. ''Well, last I knew he had a little place over on Pine. About the four-hundred block.''

''Where's Pine?''

''Take that next street down there—'' she pointed— ''then go three blocks. That's Pine. Then down two blocks. It's the third or fourth house. A little yellow one. And I mean little. You can't see the front for the bushes. It's on the left.''

Jerry in a little yellow house. Sandy had pulled her checkbook out and was scribbling the directions on a deposit slip as the waitress talked.

''But, you know, I haven't seen him in here since over a week ago. I think maybe he's out of town or something. It's too bad the other waitress isn't here. She and him are engaged.''

Engaged? Sandy did need to talk to Brigitte. ''Maybe I could call her. Do you know her number?''

''I can get it for you.''

''Thanks.'' The waitress left, and when she brought Sandy the check, along with it came Brigitte's number on a separate piece of scrap paper.

Sandy followed the waitress's instructions. Pine. The street was aptly named. The tall conifers marched down both sides of the street, bringing an early twilight. The house was indeed tiny, and from the description, Sandy was sure it was the right one, although the yellow paint was sadly in need of a touch-up. The place was like a child in a crowd of adults, the only one-story house on the block. Two overgrown shrubs flanked the porch, which sat almost on the ground. There was no evidence that anyone was home;

Jerry's truck wasn't in front and there was nothing to indicate anybody was inside, but Sandy went to the door and knocked anyway, then jiggled the handle.

She dug down in her purse and pulled out her billfold, furtively glancing both ways to see if anyone was coming down the street. A video store membership card had just the right amount of flexibility for breaking and entering. She maneuvered it between the door and the frame, then worked it a few moments till she felt the lock give. Gathering her courage, she slipped quietly and quickly into the dim house. She closed the door behind her and flipped the light switch beside it.

The serenity of the pine trees outside belied what lay beyond the door: a scene more chaotic than her own apartment last week. Furniture had been upturned, books thrown out of a small bookshelf, then torn apart. Nothing was untouched.

She moved away from the door. To her right was a tiny bedroom. Sandy recognized the old dining room rug from her mother's house. At least she was in the right place. The dresser drawers had been emptied, then tossed aside like driftwood, the bed clothing torn off and left in a heap, the mattress slit open, its innards exposed.

Behind the living room was the kitchen and off of it the bathroom. The most striking difference between what had happened here and at her apartment was the destruction. Her things had not been destroyed—the canisters had been emptied but then carefully replaced. Not so, here.

Had the intruders caught up with Jerry here? The thought scared her, and she didn't want to face the possibility. If she knew her brother better, maybe she'd have been able to tell if he'd packed up some things and fled. But time had distanced them and she had no clues.

She went into the bathroom. A toothbrush was still

hanging in the little holder inside the medicine cabinet. Could it belong to someone other than Jerry? Maybe Brigitte, if she occasionally stayed over? The dirty dishes in the kitchen suggested he'd been gone for several days at the least. Bread crusts on a plate by the sink were crispy dry. Remnants of tomato sauce in a pan were turning black along the edges. The waste container smelled awful.

Sandy squatted down and looked through a scattering of papers on the floor. There was nothing there to help her, but from this lower vantage point she saw Jerry's 35mm camera under the table and behind an overturned chair. The back was open. She picked it up and studied it. It had been dropped and the back was permanently sprung.

It seemed like an important find. Jerry probably would not have willingly left on a trip without the camera. It had been a fixture around his neck when he'd visited Washington. But, then, maybe he had two cameras. A *professional* photographer might leave one behind. . . .

She pulled an address book from the mess, looked in it, and on a hunch turned to the W section, where her name should have been listed. The page had been torn out. The page that should have had her mother's name on it was gone, too. So when they didn't find what they were looking for here, they moved elsewhere.

She went into the bedroom and, kneeling, looked through the debris, sifting through the photos scattered across the floor. As she started to get up, she noticed the corner of something sticking out from under the rug, as if it had slid under. She dragged it out with the tip of her finger and held it up.

Oh, Lord. Maybe this was what it was all about. It was a black and white photo of—she looked at the face—yes, it was Brigitte. But her face wasn't the focal point of the photo. She was lying naked on a quilt in the woods, fully exposed to God, the sky, and the cameraman—Jerry, no doubt.

Sandy had to admit it was moderately arty. The sunlight laid a sheen on the girl's skin, and the shadows made interesting patterns on the forest floor as well as Brigitte's voluptuous body. It was the girl's ripeness, the look on her face, that made it more, or less, than art.

Sandy put her hand up to her head. Maybe Brigitte's father had gotten wind of this and just maybe he didn't appreciate *art*.

There hadn't been any other pictures like this among the photos on the floor. Had someone taken them? The way this one was almost hidden under the rug suggested that perhaps it had slid under there and had been overlooked. But she was certain that this wasn't the only photo taken that day. A professional photographer took many photos in search of the perfect one. And by the seductive look on the girl's face, Brigitte had been more than willing to pose for more.

Sandy thought back to Jerry's note. What had it said? Something about being onto something big? Or was it *into*, meaning "art" photography for fun and profit. Had the pictures gotten raunchier? Was Jerry into porn?

If whoever had broken in here took most of the photos, if they took film from the camera, apparently they still weren't satisfied, because they then broke into Sandy's apartment and her mother's house. That seemed to indicate they hadn't found what they were looking for. Maybe negatives? Or perhaps they hadn't found film in the camera. Maybe it was missing. The roll that had been sent to Sandy.

Sandy shook her head. It was hard to fathom. But then, she didn't have all the pieces of the puzzle.

She'd done all she could do here, short of cleaning up, and that wasn't on her agenda, so she locked the front door behind her, glanced down the street to make sure no one was coming, then went to her car.

Heading toward the main street again, she passed the gravel alley behind the taxidermy shop. A crazy thought occurred to her, but she pushed it to the back of her mind, only to have it pop up again.

Surely it was the frustration of not knowing what to do next. She wanted to make some kind of progress, find out something. It was coloring her normally good judgment.

She made a right turn and passed Skaar's, the thought still poking at her. The shop was very dark. She turned down the next side street, approaching the alley from the other end, turning into it. Unlike D.C., there was little uniformity at the back of the buildings. Some extended right to the alley, while others had extra room for parking behind. A car was parked behind one building and lights shone through the second-floor windows. Someone must live above that shop, she thought.

Its log-cabin construction made Skaar's easy to pick out from the back. She kept driving slowly, keeping a sharp eye on the taxidermy shop as she approached. The door looked ordinary. No padlocks or anything like that. A piece of cake. She drove on by, smiling.

You can't do this, she thought. She was foolish to even try. But an excitement was brewing inside her.

Why couldn't she do it? She'd broken into Jerry's place. What was one more break-in? She needed information that might be inside the shop and she'd be in and out in no time with no one the wiser.

She parked on a side street, two blocks away, then came sneaking back, or so she hoped. It was as if the night had eyes and they were all watching her.

The flicker of a television reflected off a wall in the apartment behind the one building. She slunk along the deep shadows there, especially cautious, and no sooner had she gotten past, than headlights turned into the alley. It was a truck and as it pulled up next to the car behind the apartment, she darted behind a trash dumpster, hoping the driver hadn't noticed her. It was too close for comfort for an amateur second-story person and her heart was threatening to jump out of her chest.

The truck looked familiar, and she realized why when the driver got out. Niles. He trotted up the stairs, gave a quick rap on the door, then went in.

There was perspiration along her forehead and it wasn't because she was hot. In fact the evening was chilly. What if she was caught lurking around behind the stores? It didn't bear thinking on.

She stood there a moment, making sure everything was quiet, then started down the alley again, hugging the wall of the two-story building she was behind. The gravel crunched beneath her feet no matter how quiet she tried to be.

At last she was there, behind the taxidermy shop, reminding herself that there was still time to back out.

She glanced both ways to make sure no one was coming as she sidled up to the back door. She was going to go through with it; she'd had enough waiting around and wondering.

Her purse was locked in the car. In her pocket she carried only her keys and the utilitarian video store card. How utilitarian she had yet to find out. If there was a deadbolt, her "passkey" wouldn't work.

She eased the card in, her heart pounding in her throat, and began to work it, hoping this small shop didn't have a burglar alarm. She doubted it would. Crime was still considered a big-city phenomenon in the Midwest.

To her satisfaction, the lock gave, and she pushed the door open. Immediately, the muscles in her throat constricted at the stench that assaulted her. Her eyes began watering before she could catch her breath.

She muttered an expletive which seemed appropriate for the smell and covered her nose. She was breathing through her mouth now, but felt reluctant even then to breathe the fetid air. It was surely noxious. She kept one hand over her lips as if to filter the odor.

She had no idea that taxidermy shops smelled so bad. All those dead animals. Maybe the taxidermist had skinned one and forgotten to throw away the garbage before he went on his fishing trip. He would be really sorry. She'd always thought people probably just brought in the skins, but what did she know about it? However, if this was customary, how did anyone stand to work here?

It was almost pitch-black inside the store, but the door to the front area was open and a little light bled in from the street lights. She went toward it and came out in the front part of the building. It was like being in a graveyard, only in this place the corpses were exposed. Deer, fish, the moose she'd seen from outside, an alert-looking raccoon, other furry creatures—their eyes followed her as she moved quietly around the room, exploring. Birds with their wings outstretched hovered overhead. Several wildlife paintings on velvet hung amid the mounted fish and fish heads. It was awful, a Felliniesque nightmare.

Behind the counter there was an old rolltop desk with an equally ancient chair. Sandy sat down. The springs were loose, and she almost went over backwards. She grabbed the front of the desk and steadied herself. Sitting in this chair was an art.

The desktop was strewn with papers, as were all the cubbyholes, but it was much too dark to read anything. There was a gooseneck desk lamp at one side. Could she risk it? She glanced around, then got up and went to the front window and looked both ways. There were no signs of anyone. Not even any parked cars at this end of the block.

She returned to the desk, cautiously sat down again, pulled the lamp chain, and began to scour the desk, opening drawers, examining papers, invoices, orders. A fascinating picture of the business, but nothing that shed any light on Jerry. Just when she was about to give up, she opened a checkbook and fanned through the stubs.

Bingo! Jerry's name jumped out at her. It was on a check stub. Beneath it were dates showing a pay period. Jerry must have been working for the taxidermist. She paused for a moment and glanced at the front window as a car passed outside, then turned her attention back to the checkbook.

Jerry needed an income and she doubted that his free-lance photography was enough—although she might amend that thought, having seen the picture of Brigitte. The photo aside, though, taxidermy probably offered an outlet for Jerry's creativity that would appeal to him and provide a regular income. She went through the stubs more carefully and found other checks drawn to him.

She had just flipped the book shut, when the front door rattled. It couldn't be the wind. There was no wind. And no cars had passed in the last few moments. Someone was shaking the door.

Fortunately her position behind the counter sheltered her from a direct view from the door. Her fear galvanized her and she dived beneath the desk. Still, there was the lamp. Its glow bathed the corner of the room, but to turn it off would have drawn attention.

There were no more sounds, so after a few moments Sandy rose a bit and peeked over the counter. A police car was parked across the street. Were they just doing their rounds, checking doors?

She pulled the lamp chain and staying crouched over, ran

through the door to the back room, adrenaline pumping. The blackness swallowed her, and she tripped over something in the middle of the floor. It toppled over as she hit it. She fumbled with the furry object in the dark to get it upright, then started to get up herself, but came up under the edge of a table. For a moment she saw stars and drew a breath in through her nose. The smell gagged her, made her dizzy.

She was in a chamber of horrors, surrounded by all these dead creatures. Watchers in the dark. She crouched down and tried to get control of herself again, rubbing her head.

"I've got to get out of here," she mumbled, startled at the sound of her own voice in the dead silence of the room.

She turned and started to crawl a few feet to make sure she didn't hit the table again, when her hand came into contact with something solid. She groped to identify it, then drew back as if she had touched a hot ember. It was a leather shoe and it had resistance; she could tell from the way it had moved when she let go, which meant it was attached to something. A body. Her faintness increased and she caught her breath, forgetting about the smell.

It washed over her and she gagged again, grabbing at her nose and mouth, protecting them from the vile air. She'd never encountered decaying human flesh before, but she knew it was here with her in this room, by the smell, by the feel. Someone was lying there beside her in the dark.

12

SANDY's first inclination was to escape, to run to her car and its security. Blindly she rose and backed away from the corpse that was almost certainly there. Sharp points stabbed her in the back. She jerked away, turned, and flailed her arms out protectively, striking a set of antlers and knocking them to the floor with a crash.

She tried to calm herself. Orienting herself by the light from the front of the shop, she staggered in a half-crouch toward the back door, one hand out like a feeler before her. Her breath was coming out in frightened gasps; her stomach was churning.

But before she'd made it to the door she stopped and turned back with resignation. She couldn't leave, not until she knew who was back there, lying on the floor.

Breathing through her mouth again, disassociating herself from the horror, she groped toward the front of the shop and looked out the window and surveyed the street in both directions. The police car was gone now and once again there was no activity.

The door between the two areas of the shop was propped open with a large rock. She nudged it with her shoe and the door closed. The darkness in back seemed complete now. She was alone with the corpse and the fetid odor. Its rankness seemed to permeate every pore in her skin. She fumbled for a light switch, and at first couldn't find one, then groped farther and found it and flipped it with trembling fingers. The lights blinded her for a moment. She squinted, shielding her eyes, waiting for them to adjust, knowing they would never adjust to what was beside the table.

She slowly moved around the worktable, scattered with cans and bottles, and edged toward the shoe she could now see. Then the leg, the torso. The corpse was grotesquely bloated, the tongue protruding.

Sandy gasped at the grisly sight, then staggered against the table and clutched it to keep from falling. Her stomach churned and acid came up in her throat. She retched, choked the feeling back, retched again. It came over her in waves. Tears dimmed her vision as she tried to suppress her nausea by leaning on the table.

Mingled with her horror was a sense of relief. Even in the brief glimpses she'd given the corpse, she could see it wasn't her brother. In its deteriorating condition it would be hard to identify, but it was an old man. The hair was gray. The clothes weren't the sort Jerry would be caught dead in. She grimaced at the insensitivity of her thought.

The man was probably the taxidermist, but she wasn't going to check his pockets for identification. This was close enough to the body for her. She continued to lean on the table, weighing her options, wondering if she should call the police, then vetoing the idea.

I've broken in here. How can I explain that? She remembered Jerry's words in the letter. Don't tell anyone about the film or it would be "over" for him. Somehow his warning was all wrapped up with this shop, with this atrocity.

If she phoned the police, they would start looking for whoever made the call. The man from the café could certainly identify her. Would he tell the police about her interest in the shop? And was he somehow involved in this murder? If so, was she in danger from him when it came out that the body had been found?

She tried to mentally regroup, to think logically. For instance, why did she assume he'd been murdered? Maybe it was a heart attack.

Oh, sure, you could get so lucky, she thought. Try as she might, she couldn't buy "heart attack." Jerry's warning, the break-ins, her sneaking around, finding a body; it was all too extraordinary for it not to be topped off with murder, even though she'd seen no evidence of a weapon. Well, she wasn't going to look again; she couldn't take another glimpse of the corpse. Just thinking about it brought a new wave of nausea and a brace of tears.

Don't stand here; move. Get your mind occupied.

She knew what she had to do. She began retracing her steps since she'd come into the shop and wiped down everything she could have possibly touched, using the hem of her shirt.

The shoe. She had touched it when she lost her bearings. Steeling herself, she approached the corpse, blurring her eyes, keeping them low. She knelt down and rubbed her shirt against the shoe, her whole body cringing from the task. The bloat made the leg rigid, filling the pants leg as if it were inflated, pressing against the seam as if it would explode. She rubbed the damning shoe again, holding on with one shirttail while she rubbed with the other.

My Lord! she thought. Fingerprints on a dead man's shoe. It seemed impossible to rub away the evidence that she'd been here and touched the cadaver. She felt like Lady Macbeth washing her hands. It seemed impossible that she would ever get this out of her mind.

When she was satisfied with her efforts, she turned off the lights before reopening the door to the front room. She fumbled around in the semidarkness, trying to remember what she might have touched in front. Because of her job, her fingerprints were on file, and she could easily be traced if the police did a computer check through a crime lab. It was essential that she be careful.

When she was finished, she left the door to the street open, using her shirt on the knob like a potholder. If the police made another round, they would notice and investigate. If not, passersby would notice the stench in the morning.

She carefully negotiated the back room, not in as big a hurry this time and with a better idea of where things were, and went out the back door.

She drank in big gulps of the fresh night air as she jogged down the alley. The rental car was a welcome sight. She unlocked it almost lovingly, climbed in, and collapsed against the wheel. Her hand shook as she stabbed at the ignition with the key.

Get a grip on yourself! she ordered, holding the steering wheel a moment with both hands. *Get away from here.* She tried again and got the key in. The engine turned over and she pulled away slowly from the curb, hoping no one had noticed her. She didn't want to attract any attention.

Her knees trembled, and her breath came out in short gasps. She felt as if she were about to have a nervous breakdown. Driving the car seemed alien, as if her movements were divorced from her control. At the edge of town, she pulled under the bright lights of the convenience store and sat there a moment, unbelieving. Surely she had imagined what had just transpired. Legislative correspondents didn't find dead bodies in taxidermy shops hundreds of miles from home. It was unbelievable that she was even in Northlake. She looked outside the little world of the car and felt for a moment as if she were waking from a dream.

But the noxious smell which lingered on her clothing told her the truth of it.

13

SHE took a shower when she arrived home and threw the clothes she'd been wearing in the washer. Anything to wash off the odor of overripe death. She tried to brush her teeth, but the feel of the toothpaste in her mouth made her gag as her brain kept replaying the scene in the back of the taxidermy shop. The sight of the corpse kept returning so vividly, even when she tried to divert her thoughts, that she began to think her own mind was her worst enemy.

Several times during the night she awakened, and each time she would be disoriented for a moment in the blackness. Then memory would come back with a one-picture image of the corpse. She would toss and turn and try to blot out the scene before finally giving in to sleep again.

As morning stole closer, dreams began to riddle her slumber. Her father was in one of them. He was sitting down, plucking the feathers off of a bird, one at a time, pulling very deliberately, then holding the feathers up and admiring them before gluing them onto his arms till they were completely covered. Then he stood up. The dream was hard to reconstruct when she awoke, but there was a sense of having been on his lap, even though she hadn't been there in the prior image, and when he rose, she slid off and he began to flap his wings. Then he was on the roof while down below, her mother, oblivious to them, was telling Jerry that little boys can't fly. Jerry was running around in a Superman suit, arms extended, cape flapping. Overhead, Forrest suddenly rose and Sandy watched in awe as he circled. Then the dream changed to another scene, one her father didn't figure in.

When she finally struggled out of bed mid-morning, dark circles lay beneath her eyes, testament to a rough night and a dark mood. Even makeup couldn't conceal them. She rejected the idea of breakfast. Her stomach still felt as if it had turned over. A local newspaper seemed more important, so as soon as she dressed and put her clothes from yesterday in the dryer, she headed for town.

The *Northlake News* she picked up from a vending machine in front of a motel was almost a week old, so there was nothing *new* about it. She would have to wait till the following day to find out if the body had been found.

Actually, it didn't take that long. As she drove down the main street, she saw two police cars and a state patrol car in front of the taxidermist's. A small crowd was hovering around the front of the shop. The open door had worked like a charm. She drove by, but not too slowly—she didn't want to appear too interested. Was that the gravel-voiced man in the crowd? She couldn't tell for sure. She swung around the block and headed back for the Senator's, too uptight to do anything constructive. Her nerves felt shot.

Please, please, let me have removed all traces of my visit. She couldn't imagine all the repercussions if she was connected with the place. Why had she pulled such a dumb stunt by going in there in the first place?

She felt a strong need for human contact. She didn't want to call her mother; that was out. She finally dialed her office number and heard Angel's voice on the other end of the line.

"This is Sandy, is—?"

Angel interrupted. "Well, where are you, Sandy? Are you sick?"

"No, I'm in Minnesota." Angel started to interrupt again, but Sandy kept talking. "Is Troy there?" Even saying his name aloud gave her a safe feeling. *Please, please be there.*

"Sor-ry. He's out of town."

"Is the Senator in?" She hated to bother him, but she felt desperate.

"You're striking out, but he should be in late this afternoon. May I take a message?"

"No, that's okay." After she hung up she paced into the living room, stopping at the window to look out. It was a beautiful day. Maybe just getting out into it would untie the knots she was in.

She took her clothes from the dryer and layered them as she had yesterday for the hike—which seemed about a million years in the past now—blouse, red sweatshirt, and cardigan, then struck out along the lake shore headed in the direction of Niles's cabin, not fully admitting that she hoped she'd run into him.

The water lapping on the shoreline, the light breeze rustling the tops of the pines, the sunshine, all were therapeutic and she felt her mood lifting. She paused and looked out over the water. The wind riffled it, making intricate patterns on its surface. The corpse wasn't Jerry. For that she was grateful. Her efforts at an optimistic outlook reminded her of Angel. She realized how far away Angel had seemed, how isolated she was from her normal life. It would have been good to talk to Troy. He was so practical. He would have admired the way she'd wiped down everything she'd touched, she thought with a smile as she bent over and picked up a long slender stick and began making patterns in the soft, sandy soil as she walked.

The shoreline narrowed and disappeared, undercut by the water, and the trees encroached right to the edge of the lake. She dropped her stick and turned into the woods, noting the position of the sun behind her. It wouldn't do to get lost.

Forty-five minutes later, when she was beginning to think she *was* lost, the cabin came into sight. It shouldn't have taken this long, but at least she'd found it. The truck was there, also an old cream-colored station wagon.

Damn! He had company. And by now she was really counting on a drink of water. She started to turn away, but it was too late. Clyde, inside the cabin, was raising the alarm.

Sandy expected the door to open, but it didn't and Clyde continued his concert. Apparently no one was there after all.

She tried the door. It was unlocked. She didn't want breaking and entering to become a habit, but she didn't think Niles would mind if she got a drink. Clyde was going crazy and she began talking to him, hoping he wasn't secretly trained as an attack dog. If he was, he was well disguised in his sausagelike body. She pushed the door open and Clyde's barking turned to slavishness as he sniffed at her feet with his tail down between his legs.

"I'm just getting a drink," she told him. Even talking to Clyde was better than no one. She went into the kitchen. The dog followed and hovered over his food dish in one corner as if to protect the contents from her. She drank her fill, then with a few more words to Clyde, left.

It hadn't been a wasted trip, even if she now admitted her disappointment at not finding Niles at home. The walk had helped her mood and she decided to explore some more.

She followed a path that struck out north of the cabin. Clyde's barking had stopped behind her, or at least she had moved out of range. Even the fussing of a nearby bird couldn't disturb the peacefulness of the forest. It was like being in a cathedral, the pine tree spires pointing heavenward, and she was filled with a sense of reverence.

The path forked as it started downhill, and while she stopped to rest, she made a mental note of landmarks so she wouldn't get lost. The upper path continued through the pines; the lower one went down into a valley of aspens and birches. She chose the latter.

Sunlight filtered through the canopy of yellow foliage, making an ethereal world beneath them. Leaves drifted silently down to add another layer to the earth's blanket against winter's cold. This was the perfect antidote to the cares of the world. Even the air out here smelled pure, the scent of the earth underfoot, pine and balsam in the breeze.

She took off her cardigan and tied it around her waist, then continued through the woods. In an open area, she stooped to examine a determined white flower, a late bloomer, poking its head up amid the dried grasses. As she rose, she heard a heart-rending cry. Something was in distress.

Without thinking, she ran.

Suddenly a bulky shape charged across her path. A bear! Fright paralyzed her. Fortunately the bear wasn't zeroing in on her, but on the call of distress that still sounded intermittently through the woods. Close behind the bear came a cub, both of them crashing through the underbrush till they were just dark shapes moving among the trees. They disappeared from sight, and Sandy caught her breath, her heart pounding.

Her reflexes were working again and she turned to leave as quickly as possible. So much for the peacefulness of the forest. She felt very defenseless. If she were lucky, she could get home without any other encounters with wild animals. Once was enough, even if it was only a close call.

Suddenly, a gunshot split the air, followed by a mournful cry.

Sandy ducked behind some bushes for cover and waited, heart pounding. First animals, now guns, although bullets flying haphazardly through the woods were far more dangerous than a bear. She cocked her head and listened. Where before there had been no human sound, now there was human babble.

She started to call out and announce her presence to keep them from shooting again, but had second thoughts. A woman alone in the woods. A group of men from the sound of the voices, maybe drinking. Better to keep quiet.

She wondered about the first call of distress she'd heard. Had the men wounded an animal and its cry had attracted the bear? She knew that one animal sometimes attacked another when it was down. Is that what had happened? The cry had certainly attracted her.

Another shrill cry pierced the air. She frowned and moved ahead stealthily, following the sounds of the voices till she saw movements through the trees. A group of six men were just ahead, dressed in camouflage, and now she could hear them more plainly. Three of them were bending over the bulk of the bear's body, speculating about her weight.

"Finish it off, Maris. You and your goddamn bow hunting," one said over his shoulder toward another cluster of three men farther away. "You can't leave it like that, squealing in pain."

She ducked lower to see what they were looking at. Beyond them, the cub clung to a pine trunk fifteen or twenty feet above the ground. An arrow stuck out of its shoulder. The cub tried to climb, faltered and slid back. Again it wailed. A youngster crying for relief. *A tree bear.*

Tears blurred Sandy's eyes and she felt weak with anguish. She covered her mouth to keep from crying out.

One of the men lifted a bow, pulled back on the string and let go. The second arrow struck the cub in the nose, driving the frantic animal upward a few feet, where it wailed again, knocking against the arrow as it shook its head trying to dislodge it.

"Shit! Can't you do better than that?" someone asked.

One of the men at the bear carcass looked over, then picked up his rifle, and walked over beside the man with the bow. The archer made a futile attempt to stop him from shooting, but he sighted and pulled the trigger. The cub crumpled and fell from the tree as the blast hit it.

"It was mine, shitass," the bow hunter said, glaring at the man with the rifle. The two other men hurried over to the cub, now at the base of the tree. One pulled his knife and plunged it into the body, extracted it and repeated the gesture, letting out a bloodthirsty cry each time.

"Learn to shoot," the man with the gun said as he turned and walked back to the mother bear's carcass. Sandy's heart sank. It was Niles. He'd said he killed to survive, that hunting and trapping were his livelihood. Then what was this? This butchery had nothing to do with survival.

She sat back on her heels and closed her eyes, clamping her teeth together, making fists of her hands. If she had a gun, she would shoot them all!

The hunters were all talking at once now, energized by the kill. "Boy, I thought she had me, the way she came running in here," Sandy heard one say, his voice at fever pitch above the others.

Their excitement seemed to be growing. She hunkered forward and chanced another look from behind her cover. The three men were still struggling with the mother bear; two of the others had the cub's lifeless body and were dragging it nearer. Over his anger now, the bow hunter wasn't occupied except with moving to music only he heard. He stomped his feet and gyrated in circles.

"Let's hurry this up," one of the kneeling men said, "before the game warden stumbles onto us."

"He comes out here I'll blow his balls off." It was the man from Hurd's; Sandy recognized his gravelly voice. "I'd just like an excuse. That son of a bitch was by my place last night, snoopin' around."

"You're a regular Claude Dallas," Niles said, referring to an Idaho poacher who had killed two conservation officers, then had become a legend when he evaded capture for months.

Gravel Voice snorted. "Claude Dallas had balls. Those wardens were askin' for it. Jimbo, open 'er up there."

The others came over and they all stood or knelt and watched. Sandy was glad their bodies masked her view of what was happening. Her imagination made it graphic enough and she bit her lip at the thought of what was going on.

"You got the hands of a surgeon," one of them remarked.

Someone let out a banshee cry. It must have been the bow hunter, because he leaped up from the squatting position he'd taken, his hand in the air. It glistened red with the blood of the bear. He wiped two streaks of it down his cheeks, then began to whirl and hop around wildly, hooting like a crazy person.

Several of the others cursed at him. One man laughed.

Sandy crawled closer, crouching behind some low brush to watch the sickening spectacle. Another of the men stood up and started hopping around, licking blood from his hand, and cackling. "Hmmm. Turns me on."

"Shit, let me get it—" Gravel Voice grunted, on his

haunches. "—there it comes." He held up a mass of tissue the size of a tennis ball in one bloody hand. "Here, Maris. Quit that damn crazy dancing, you fag bastard, and take this. Put it in a bag. Then get to work on that cub."

Maris took offense and shoved Gravel Voice off balance. "Don't call me that, you shitass. Don't ever call me that." The other dancer, who had blood around his mouth, stood behind Maris in a belligerent posture.

The man from the café stood up and grabbed Maris' shirt with his free hand. Two of the others stood up, as if anticipating trouble, and Maris seemed to wilt. The man behind him backed off.

"I oughta shove this down your throat," Gravel Voice said, holding the bloody mass near Maris' mouth. "Give you some balls."

"Lay off, Hurd," one of the men said.

Hurd. So Sandy had been right; Gravel Voice was Hurd.

"Stay out of this, Anderson," Hurd said, but he dropped Maris' shirt. "It's none of your concern."

"Maybe we could all eat us a little sample of this gall bladder," Jimbo said from his position by the carcass. "I hear it's an aphrodisiac"

"You can have my share," Niles said. He'd stood up when the fracas began. Now he dropped down beside Jimbo.

Maris took the small pouch, and Hurd turned back toward the bear again, saying, "You don't need nothing to make you horny, right, Benson? You've probably got a hard-on for that ripe little piece of ass over at the Senator's. Get that paw off, will you?"

The man with the bloody mouth reached out for the gall bladder Maris was holding. "I'll take a little piece of it. My old lady sure don't turn me on no more."

Maris sidestepped away, beginning to whistle and dance, holding the gall bladder in the air.

"God, you two are disgusting," the one called Anderson said. He wore a camouflage rain hat pulled low over his face.

"Don't even think of putting your flabby lips on that," Hurd growled. "It'll bring a couple of hundred bucks. Maris, would you do something useful?"

"Man, I'm just appeasing the gods for killing a bear."

"You didn't kill a bear, you tortured it," Niles said.

"Hey, I'm gettin' better. I hit it, didn't I?"

"Yeah, you hit it, Maris, you hit it," Jimbo said. "Just barely."

Hurd was grumbling. "A guy has a little Indian blood and he thinks he knows how to talk to the gods. What are you, Maris? About a thousandth part Chippewa?"

"An eighth."

"Well, they wouldn't claim you. You don't know your ass from a hole in the ground."

"I think you're supposed to put the skull on a tree to show respect for the bear, not to appease the gods," Niles said.

Maris went over to a pack that was sitting on the ground and took a plastic bag from it, then moved so that Sandy's view of what he was doing was blocked.

"This is where I baited during the season," Hurd said.

"I thought you were further north," Jimbo said.

"I bait up there, too. I took this one ol' pussy in. Took a couple of hours and we're sitting there maybe an hour and it starts to rain. Damn miserable. About the time I'd like to quit and go get drunk, up comes this big cinnamon-colored bear. A boar. I mean that sucker musta weighed five hundred pounds."

Several of the men laughed at that.

"I mean it. It was huge! So this guy I've got with me gets all nervous. I thought he was gonna shit his pants and—you aren't gonna believe this—biggest damn bear I've seen in years and this guy tries to shoot with the safety on. He's shakin' and fumblin' and the bear sees him."

"Where were you all this time?" someone asked.

"Shit. I'm over here makin' like a movie producer. The asshole wants the whole thing videotaped even in the rain—so I'm tryin' to shield his lens and take pictures because this mother wants to show his family what a big brave guy he is, and I'm not even holding my damn gun."

Snorts of laughter again.

"So here I am, lookin' through this little viewfinder and I see the bear look right back at me. Man, I got rid of that camera fast and grabbed my gun. I squeezed off a shot and hit him, but the bear'd already turned tail from all the commotion. We trailed him a while, but this asshole gets tired and says he wants to quit. He's huffin' and puffin' so I think he's gonna have a heart attack on me. I went out the next day, but never did find the bear, so I figure he's still alive. Somewhere there's a big ol' boar carrying my slug."

"Here. Catch," one man said, tossing a bear paw to Maris.

"So what's the guy tell his family when he goes home without a bear?"

"He bought that dusty excuse for a bear Skaar had in his window for so long," Hurd said.

There was some appreciative laughter. Maris had joined them at the bear again. "They found him dead in his shop this morning."

"Skaar? No shit," Niles said. "What do you think happened to old Gus?"

"He'd been garroted."

"Jesus Christ," someone said.

"They have any notion who did it?" Niles asked. "That guy was so docile, it's hard to think of someone murdering him."

"Probably some jilted lover," Hurd said, his voice dripping with sarcasm.

Gus. His tone touched a memory, and she recalled what had been eluding her since she'd read the return address on the envelope Jerry had sent her. Skaar was Gus's name, her father's old friend. The bloated body in the taxidermy shop was her old friend who had swung her in circles in the back yard, letting her down gently on the newly cut grass.

"Shit, Hurd, you'd come nearer to being garroted by a former lover."

Everyone but Hurd laughed.

"You're a riot," Hurd said. "Remind me to laugh when I got the time."

"That wounded-rabbit call worked real good," Niles said.

Murmurs Sandy couldn't decipher.

"My cousin put me onto that. Damn sight better than a steel jaw out here that some hiker would stumble into," Hurd said. "God, this was a beautiful kill."

Another man with his back to Sandy held up a paw he had cut off the animal. He tossed it to Niles, who was now facing her way. "Here, Benson, now you got a mitten."

"You're a helluva guy for thinkin' of me," she heard Niles say as he held the paw up. Sandy could see his red-stained hands and the sight made her feel sick.

"When we goin' out again?" Maris asked. "I can use some Christmas money."

Hurd answered. "The bears are gonna be dennin' up soon. This cousin of mine's got some bear hounds. He lives down South, but I think I can get him to come up here 'cause him and his ol' lady have split the sheet. That way we can keep operating clear into winter.''

"You trust him?''

"Shit, he's been poachin' all his life. He took me out fish-dynamitin' when I was thirteen. You ever done that?'' There were murmurs from the others. "It was something to see. Easiest fishin' I ever done. There were fish floatin' everywhere. Here, Maris, bag this.'' He handed over the last paw as he stood up. "Now, who wants to play doctor on the cub so we can get back to town and do some serious drinking?''

They all laughed, but Sandy had seen enough. She couldn't handle watching them eviscerate the baby. She edged out of her cover and crawled a few yards back the way she'd come, then took off running, keeping her body in a crouch.

"Hey, someone's back there,'' she heard one of them say.

She put herself in gear, thinking, *Damn this red shirt*.

"Shit, there is.'' That was Hurd.

By now she was running, upright, staying under cover as much as possible. She could no longer hear them talking. Although she was trying to be quiet, her movements and her breathing were enough to mask any sounds they were making, so she had no idea if they were in pursuit.

She had made it to the fairyland of birch and aspen when a shot rang out.

My God! she thought. They're willing to shoot me over a gall bladder.

She plunged ahead, ducking under a low limb, struggling at the same time to undo the cardigan that hung around her waist. Her red sweatshirt needed camouflaging. Intent on getting the sweater on, she failed to see the exposed root in her path and she tripped, sprawling onto her face. Hurriedly she picked herself up and kept going; there wasn't time to even think she was hurt. She looked around frantically as she ran. Everything seemed so open; there were no dense stands of brush here to hide in. Another shot pierced the air. Did she imagine that it had swooshed by her? Or were they shooting in the air to scare her? She had to get beyond this area. Her legs pumped faster.

Up ahead, if she was going in the right direction, there was an area where huge boulders lay tossed like pebbles. If she could only reach them. Her lungs burned from the unaccustomed exertion; she could feel her pulse throbbing in her head. Still she pushed on, hoping to find the welcome shelter of the rocks.

At last, she saw the first of them. Relief welled in her, bringing tears to her eyes. It was like being welcomed by a friend. She scrambled up and across the first tier and dropped into a channel formed by their bulk, working her way farther in among them, keeping her body hunched down. Her feet wedged into the vee at the bottom where they came together and the going was difficult. The slot between the rocks narrowed as she went along until she finally came to an impasse. Nervously she edged up the smooth side of the boulder that blocked her way, scampered across its top on all fours, keeping as low as she could, and dropped down on the far side. Her ankle twisted as it slid into the space between the rocks and she grimaced at the pain. After a moment it subsided and she scrambled on.

She could hear water now and surmised that the boulders followed a stream that tumbled from one lake to another. Maybe she could cross it. She cut over toward the sound.

The waterway was as rocky as the shore, but there was no way she could cross it, at least not here. This was more treacherous than the stream she and Niles had crossed the day before. One misstep and she would end up in the swift river. Even if she didn't get dashed to death on the rocks, the cold water would freeze her into immobility at this time of the year.

Glancing behind her, making sure there weren't any pursuers in sight, she picked her way upstream a short distance, then headed back into the woods where the forest was more dense.

Fear and fatigue were taking their toll, the first charge of adrenaline having dissipated. A dense stand of alders invited her in and she crawled under them and collapsed on the ground, face down, and tried to quiet her breathing.

She lay there for quite a while, pondering her options. The enemy was out there and she might walk right into them if she left this hiding place, so it seemed best to stay put until dark.

A faint sound made her look up. A pair of legs clad in camouflage showed through the alders.

She closed her eyes and held her breath. Had she gone in a circle that they found her so easily? Her body relaxed against the ground in hopelessness as she exhaled. Thank God she'd covered the red shirt!

"See anyone over there, Benson?" someone shouted.

"No. Nothing over here," he answered. She heard his footsteps moving away.

It was at least an hour before she had the courage to crawl out from under the alders. Struggling swiftly to her feet and looking back at her hiding place, she wondered how she'd evaded capture. Niles had strong powers of observation, of reading woods. She'd even seen evidence of them the day before on their hike. So how had he missed her? She was grateful, whether it was intentional or if he was just careless.

The sun had dropped below the trees, but she could still see its aura. She decided she should head east to run into the road.

The woods were getting cold and she began walking.

After dark, the road would be a safer bet for finding her way back to the Senator's than a path through the forest.

She was relieved when she stumbled out onto the road half an hour later. She no longer felt lost. Roads meant civilization. She'd been on it for thirty or forty minutes—maybe she'd gone a mile because she was footsore and weary—before she realized it was more primitive than the one that went by the Senator's place.

She stopped and looked around, clutching her sweater closer. Could she be going in the wrong direction? It was a frightening thought.

She'd always been well-oriented, and knowing where the sun had gone down had given her an initial idea of where she was, but now it was dark. She glanced up in the direction she thought was north, hoping to see the North Star. She knew it would be bright and in one of the dippers. The trees kept her from seeing the stars in that direction. She moved across the road. There it was, sentinel and guide for centuries, shining clearly. Old friend. And there were the four hunters of the Great Bear, turning October red with blood.

A cold finger of fear ran along her spine, radiating out along her arms. She shuddered and started walking. If the road from the highway went straight north, it must still be to her east. The trouble was that all these roads twisted and turned. Maybe the road bent to the east somewhere south of here.

She felt safe, however, as long as she kept going south.

She kept a determined if not fast pace. From the forest, which flanked the road, she heard strange sounds from time to time, ones she couldn't identify, but for the most part the only noise was the soft pad of her feet on the road.

The light changed. To the east, a gossamer curtain folded into a rosy-colored ruffle. Streaks like searchlights shimmered upward from the northern horizon and she remembered, not the words, but the essence of a poem she'd read in high school: that when a Chippewa Indian warrior died, he and his ghostly friends danced on the northern horizon, and the colors were their headdresses. Those ghost warriors, Sandy thought, were surely stirred up by the barbarity they'd witnessed in the forest today.

She'd lived in Minnesota most of her life, but she'd never seen the aurora borealis like this. Sometimes there'd been color shows, but this was spectacular, like a soundless Fourth of July.

The lights danced, changing to a greenish tinge, then yellowing, dancing across the sky, becoming a restless butterfly, rising with a drift of a breeze.

The grandeur of the display made her feel inconsequential. She shuddered and averted her gaze, feeling as if she were witnessing something secret and beyond her ken, and she began walking again, glancing only occasionally to see what strange shapes had formed in the cosmic light show.

The pumpkin moon floated up over the eastern horizon, its light dissipating the effect of the aurora as Sandy went over a rise and came to another road. This was gravel like the one that passed the Senator's. From far away headlights were coming toward her. She darted into the tamaracks that lined the road and dived for cover. This might be one of her pursuers.

The truck drove by slowly, and she could see the driver's face in the light from the dash as he went by, scanning the trees as he passed. It was Niles. There was no chance of his seeing her; she was deep in the shadows. He was alone, and she toyed with the idea of running out and catching a ride to the Senator's. If he'd seen her hiding in the woods earlier, the fact that he hadn't given her away to the others meant she would be safe with him now. But it was also possible that he'd just been unobservant and that he, like the others, was worried about the threat she posed to their poaching. So she didn't run out.

Niles was headed south. Was he just returning from where the hunters had rendezvoused? Were the others going to come along in a moment? But then she remembered his truck was at his house earlier when she'd stopped there. So he'd been home, then driven north—searching for her?— and now was returning.

She returned to the road and padded softly along, wrapping her sweater more tightly around her against the cold. She could understand subsistence hunting, even poaching perhaps. Someone killing for what he and his family needed for food. But hunters who spent hundreds of dollars to go on hunting trips, then tried to say they did it for the food—she thought it was a travesty. It was a blood sport. Justifications came after the fact.

The hunters she'd seen today weren't even taking the whole bear, just an organ and the paws. It didn't even rise to the level of blood sport; it was senseless depravity.

And Niles Benson was one of them. She had to face that, no matter how physically attracted she was to him. The only positive thing to hold onto was that he had put the badly wounded baby bear out of its misery. His act seemed to show some spark of decency.

14

I<small>T</small> was almost ten P.M. before Sandy saw the howling wolf sign marking the Senator's lane. By that time the cold had insinuated itself deeply into her body and she had begun shivering uncontrollably. Her fingers groped numbly for the key in her pocket, and she unlocked the door.

She felt as if she'd stepped into the tropics. The warmth of the house prickled her skin, but it didn't stop her shuddering.

She went to the kitchen and got a glass of water and drank it slowly, leaning on the counter. What was she doing here, why she was putting herself through this game of cat and mouse with her brother, who had given her nothing but trouble since he was a child?

She slogged into the bedroom, tired and depressed, removed her contacts, stripped off her clothes, and climbed under the blankets. She'd just barely drifted off when the phone rang. The sound became part of a dream and it took several rings before she realized it was real and pulled herself awake. She shook off her fogginess, then rolled over and shoved one arm out from under the covers.

It was Niles. The memory of the dead bear and the men

working over it popped into her consciousness when he said his name.

"I just wanted to see if everything's okay over there."

"Sure," she answered. "What could be wrong?" Her voice lacked warmth as she pictured the men hovering around the dead bear. Could that have really happened?

"I called earlier and you weren't home."

And you knew where I was, she thought. "Well, I'm here now. But thanks for your concern."

There was a long, uncomfortable pause and after a few more perfunctory comments, Niles ended the call.

It was raining the next morning. A gusty wind whipped the lake into choppy waves. Sandy blew on her instant coffee as she looked outside, thinking that the day fit her mood perfectly.

She put on a pair of jeans and a blue chambray blouse, then slipped the red sweatshirt over her head. She was getting tired of it, but she had packed so few warm things. She planned to remedy that situation today.

Before she left the house, she phoned her mother. Pauline's first question was whether or not Sandy had found Jerry.

"No, Mom. I've been occupied with business for the Senator." Just a flat lie now, no half-truths. She couldn't tell her mother Jerry wasn't to be found.

"Sandy, are you going to try to locate—your father?"

It was a question Sandy had avoided asking herself. Knowing his last known address was Northlake, did she want to look for him? How long had it been since he'd been here? Could he have been one of the crowd standing outside the taxidermy shop the day before? The thought had occurred to her.

Sandy was ten years old when her father had left, and ready to believe his defection was her fault. Since then, her adult mind had tried to redirect the blame. She knew marriages didn't work out. Look at her own.

But reason was about as good for guilt as regret was for a hangover. The doubts would always dwell in some little-girl place inside her. Somehow she hadn't been good enough to keep her daddy at home—that's how it felt.

The revelation that her father was gay didn't change anything. The weakness in his character had nothing to do with sexual preferences. Her mother had admitted forbidding Forrest to see them, but what sort of person would *accept* that? To leave behind his children and never have any more contact? Could they—*could she* was more to the point; after all he hadn't ever known Jerry—could she have meant so little to him?

"I don't know yet, Mom." She quickly changed the subject and promised she'd call her mother as soon as she tracked down Jerry.

If and when, she thought, *if and when*. She gave her mother the phone number for the Senator's house. It didn't reveal where she was. Duluth had the same area code.

She hung up and made another cup of coffee. The waitress was on her agenda today. Sandy felt sure Brigitte knew something about Jerry.

Fifteen minutes later, she pulled on her cardigan and made a dash to the car. It was locked, a city habit, and she stood there getting soaked while she opened the door.

A water-repellent coat would be nice, she thought, as the windshield wipers struggled to keep up with the deluge.

There was a trading post on the corner across from the café. Its sign read YOUR COMPLETE OUTFITTER. Sandy understood that the words often meant a canoe and provisions for a wilderness trip, but this window had mannequins wearing a wide assortment of attractive winter clothing.

She looked around for a policeman, and seeing none,

made an illegal U-turn and parked in front of the store. Two tries. She made a run for the covered porch, shielding her head with her hands, but not avoiding a drip off the roof that went down her neck. After her adventure last night, she was going to buy a warm coat in an unobtrusive color—and it would be water-repellent, too.

The store had a nice outdoorsy flavor. Pine floors, log cabin interior, both glossy with varnish, beamed ceiling, hunting trophies, posters of wolves and loons and mist-covered lakes, camping supplies on one side of an aisle, outdoor wear crowded on round racks on the other. Mukluks, paddles, packs, lots of wools. Seeing such an abundance of stuff for roughing it in the Northwoods made her almost want to try it again. She could live without the telephone and a curling iron now.

A woman popped up from behind the counter. "May I help you?" she asked.

"No, thanks," Sandy said. "I just wanted to look." She hated to have someone hovering over her while she tried to shop.

"Okay. Just holler if you need me." And she disappeared again. Sandy found the coat rack, pushed several aside till she found one she liked, and tried it on. It felt good, so she carried it over to a three-way mirror to get a full look. The coat had a drawstring just above a flounce and Sandy felt as if it made her look fat, so she returned it to the rack and found another.

Several people entered the store behind her as she turned this way and that to size up her second choice. She heard them clomping toward the counter, heavy boots on the pine flooring.

The second coat was better. It was a mauve color with a pink lining. Fiberfill sandwiched between. A hood which folded into a collar. Nice, but maybe it was overkill; she wouldn't need anything quite this heavy in Washington. Not that it didn't get cold there; the coat was just too sporty to justify its price, considering how little she would wear it.

She slid several more coats aside, holding them out and examining them. An electric-blue with a touch of chartreuse and shocking-pink hollered at her. If she'd had it on yesterday, she'd have been even more of a target than she'd been in the red sweatshirt. Still, she thought as she surveyed herself in the mirror, she wasn't planning to get into any more situations like that and this style was flattering and the price reasonable—at least compared to the mauve one.

She took the coat off, gathered her cardigan and purse and went over to pay. Only when she heard a gravelly male voice did she realize who had come in behind her. She glanced briefly down the counter toward Hurd to see if he'd noticed her.

Oh, no. It wasn't only Hurd. It was three of the poachers. Niles wasn't with them or the one they'd called Jimbo. The three were preoccupied, examining something, mumbling among themselves.

And here she was wearing the red sweatshirt again! The one they must have seen a flash of in the woods. She shrank into herself, put the coat she wanted to buy on the counter, and tried to nonchalantly slip into her cardigan before they glanced her way.

"Did you decide on this one?" the woman asked, her voice so loud Sandy wanted to grimace.

Out of the corner of her eye, she saw Hurd look up.

"Well, boys, look who's here. One of Senator Mattingly's girls."

Sandy acknowledged the woman's question, then looked around. The "boys" weren't responding with much curiosity; they were rather preoccupied with whatever it was they were looking at.

This was the first time Sandy had gotten a good look at them. There was Maris, facing her from the end of the counter, looking relatively normal—now that he wasn't dancing around and streaking blood on his face—flat, tanned face, dark stringy hair under a red ball cap. The other one, just beyond Hurd—she couldn't remember his name—had reddish-blond hair sticking out from beneath his camouflage rain hat. He finally turned his head to give her a cursory look.

She did a double take. She knew his name all right, but not from yesterday. From a year ago when she'd sat across a restaurant table stifling a yawn as he told her all about fresh water mussels. "Dave Hale!" she blurted out.

He did his own double take. Momentary astonishment registered on his face before a mask dropped over his eyes. He raised his eyebrows to show puzzlement, glanced at his companions, then back at her as he pointed at himself. "You mean me?"

She nodded, slowly, confused by his confusion.

"You're mistaken, ma'am. My name is Anderson. Kevin Anderson."

She remembered the name from the bear slaughter, but she hadn't really seen him. His back had been to her the whole time as he sawed off parts of the carcass.

Maris and Hurd looked at her, then at Anderson. Hurd especially seemed interested. His eyes had narrowed even though an open-mouthed grin remained on his face.

"Sorry," Sandy muttered, looking away, embarrassed and perplexed. That *was* Dave Hale; she was sure of it. She couldn't forget his face. She specifically remembered the flat wart that hovered between his eyebrows. Not that two people couldn't have a wart in the same place. But the hair, the gangly height.

Dave—Kevin Anderson—moved away from the group

and went to look at a camping equipment display. Maris joined him.

"You havin' any luck finding your brother?" Hurd asked, moving closer to Sandy. She could smell the damp wool of his jacket.

She gave a nervous laugh. "No. I guess he's moved on." She fumbled for her MasterCard.

"I see you're not the only one looking for him," Hurd said.

She jerked her head around toward Hurd. "What do you mean?"

"You haven't seen? Got a paper, Naomi?" he said to the clerk.

The woman looked under the counter, dragged a newspaper out, and handed it to him. He, in turn, passed it to her.

LOCAL TAXIDERMIST MURDERED, the headline shouted. Sandy scanned the story. It said the police were looking for Gus Skaar's missing employee, Jerry Cochran, for questioning.

She steadied herself against the counter. My Lord, she thought, she'd never even considered that maybe Jerry murdered Gus Skaar. How naive was she?

Her mind was bombarded with recriminations. She should have never left that door open at the taxidermist's shop; then there would have been more time to find Jerry, more time to get to the bottom of this. But earlier than that: she should have never come here, should have never opened that envelope.

But that was ridiculous. Even if she hadn't become involved, the script would have acted itself out. She'd had no impact other than to hurry things along by opening the door to the taxidermy shop.

Even if she now found Jerry, she wasn't sure she could get a straight story from him. She'd always wanted to believe him, give him the benefit of the doubt, but he lied adeptly, and she knew it.

She shoved the newspaper toward the clerk, then signed the credit card receipt, feeling dazed, as if all her realities had just shifted 180 degrees. She just wanted to get out of there, away from the prying eyes of this loathsome man.

Clasping her bulky package against her, she hurried out, avoiding the other men as she left the store. As she unlocked the car door and threw her package in, she glanced up and saw Anderson watching her out the window. Anderson, phooey! That was definitely Dave Hale. She relocked the door and hurried across the street and down several doors to the café. Finding Jerry had taken on new importance.

The crowd and noise inside the café felt like a sanctuary from her thoughts and Sandy would have loved nothing better than to push Jerry out of her mind, but she had a job to do here. Question Brigitte. She sat down at a table halfway back into the room which still had dirty dishes on it. A waitress went by, her hands full, and said, ''I'll be with you in a minute.''

Sandy nodded, keeping her eyes toward the front, hoping to see Brigitte, but the girl didn't seem to be there.

As she watched, Hurd walked in, Maris with him. Kevin—Dave—wasn't with them. They both pulled their coats off and hung them on a rack and Maris slid into a booth. Hurd saw someone he knew and walked over to the first table, slapped the man on the back and shook his hand. The two of them laughed and talked.

After a moment, as Hurd started to move away, he raised his eyes and seemed to notice her. She was sure he'd seen her because his eyes narrowed slightly, but he didn't acknowledge her. He went over to Maris and leaned on the table, his back to Sandy now. Maris looked her way, a sure sign they were talking about her. Hurd stepped aside, and

Maris slid out of the booth, grabbed his coat, and left the café. Hurd disappeared from her view around the corner into the next room.

The waitress cleared Sandy's table, then gave it a swish with a wet cloth, leaving a line of crumbs behind.

"Is Brigitte here today?" she asked as the waitress handed her a menu.

"She's sick. I'll be right back to get your order."

Sandy was disappointed. She consoled herself with the fact that with the café so crowded chances were she wouldn't have gotten to talk to the girl anyway. Especially with Hurd up front.

Realizing her appetite had returned—she hadn't really had anything to eat since before she found Gus Skaar's body—Sandy ordered a big breakfast, even though it was already noon.

After her meal, she had another cup of coffee then left the café. By then the wind had picked up and the rain undulated across the pavement. She ran along the sidewalk, trying to stay under the overhang of the buildings, her head ducked into the wind. She wished she'd taken the time to remove the tags and put on her new coat. The weather was definitely getting colder. Or maybe she was just damper.

A tall figure emerged from a doorway and fell into step beside her. Alarmed, she glanced over. It was Dave Hale, his hat as low over his brow as it would go.

"What's going on?" she asked, stopping abruptly and facing him. At least his presence acknowledged that she wasn't mistaken about his identity.

"Come on," he said, looking around nervously. "Let's get in your car. I don't want to be seen with you. It's not safe for either of us, not after that little exchange in the store."

The urgency in his voice made her do as he said unquestioningly. They darted across the street; she unlocked the car and they got in. The rain washed down the windows, distorting any view the outside world might have of them. The car was a safe little shell.

"I was surprised to see you in there," he said over the staccato sound of the rain beating on the car. He smelled like a wet dog.

"Same here," she said. "I saw your mother in Minneapolis the other day. She thinks you're in Arizona."

He didn't reply.

"She was going on about not hearing from you."

"I've been pretty absorbed." He leaned forward slightly, squinting his eyes to see through the windshield, then darted a glance out the window. "Go ahead and start your car. You can drop me off at my place around the block."

Yes, boss, anything you say, boss, Sandy thought, but she did as he ordered.

"What are you doing in Northlake?" he asked as she pulled out.

She turned on the windshield wipers, then the headlights. "It's a free country. So what are you doing here?"

"It's a free country," he countered, indicating that she should turn right. "Go around this block."

"Yes, but *I'm* using my real name."

He grunted and she turned south.

"I saw you out in the woods," she said. "Bear hunting."

"That was you?"

She nodded, turning at the next corner.

"It's a wonder you weren't shot. What were you doing out there?"

"Hiking. Watching a bunch of barbarians slaughter a bear."

"Turn right again and let me out at the alley."

"I presume you would have saved me if it had come down to my getting shot?"

"That would have really blown my cover. As it is—" he sighed. "If we meet again, please remember I'm Kevin Anderson. It's important. If any of those guys ask you anything, tell them you made a mistake." She pulled up to let him out. So he was the one who lived in the apartment on the alley.

"Listen. What I'm doing is confidential. I can't explain, but it's important." His voice was grim. "I hope you haven't already blown it."

Her? What was his problem? She was just in Northlake, a tourist for all he knew. He was the one who was doing the cloak-and-dagger number.

"Is my mother okay?" he asked, his hand hesitating on the door handle.

"She seemed fine."

"Like I said, uh"—she could see him searching for her name—"Sandy. Forget you know me."

He jumped out, and she watched through the rain-streaked window as he disappeared into the gray of the alley. When he was out of sight, she pulled away and headed back to the Senator's, preoccupied with trying to piece the puzzle together.

An insistent ringing met her when she opened the door. She hurried over to a beige extension phone on an end table, tossed her package onto the couch, and picked up the receiver.

"Sandy! It took a long time for you to answer. Did I catch you in the sauna?" A short laugh, a call from another life. It was almost as if he were here.

"No, I haven't even taken a sauna. Oh, Troy, it's so good to hear your voice!"

"I've been worried about you, wondering where in the hell you were."

"I kind of left in a hurry, but Jim knew." She shrugged off her cardigan and slung it across the back of the couch.

"Yeah, but our paths haven't been crossing much until this morning. What are you doing out there?"

"He didn't tell you that, too?"

"No."

"Well, someone broke into my apartment and stole that film Jerry sent me. It was after you went to New York." It seemed a long time ago since that evening when she and Troy had eaten spaghetti. "I figured Jerry wasn't imagining things, so I'm looking for him."

"Sandy, I told you not to involve yourself. It makes you an accessory." Troy sighed audibly.

"He's my brother. I can't just let something happen to him."

"Well, have you found him yet?"

"Not a trace."

"He's a real pain to you sometimes. So what *have* you found out?"

"Well, now he's wanted for questioning in a murder. Things are going from bad to worse and I'm not doing a bit of good. I'd never make a detective." She gave a short laugh.

"Well, in one way I'm glad. I don't like you out there running around in the wilderness alone. Let the law deal with it. If he's involved in something illegal, they'll take care of it."

"Troy—"

"Besides, I need you here."

"I'd like to stay the rest of the week anyway. I have the time coming," she said a little defensively. "Jim said it would be okay." She hoped Troy didn't mind that she hadn't cleared it with him. He was, after all, her immediate boss.

He chuckled and his voice became soft. "I was thinking of a more personal kind of need. I mean—maybe I came on a little strong the other night, but the truth is I"—he cleared his throat—"miss having you here, just knowing you're in town."

"It's nice to hear that, Troy."

"I mean it. I want you to hurry back."

She couldn't promise that, so she changed the subject. "The Senator's place is magnificent, Troy. Have you ever seen it?"

"Yeah, I was up there once," he said offhandedly, then, "Sandy, what kind of trouble is Jerry in? Do you have any idea? Maybe I can pull some strings, help him out."

"I don't know. But now the police are looking for him, too. The man he worked for has been murdered."

"Oh, no, that sounds bad. Tell me about it."

She told him briefly, omitting her own involvement. "I really don't even like talking about it, so you catch me up on what's happening there," she said. "How are the hearings going?"

He spent several minutes bringing her up to date; then they ended their conversation with Troy telling her to keep in contact. "If you find Jerry, let me know. Like I said, maybe I can help talk some sense into him."

Troy's mention of the sauna gave her the idea. It was the perfect way to throw off her worries temporarily. She went into the master bathroom and studied the controls a moment, then adjusted the dial to turn on the heat. It would take thirty minutes or so to get up to temperature. Meanwhile, she'd fix herself another cup of coffee—real coffee, not instant. She'd seen some in the cabinet.

She'd just inserted the filter in the coffeemaker when the

phone rang again. This time she picked up the kitchen extension.

A female voice identified herself as Brigitte Hurd. So, Sandy thought, she was the café owner's daughter. It would be Hurd who would be upset about Jerry's photos of the girl—if he knew about them. The waitress spoke very quietly, as if she had her hand cupped around the mouthpiece.

"If you can come to the café about eleven tomorrow, I think we might be able to talk. My father won't be there."

"Do you know—?" Sandy started, but the line was already dead.

Eleven tomorrow. So long to wait. She turned on the coffeemaker, then sat at the dining table and stared out at the rain through the window wall, wondering what the wolves were doing now. Did they continue to roam around, or did they huddle together under cover, waiting for the weather to pass. How difficult life was for animals in the wild through no fault of their own. She sighed. Life was difficult for humans, too, but it was as if they went out of their way to make things complicated.

The rain seemed to be letting up as she watched, and the gray lake became more distinct. She was glad to be inside where it was warm. She pushed her shoes off with her toes, then pulled her legs up in the chair and hugged them against herself waiting for the coffee to drip through the filter.

She ought to give up the coffee habit; she drank far too much, but she loved it, not just the stimulant of the caffeine, but the taste as well. It conjured up a lot of pleasant times with friends—when she had friends. She frowned. Since she'd moved to Washington she'd been rather isolated, except for Troy. There was no one there she could truly call a soulmate.

The sauna seemed ready enough after she finished her

coffee. She took a wooden bucket and filled it with water at the lavatory, then put the bucket and a ladle in the sauna before stepping into the shower. The shower itself was larger than her so-called walk-in closet at home. Step-in closet would be more accurate.

After a brief shower, she stepped into the sauna, and closed the door. A dipper of the water poured on the hot stones sent up a billow of steam. The warmth felt good as she lay down on a large towel she'd draped on the sauna bench. She tried to empty her mind of all the things which had been weighing upon it. Gradually she relaxed, slipping into a fantasy that she was rich, that this was her house. After pouring more water on the stones, she was perspiring freely and decided it was time to take another shower, then maybe spend a few more minutes in the sauna. Of course, a Finn would probably run outdoors now and jump into the cold lake, she thought with an audible laugh. The sound almost startled her.

She pushed on the door, but it didn't budge. Her tranquility vanished. She was trapped. Someone had locked her in. She would die in here, in this sweltering heat. The sour taste of panic rose in her throat.

She heaved her weight against the door and it gave way, and she hurtled across the room to the lavatory. She leaned there heavily for a moment, feeling sheepish, till she glimpsed her eyes in the mirror. Her fear-filled eyes looked back at her.

Fear was a natural, reasonable reaction, she told herself. If Jerry was involved in something, then by coming here she was, too.

She calmed herself down, turned off the sauna and considered a final shower, but no. She'd seen *Psycho* once too often. Even though there wasn't a shower curtain here, her nerves couldn't take it.

She put on a pair of whipcord slacks and a long-sleeved, striped T-shirt, then padded barefoot, carrying a pair of socks, back to the main part of the house. Her shoes were still under the table where she'd kicked them off.

No sooner had she gotten to the living room than she heard a shuffling sound at the door to the side porch.

Clyde! Niles must be here. She felt her heart lift with anticipation, then stifled the feeling. He wasn't for her. Think of Troy, who worried about her, who was more her type.

She went to the door and opened it, but there was no sign of Clyde. She took a step or two outside, pulling the door shut behind her to keep the cold air out and the warm air in.

"Clyde?" she coaxed in her talking-to-dogs voice. "Is that you?"

A low, rumbling growl caused her to look around the end of the woodpile. She should have taken it as warning.

A wolf stood there, its teeth bared. The hair on its neck stood up.

Sandy started backing up, but the animal moved toward her.

She turned to bolt, and the wolf sprang. A searing pain shot through her arm as the animal sank its teeth into the flesh of her upper arm.

She staggered sideways at the thrust of its massive weight and fell against the woodpile, scraping down it, embedding slivers in her free arm.

From inside, the doorbell faintly sounded.

"Help!" she yelled, hoping that whoever was ringing the doorbell could hear her from where they were in front of the house. "Help me!"

She caught her footing momentarily and groped for a stick of firewood, wrapped her fingers around a small log, and wrenched around and struck out at the wolf. She felt a dull thud as the makeshift club made contact with its back, but the impact jarred the wood from her hand and she fell forward, catching her weight on her free forearm. Her knees slammed onto the concrete.

She grabbed at the wolf, but it was behind her and she could barely get hold of its fur. The animal was shaking its head, her arm still gripped in its teeth like a toy.

Play dead, she thought. *Maybe it will stop*.

She went limp, just as she heard someone coming, heard the screen door rasp against the concrete, heard the gunshot. Her ears rang from its nearness.

The wolf let go, its body dropping over her at the same time. The air went out of her in a gasp at the weight.

"Are you all right?" a man's voice asked as the weight was dragged off her, allowing her to breathe.

She sucked in a noisy breath, then tried to nod her head. She took several more deep breaths, then pushed herself up shakily.

A glaze of moisture in her eyes kept her from focusing, but she could vaguely make out a military-type cap with a bill. The man's raingear made a swishing sound as he moved.

Again he asked if she was okay.

This time she came out of her fog and answered. "I don't know. My arm." She twisted her neck around and looked at it. Blood was seeping through her shirt.

"Let's get out of this cold and I'll take a look." He helped her into the house and sat her down at the table.

Thank God he had come. Her stomach felt queasy at the thought of what would have happened—

He pulled the shredded shirt sleeve apart and examined the wound. "I think you need some stitches," he said, "and definitely a tetanus shot if you haven't had one lately. Now let me get a wet cloth and clean that up."

"I can do it," Sandy said. She went down the hall to the bathroom, pressing the wound with one hand. There were no first aid supplies, so she settled for washing her arm with soap and water, cringing as she did it.

"What about rabies?" she asked when she returned to the living room. "Could that wolf have been rabid?"

"That wasn't a wolf; it was a hybrid."

It had looked like a wolf to her, but she took his word that it wasn't. At the moment she wasn't terribly curious.

"I'll get one of my people to come out and get it; then we'll make sure it didn't have rabies. Oh, by the way, I'm Chief Breton. Northlake Police. Why don't I drive you into town, to the clinic? Let them take a look at that arm."

She nodded. "I'm Sandy Wilson. Pardon me if I don't shake hands." She knew her voice sounded tight and unfriendly, but her arm was beginning to throb. She fished her shoes out from under the table with her feet, put them on, then picked up her cardigan off the couch. Her new coat was there in the bag, but she wasn't going to risk bleeding on it. She awkwardly got one arm in the sweater, but couldn't manage farther than that. The chief noticed and helped her get the other side over her shoulder. "Thanks," she said. "I'm kind of incapacitated. What was that—that hybrid doing on my porch?"

"Screen door must have blown open and it got trapped. There's nothing more unpredictable than hybrids. People want to treat them like dogs, but when it gets down to it, instinct takes over. You can't domesticate wild animals just by raising them in captivity. Anyone says you can is mistaken."

They went out the front door and she felt as if she were walking in a dream. The rain had turned to a silent mist, but nearby in the woods, water dripped heavily from the trees.

Chief Breton helped her into the police car which was

parked on the circular drive, then went around and slid under the steering wheel.

She clasped her injured arm against the pain. Perspiration formed at her hairline, even though it was cold outside. She didn't like to think of what would have happened if Breton hadn't heard her cry for help.

The chief turned on the windshield wipers and they began their patient slap, slap, slap. Sandy focused on them, trying not to think of her arm.

The emergency room at the clinic was occupied, and after a quick assessment of Sandy's wound, a nurse told her to have a seat in the hall.

Chief Breton sat down next to her. "I was coming out to see you to ask a few questions. Do you mind if I go ahead now?"

"No. That would be fine."

He removed his cap and placed it on the chair next to him. Then he took out a small memo pad and a pen from his pocket. "I understand you're Jerry Cochran's sister. Is that right?"

"Yes."

"And your name again?"

"Sandy Wilson," she said. "S-A-N-D-Y."

"S-A-N-D-Y Wilson," he said as he wrote. "And your permanent address?"

She told him.

"Maybe you know that we're looking for your brother in connection with a homicide investigation?"

"I saw the paper, yes." She gripped her arm tighter and winced at a sharp spasm.

The chief noticed. "Sorry. I thought maybe answering these questions would help keep your mind off your injury."

"It's okay. Go ahead."

"Do you know where your brother is?"

"No, I don't. I didn't even know he was working for the taxidermist until I saw the paper."

"What brought you here?"

"I just came to see my brother."

"Seems odd that you made the trip and didn't even know where he lived."

"I had business in this area and thought I'd drop in on him. A surprise, you know? Only when I got here, I realized"—she gave a humorless laugh— "that I only had a post office box number."

"What kind of business did you have up here?"

She was on shaky ground here, but she thought Jim Mattingly would back her up if the policeman called him. "I work for Senator Mattingly. It was political business—not here. In Duluth. But when you're that far, what's a little farther?" She was doing Jerry proud the way the fabrications were slipping off her tongue. "I'm curious. How did you know I was here?" she asked Breton. Had Hurd told him?

"My daughter works at the convenience store at the edge of town. Once this homicide thing got underway, she remembered the name, said you were asking about your brother."

Sandy vaguely remembered telling the girl at the convenience store she was staying at Senator Mattingly's.

"So you haven't seen your brother since you got to town?"

"No."

The nurse called her name as if there were scores of people waiting, and Sandy stood up.

"Well," Chief Breton said, also rising, "I have to ask that if you do see your brother, to please let me know. We want to question him, that's all, and it would be best if he came in willingly. Now, I'll be waiting when you get out of there.''

After five stitches, a pain killer, a tetanus shot and a few extra pills in a bottle for later, Sandy rejoined the chief, who took her back to the Senator's.

''I'm curious,'' she said as they neared the turnoff. ''How could you tell that wasn't a wolf?''

''Its tail had a curl in it. Noticed it as soon as I came around the corner of the house. Wolf tail is straight.''

Interesting. Frankly she didn't remember; she'd been too busy to see anything except the snarling mouth. ''Do you have any idea who owns it?''

''No. There are several people around here who breed them and, of course, they go on and sell them. Were you thinking of trying to press charges?''

''If you could find out who it belonged to.''

He shook his head. ''Be mighty hard. It didn't have a collar or anything.''

He deposited her on the circular drive at the Senator's. ''You take it easy,'' he said as she climbed out.

She thanked him again and watched as he drove away, then slowly went into the house, kicked off her damp shoes, plopped down on the couch, and stared at the dead fireplace. She felt lousy. Her arm ached, her head ached. And she was getting absolutely nowhere.

What a day it had been! What an extraordinary few days! And it had all started with that damn letter from Jerry. But despite how bad things looked, she couldn't believe her baby brother was a murderer. He was spoiled and self-indulgent, but he couldn't have killed someone.

She sighed and went to the kitchen. *What I need is a cup of coffee.* Maybe it would help her aching head; it would at least lift her spirits. She headed toward the kitchen, pausing at the door to the porch as she considered looking to see if someone had come to remove the dead animal. But no—she withdrew her hand from the knob—she wouldn't look. She didn't want to see the lifeless creature lying there. She brewed the coffee, then headed out the other end of the room.

"Yuck," she muttered, as she stepped in a puddle of water near the refrigerator. What was that doing there?

Had she come through this way earlier today, when she was dripping wet? She thought back, retracing her movements. No, she hadn't. And Chief Breton hadn't been in here.

Maybe the freezer was malfunctioning, bad news with all that bait—She paused mid-thought. Those plastic bags weren't full of bait. They were gall bladders, each worth a couple of hundred dollars and representing a dead bear. She couldn't begin to imagine how many were stuffed in there.

She pulled the freezer door open.

It was still frosty, but it was also empty. All the plastic bags were gone.

Someone had been in here. But when? She examined the floor. It was still wet only in front of the refrigerator, but she could see where water had evaporated, leaving a slight haze of minerals in a track to the entryway.

A shudder rippled down her spine, and she thought again about the fears that had raced through her mind in the sauna. But no. The sauna door had just been stuck. No one would have come in while she was here and her car was in front. It must have been earlier, when she was in town. Had someone removed the gall bladders while Dave Hale kept her busy in town? She remembered Maris' glance toward her in the café when Hurd was talking to him. Then he had left abruptly. Had he come out here? Or had he called someone? Niles? She frowned. Niles hadn't been with the others. Had he come over while she was gone and unloaded the freezer?

She paced into the living room. She'd better just call the Senator and tell him Niles and his poacher friends were using the house for storage. After all, Niles had a key and free access.

She paused at the phone. But did Jim Mattingly already know? Was he involved? He seemed to know there was something in his freezer. And she'd accepted that a whole freezer could be full of bait! She was so gullible! She grimaced. He'd practically pushed her into coming here, offering his house. Why? Was she the lure to help them find Jerry?

And what about Jerry's meeting with the Senator? Was this the help he gave Jerry? Getting her brother involved in this dirty work?

Sandy's head hurt. She pressed her temples and dropped down on the couch. Tomorrow she would contact Dave Hale again. He could help her get to the bottom of this.

15

A loud *crack* snapped Sandy upright in bed early the next morning. The memory of the shot fired at her in the woods rushed back to her. She pulled the covers back, alert for other sounds, but there was only the wind wrestling with the trees outside.

She opened the bedroom drapes; outside the world was white. An almost horizontal blizzard concealed the nearby woods and the lake. The trees near the house drooped with their heavy burdens, and as she watched, a limb broke and plunged to the ground with a sodden plop.

Where are you, Jerry? she thought. Are you out in this? Or are you in Duluth with some new girlfriend.

She dropped the curtain back in place and returned to bed, hoping to drop right back to sleep, but her arm was aching, and after a few uncomfortable minutes, she went into the bathroom and swallowed two painkillers. Before long she was in a drug-induced sleep.

By the time she woke again, the wind had subsided, leaving high drifts of snow piled against the side of the house. She got up and headed for the kitchen and that first cup of coffee which was going to revive her. The house seemed extra cold and she stopped at the thermostat to turn up the heat. She moved the indicator, but didn't hear anything happen. She gave it another jiggle, but it still didn't respond.

Frowning, she went into the kitchen. The clock on the stove was frozen at three. No wonder it was cooling off in here. No electricity. That meant no heat, no pump, and worst of all, she thought glumly, no coffee. She picked up the phone—no dial tone.

She poured some of the orange juice she'd made the day before and took two more painkillers, thinking about her options. There didn't seem to be but one. She would drive to town and get a motel room where it would be warm, and from there she could go talk to Brigitte.

She put her clothes on carefully, trying not to hurt her arm, put in her contacts, then packed her things in her suitcase and headed for the door. When she opened it, a wall of snow remained upright where it had drifted. She would need more than her running shoes to even make it off the porch. Then she looked at her car on the unplowed driveway. She wasn't going to get to town. The car was boxed in by the heavy wet snow. Even if she could get it out, what if the highway had not been plowed? She closed the door. She remembered why she liked the city; someone took care of you.

She wished now she'd had Niles lay a fire ready for her to simply touch a match to. But she hadn't and now she would have to remedy the situation or freeze. She went to the door out of the dining area, took hold of the knob reluctantly, opened it a crack and peeked out, every muscle tensed.

The animal's body was gone. Only a dark stain on the concrete gave evidence as to what had happened the day before. Apparently Chief Breton had sent someone to pick up the body while they were at the hospital, because there were no tracks in the snow. Even so, she stepped out warily, listening carefully for any growling or other warnings.

The screen door was shut and holding back several feet of snow. On an impulse she went over to it and pulled it open. It rasped against the door. There was a scrape mark where it had etched the concrete. She shoved it closed with difficulty and went over to the woodpile and selected two small logs—all she could manage with her arm in the condition it was.

Someone had let that dog on the porch. She knew it for a certainty because she had suddenly remembered closing the screen door, which had been stuck open, after she'd let Clyde come in, and no wind could have pushed it open if the wind last night hadn't. It was a tight fit.

She carried the logs in, then made a second and third trip. She tore the paper bag her coat had been in into pieces, and wadded each one up and tucked them under the three logs she stacked in the fireplace. Luckily, there was a book of matches on the hearth. She struck one and lit the paper. It quickly burned up, and she felt quite successful as the edges of the bark on the logs flickered, but after the initial flare of warmth, the paper turned to ash and the logs remained cold.

She frowned. *More paper.* She looked around the room. Nothing there, but she remembered seeing a stack of grocery bags in the kitchen under the sink. She got them and returned to the fireplace. She had to get this thing started soon; she was freezing to death. Her hand shook as if to give truth to her thought.

Once again, she rolled the paper into wads, then looked for the matchbook. What had she done with it? She looked on the mantel. It wasn't there, but there were some fireplace matches. She opened the box and at the same time noticed some little cube-shaped fire starters.

Ahhh. These I know how to use.

Soon the logs caught.

She stood in front of the blaze, stretching her hands toward the warmth. Somewhere in the distance came the rather preposterous sound, considering the weather, of a motorcycle. It grew louder and she went to the window. It wasn't a motorcycle after all, but a snowmobile. The person on it was unrecognizable because of a ski mask and goggles, but she presumed from the direction it was coming, it was Niles.

"Niles? Is that you?" she said as she opened the door to admit him.

"Don't recognize me, huh?" He stomped his feet on the porch, then came on in, sliding his goggles up over his head, and pulling his ski mask off. "I can't understand why not."

She laughed. Right now, she was glad to see him, even if he was involved in all this poaching business. He was like a knight riding up to save her, although his trusty steed was a snowmobile.

"We kind of had a blizzard during the night," he said.

She bit her lip to suppress another laugh. His hair was standing up crazily. As if he detected her thoughts, he ran his fingers across his hair to smooth it down.

"I thought you might need help," he said, meeting her eyes for only the briefest moment, then focusing on the suitcase.

"I was going to a motel."

"I don't think so. Your car is kind of socked in out there."

"Yes, well, that was my plan before I opened the door." She looked toward the fireplace. "I—uh—built a fire." She wanted him to think her competent.

"I noticed, but that fireplace isn't really designed to heat the house." He appraised her. "Good job, though."

"Thanks. Could you take me to town?"

He made a face as if she were crazy. "You want me to take you to town on the snowmobile?" He laughed. "I had in mind to take you back over to my place."

What would they do, trapped in his cabin together for who knew how long? Read *Field and Stream*? *National Geographic*? The physical attraction she felt for him was so intense—well, she didn't like to think about having to deal with it for hours. But what could she say? That she didn't trust herself with him? "Isn't your electricity off, too?" she asked.

He nodded. "But I heat with wood and I cook on propane. And I've got a Coleman lantern if they don't get the power restored by dark."

"Sounds like you're ready for anything." She tried to keep her voice even, not showing the edge of involuntary excitement she was feeling. "I think I'd better just stay here, keep the fire stoked and—"

"That's not a good idea," he said. "The power may be off for a long time. And you know what that means."

She looked at him, puzzled.

"No coffee." He said it very seriously, without a hint of a smile.

But she smiled. "You got coffee, huh?"

He met her eyes for a second; a smile played at the corner of his mouth and she wondered what he was thinking, but all he said was, "Sure." His eyes wandered over her shoulder, scanning the room as if he were looking for something.

"Do I need to take any food?"

"No, I've got plenty of everything. You might need some boots, though."

"I don't have any. Maybe there are some here somewhere."

"I think there are some in the utility room off the kitchen," he said. He led the way.

"They're huge," she said, making a face when she saw the man-sized black galoshes.

"Just stick your foot in, shoe and all."

He knelt down and held one boot while she shoved her foot down in it, balancing by putting her hand on a chest-type freezer that sat along one wall of the utility room.

"The slipper fits," he said, looking up into her eyes, holding them for a moment, then getting back to the task.

She clumped around in a little circle once she got both boots on. "Am I fetching?"

"They'll keep your feet dry. That's what's important."

The world outside the house was muffled, wrapped in cotton batting. The evergreens at the edge of the woods drooped in resignation at sudden winter. Only the crunch of their footsteps broke the peace.

Niles climbed on the snowmobile and directed her to straddle it behind him.

"Here take this," he said, handing her his ski mask.

"No, you use it," she said, pulling on her gloves. "You're in front and I can keep my face down against you."

"Okay," he said, putting it on.

He started the engine, then turned the throttle and they shot across the white expanse that yesterday had been the lawn and headed through the woods. He followed his earlier track through the trees.

The woods looked like a war zone. The combination of wet snow and high winds had been devastating. Hundreds of limbs had broken and lay scattered on the forest floor. Several trees had blown over.

He plowed toward his cabin. Even at a low speed, the

wind chill must have made the temperature below zero. Sandy buried her face against his back and clung tightly to his parka as the machine rocketed over a rise.

At last they were there. She crawled off, stiff with cold and followed him into the cabin, which was toasty warm and welcoming. Clyde acted glad to see them.

"Just hang your coat on one of those pegs," he said as he pulled his own coat off. "How about that coffee?"

"Hmmm. I'd love it." She grimaced privately as she struggled to get her sore arm out of her new coat.

"Nice coat," he said.

"Got it yesterday. None too soon. I had no idea we were in for this."

"Nor did anyone. It was predicted for further west. You know how that goes."

He went into the kitchen and a moment later she followed. He was pouring coffee into a mug.

"You already had it made," she said, gratefully accepting the steaming brew.

He didn't say anything.

She lifted the mug and let the strong aroma waft into her nose. How could a smell be so comforting. She closed her eyes and savored the feeling for a moment.

It was too hot to drink, so she carried it into the main room and stood near the stove, warming up.

"How about some scrambled eggs and bacon?" he asked, rubbing his hands together. He hadn't poured himself any coffee.

She hesitated. "I don't want to put you to any trouble."

"It's no trouble. There's nothing else to do."

"Okay. If you're sure."

Sandy went back to the kitchen door and watched as he took eggs and bacon from the refrigerator. He peeled off half a dozen slices of bacon into a cast-iron skillet on the stove, then rewrapped the package and put it away.

As the bacon began to sizzle, he cracked an egg with a solid rap on the edge of a graniteware bowl, then one-handed, pulled the shell apart and let the contents slide out.

"Very neat trick," she commented.

"What?" he asked, looking over at her. "You mean this?" He cracked another one and repeated the gesture, this time with more flourish.

She gave him an arch look. "Showoff."

"It's easy."

"I've tried it and ended up getting egg all over my hand and shells in the bowl."

"Here, come try," he said, holding an egg out to her.

She put the coffee mug on the counter and took the egg. She tapped it, but it didn't break. Another harder tap. The shell gave way and the egg came sliding out prematurely, getting on her hand. "See?"

Niles took the shell from her and looked at it. "No wonder. You've pulverized the shell. You're not supposed to smash it."

She turned on the water to rinse her hand.

"Don't let it run. Once the pressure tank is empty, no water until the power's back on."

She watched him successfully crack another egg.

"A big hand helps," he said. "My father always did it like this. He liked to make breakfast for the family." Niles whisked the eggs with a fork, then added a tiny bit of milk and whisked again.

His words brought Sandy up sharply with a clear memory of her father cooking breakfast. Pancakes with happy faces on them. She could see him pouring three circles for the eyes and nose, the batter dribbling out into a smiling line for a mouth. Then he covered them with a circle of batter, only to have the more heavily browned features reappear when he flipped the pancake over.

She frowned and turned away from Niles and went into the other room. She didn't want to remember her father in happy times. It only confused her. Anger was healthier. So what if Forrest Ahlgren had cooked an occasional breakfast of happy-face pancakes for his daughter? What did it mean? He hadn't cared enough to stand up and fight for the right to see her. He hadn't cared enough to do that.

"It's ready," she heard Niles call in a few minutes. He handed her a plate as she came back to the door of the kitchen. "Help yourself."

She took two pieces of bacon and almost half the eggs. He'd made toast in the oven and she took a slice of it, then went to the table. After a moment he joined her.

They ate silently, her anger toward her father smoldering, bleeding over onto Niles for reminding her that there had been good times.

"So," she said. "Did you kill all these animals hanging on the walls?" Her voice held a disapproving edge.

He hesitated a moment, looking around at them, his fork suspended in front of him, then nodded.

"And bears? Do you kill bears?"

"If I get lucky in the lottery."

She looked at him, puzzled. "Lottery?"

"There's a state lottery each year. They draw numbers to see who can legally take a bear that season."

"Is it bear season now?"

"No." He looked at her sharply, then got up and went into the kitchen and came back with the coffee pot. "More?" A friendly gesture, but there was an uneasiness between them.

She nodded and held out her mug. So they weren't going to admit what each one knew about the incident in the woods—that he had participated and that she had witnessed.

Things didn't improve after breakfast, probably because she was so aware of his physical presence. He gave her some magazines and she settled down to read. He disappeared into the kitchen for a while, then reappeared and said he was going to go and cut some wood to clear off the drive.

With Niles out of the cabin at least she could relax. Finally, she fell asleep on the couch to the distant chir-r-r of the chain saw.

She drifted in and out of consciousness until she realized she was no longer hearing the saw. She sat up, assuming Niles would return soon.

She heard footsteps come up on the porch, then a heavy thump on the door. He didn't come in. She waited a moment, then there was another thump. Maybe his hands were full. She got up and went to the door and opened it. There was no one there. Uneasiness gripped her. What had hit the door?

She took a cautious step outside to take a look around.

Whap! A snowball zeroed in on her, spraying snow on her as it hit her good arm.

She shrieked, stepped back inside, and closed the door, dropping snow onto the floor.

Hurriedly she put on her coat, then struggled into the huge boots, handicapped by her injured arm, although it was feeling better. She pulled on her gloves, then peeked out the door. There was no sign of Niles, so she went on out and started across the yard. She glanced back and saw him at the corner of the house, stacking wood onto a carrier, getting ready to bring it in.

She bent down and scooped up a pile of snow with her

good arm and packed it into a ball, then went clumping toward him gracelessly, hollering, "Revenge!"

He turned slightly and she sent the snowball flying. He dodged, and it missed him. He swept over and scooped up some snow, packed it, and threw. She sidestepped and sent one of her own back toward him. Her boots hindered her flight, and a snowball caught her on the back.

She got behind a tree and picked up some more snow and peeked out. Niles was coming toward her, carrying a big snowball.

"Truce!" she hollered. "Truce!"

"You sure?" he asked.

She nodded, her head sticking out from behind the tree. "Drop your weapon."

He lowered his hand, letting the snow fall.

She jumped out from behind the tree and let her snowball fly, then darted away.

It missed him. "Traitor!" he yelled, coming after her.

She laughed, her frosty breath coming out in gasps and shrieks. "No, no. Stay away." She tromped among the trees.

He kept closing in, and finally she let herself be caught in front of a big birch. He grabbed her good arm with one hand. His other hand held a gargantuan pile of snow.

She closed her eyes and twisted her head from one side to the other, knowing what was coming, expecting to feel the cold snow on her face any moment. Then she realized that he had put both hands around her face, that he'd dropped the snowball.

She opened her eyes just as his mouth covered hers, the warmth of his lips crowding out the cold. She was pressed against the tree, encapsulated by it and his body and she relaxed, returning his kiss. It had been too long since she had felt this way. Never with Troy. Even with so simple a thing as a kiss.

Niles explored her face with his lips, then pulled away. His eyes tried to search hers, but she looked away.

With one of his gloved hands he wiped her damp hair aside. She gazed up at him and he tipped her chin up with his other hand and kissed her again, a light kiss this time. "We'd better stop this," he said.

Yes, good idea. But her body didn't believe it.

16

NILES detoured to pick up a load of wood on the way into the cabin, and handed her several sticks to carry. After being outdoors the cabin seemed sweltering.

They peeled off their soggy coats and gloves. He helped her pull off the oversized boots, then opened the door of the woodstove and laid some wood on the fire. He stepped away from it, watching, and rolled his sleeves up.

Don't do that, Sandy thought, catching a glimpse of the contour of his forearms. She closed her eyes and willed herself to resist temptation.

She picked up her mug where it sat on the table and went to the kitchen. There was still some coffee in the pot. She poured herself some and hollered at Niles, ''There's coffee left. Do you want some?''

''No,'' he answered. ''I'm going to have a beer, then go cut some more wood.''

He came into the kitchen and took a beer out of the refrigerator, popped the top and took a drink, observing her over the rim. She looked back at him steadily. She knew she was being slightly challenging and at the last minute lost her nerve and looked away.

He lowered the can and put it on the counter after only one swallow. "Listen, you make yourself at home. I've—uh—kind of got cabin fever. I'm going out." A moment later she heard the door slam.

"Well, I've got cabin fever, too," she muttered to herself. But it wasn't cabin fever that made her want to run back to the security of the Senator's cold house; it was a different kind of heat. And she needed to douse it.

She scribbled a note on a piece of paper, telling him she'd gone back to the Senator's and not to worry about her, propped it up on the table, put on her coat and gloves, worked her feet into the boots, and went out. Down the road she heard the chain saw, but she wasn't going that way.

Instead she clomped along the path the snowmobile had made earlier, her legs soon aching from carrying the extra weight of the boots through the deep snow. Surely the utility company would get the electricity on soon. They were good at this sort of emergency. Meanwhile, she could build a fire, now that she'd found those handy little fire starters.

Why now? Why do I have to meet someone out here who awakens all these feelings in me? Why not Troy? Because that would be too simple. *I'm like some teenager with a crush.* "Crush" was a good word for it. Her chest felt as if a crushing weight lay on it.

She followed the track through the silent woods, squinting against the brightness. The buzz of the chain saw was more distant now. The slight breeze felt frosty on her cheeks and nose. Her eyes watered from its bite, but already the snow was beginning to get slushy under the mid-afternoon sun. It was too early in the season for the snow to last long.

Movement beneath some bushes startled her, but it was only a ruffed grouse. She startled it as well, and the bird flapped out of the undergrowth and took off. It was the only sign of life she'd seen. *Everything is holed up,* she thought, *as I would be if I had any sense.*

When she got to the Senator's, she rekindled her fire, then brought all the blankets into the living room. She made a bed of cushions from the couch, then lay down in front of the fireplace to think. It was Thursday. Only a week since her apartment was ransacked. Mrs. Purvis would be watering her plants today. Sandy wondered how the weather was in Washington, wondered about Troy, what he was doing, thought about Chinese food—anything to keep her mind off Niles.

Before dark she got up and made a sandwich. It wasn't cashew chicken, but it tasted good. The bacon and eggs seemed a long time ago. The food in the refrigerator was still good and cold, but why wouldn't it be, she thought, so am I. She flipped the light switch near the door. No electricity yet, but when the power came back on, she wanted something to let her know.

She returned to her pile of blankets and huddled before the fire like a cavewoman in a pile of skins, waiting for darkness to swallow the room, realizing that all afternoon she'd harbored a secret hope that Niles would pursue her, like the hero in a romance novel. She wasn't proud of the thought, recognizing it as childish, but there it was.

But he didn't come. Not until the next morning. She heard the snowmobile for a long time before it really registered. She stuck her head out from beneath her blankets.

Damn! Her fire had gone out. The house was cold as a tomb. She struggled out and poked at the ashes. There seemed to be a little heat left in it, so she placed one of the little fire starters on a clump of embers that seemed to have a little life. Then one-handed, clasping her blanket with her injured arm, much better today, she went out and got several logs and put them in the fireplace. By the time she got back inside, her teeth were chattering like a typewriter.

The sound of the machine outside continued, growing louder, then receding, repeating the sequence. Once it stopped for a while, then started up again. What in the world was he doing? Finally, it receded even farther and disappeared. Her curiosity got the better of her and she went to the door and looked out. A trail had been beaten down up to her car. The snow had even been cleared off of it and from in front of the wheels. She would be able to get to town, providing the road had been cleared. Niles was nowhere in sight. Obviously he wanted to avoid her, for whatever reason. Well, good. That was for the best.

She'd slept in her coat and shoes, so there was little to do to get ready to go. Her bag was already packed from yesterday. She folded the blankets and put the cushions back on the couch, then went to her car, without the boots, stepping carefully in the footprints left from the day before.

The blizzard had been inconvenient, but in a way she was glad it had happened. It had given her time to think before she went running off to talk to Dave Hale—or rather, Kevin Anderson. She needed to think of him that way.

What if Niles and the others were using the Senator's house without his knowledge? What if Senator Mattingly wasn't involved? It sure wouldn't do to sic Kevin on him. What a stink it could make either way! She was caught in between and the only thing to do was try to unravel things herself.

The snowstorm had intruded on the familiarity she was beginning to develop with Northlake, leaving her feeling disoriented, as if she'd awakened in a new time and place. The town looked strange to her with its mantle of snow. But it wouldn't last long. The temperature sign on the bank said it was already 33° degrees fahrenheit, and the sun was shining. Rivulets of water were beginning to trickle here and there.

Sandy parked in front of the café, as close to the curb as she could, then negotiated the ridge of snow piled up by the plow.

The café was busy, and after her forced isolation she welcomed the hubbub. Brigitte was there. Unfortunately so was the girl's father.

When Brigitte approached the table, Sandy's eyes widened. "What happened to you?" Sandy asked.

The girl's hand went to her face. She had a bruise on one cheek. "I ran into a door," she said, glancing over her shoulder.

I just bet you did. That bastard had beaten his daughter up. "I couldn't get in here yesterday," Sandy said. "I'm sorry."

The girl, with her back to Hurd, pulled her eyebrows together and pursed her lips in warning, thwarting any further attempt to question her.

Hurd came over and leaned on the back of the next booth. "Found your brother yet?" he asked.

She shook her head, trying to quiet the pounding in her head at the sight of him.

"I guess the police haven't had any luck yet either. How d'ya like this weather? Did it lock you in out there?"

She nodded. "I didn't expect it. Tell me," she said, her eyes narrowing, "just why are you so interested in whether I find my brother? And what were you doing over at the taxidermy shop the first night I got to town? You didn't go in there, did you? And what happened to your daughter's face? Did you have something to do with that?"

The smile left his lips and he glowered at her. "You better not be sticking your nose where it doesn't belong. Outsiders aren't appreciated here. Your brother should have kept that in mind.'' He turned on his heel and went over to the cash register, where a customer was waiting to pay.

Sandy's heart sank. His words sounded so final, as if Jerry was—No, she wouldn't even think it.

Brigitte passed him and brought Sandy her breakfast. She put a napkin on the table beside the plate, then left. Sandy picked up the napkin to spread it on her lap and noticed it was dirty. But it wasn't soil; it was handwriting. Brigitte had scrawled three words on it. Early Dawn Lake.

Sandy wanted to ask her to explain, but the girl managed to stay out of sight until she brought the check, and it was Hurd who took Sandy's money.

Back in her car, Sandy looked at the note again. Did it mean that's where Jerry was? That was the only conclusion she could draw.

She couldn't find Early Dawn Lake on her road map but noticed that the names of many other lakes did not appear on the map either. Maybe just the major ones were listed.

She got back out of the car and picked her way across the patchy slick street to the trading post where she'd brought her coat. She dodged under the dripping overhang and went inside.

''Do you have a map that shows every lake in the area?'' she asked the woman who'd helped her the day before. She was going to ask if the woman knew where Early Dawn Lake was, but then remembered that Hurd had called her by her first name. Who could tell how chummy they were?

The clerk handed her a map. Sandy paid, then took it to a bench in the shoe section. There was an index and she found the coordinates, then targeted them on the map. There it was. Quite a way north of town, and only one road to the eastern side of it, and that was a logging road, according to the key.

Where would Jerry be staying? If he was camping out,

this snowstorm might have put him in serious physical jeopardy.

She glanced outside. The melt was underway. With any traffic at all, the blacktop roads should be passable soon, even if they hadn't been plowed. She would just have to take a look at the logging road to see if it was usable.

The drive up to the junction of the highway and the secondary road was fairly clear, but after she turned, conditions deteriorated and the logging road was still a good twenty miles north. The ice was patchy. There would be a clear stretch in full sun, then a shady area where the ice was treacherous, forcing her to keep her speed down. Piles of snow bordered the road.

The resort signs became more scarce as she got farther from Northlake, and she encountered only one car. She pulled over once at a wide spot—the entry to a fishing lodge—to study the map again, then she peered out the windshield. The highway veered to the northeast just ahead and that, according to the map, was where the logging road headed west. Almost there.

She pulled back onto the highway, sure enough, as the road eased to the northeast. She saw a break in the trees that indicated the turnoff. But there was no break in the snow along the highway. So much for that idea, she thought, slowing. She would have to wait for another day.

Or better yet, she thought, looking at the crystal blue sky. She could hire someone to fly her in. She'd seen a sign on the way into town announcing fly-ins for fishermen. So why not her? Surely she could hire someone to take her in.

She could scout the lake quickly that way, looking for signs of life. She'd be better off reconnoitering first. That was decided, then.

She continued northward till she found a long stretch where she could see traffic coming and going—if there happened to be any—and there she executed a U-turn, although it took two tries since there was no shoulder because of the snow.

She started back toward town, preoccupied with thoughts of Jerry alone out there in the wilderness during the blizzard—he was a city boy. Suddenly a deer bounded across the snow ridge along the highway. Her foot hit the brakes and the car went skidding out of control. It careened against the snowbank, tipping till she thought it would go over. At the last moment it righted itself, and careened to the opposite side of the road, where the plowed ridge sent it into a spin, which ended in the bank of snow on the opposite side of the road.

She took a deep breath and sat there a moment, leaning on the steering wheel, gathering her wits. The engine had died during the spin so now she started it, but when she tried to back away from the snow, the wheel wouldn't turn.

She got out and took a look. The fender was crushed against the wheel.

Great! she thought. Here she was stuck in the middle of nowhere again. She wrapped her arms around herself. At least she had a warm coat this time.

She took her purse from the car and started walking. She would find help at one of the scattering of lodges along the road. Fifteen minutes later she heard the sound of a vehicle behind her. She turned and flagged down the approaching truck.

"That your car back there?" the middle-aged driver asked as he rolled down his window.

"Yes. I almost hit a deer. Could you give me a ride to Northlake?"

"Sure. That's where I'm going. You want to go to a garage that has a tow truck?"

"Yes, please." She climbed in beside him, glad to be out of the cold. "Do you live out here?" she asked.

"My wife and I have a lodge up north of here. Red Feather Lodge."

"Do you know Early Dawn Lake at all?"

He nodded. "You betcha."

"Are there cabins on it?"

"No. It's undeveloped. Well, there is one cabin up on the northwest side, but there's no good way in there. Great lake for fishing, though. I take folks over there sometimes, just because it isn't developed."

"The map shows a logging road that goes up to it."

"Yeah. It goes pretty close to the lake. That's how I get in there when I go. You been out there today?"

"Well, I tried, but the road was impassable."

He snorted. "I guess so. Why you interested in Early Dawn?"

"I just heard the name and thought maybe it would be a good place to look at property."

He shot her a sideways glance that said it was a strange time to be looking at property, but he didn't say anything. Instead he asked, "You thinking of buying?"

"I don't know—I just think it's a beautiful part of the world."

They reached the outskirts of town and he pointed out a garage. "That do ya?"

It had been a service station. A concrete island devoid of pumps stood in the middle of the wet expanse of driveway in front. Someone had shoved the snow into huge heaps at the side of the lot. There was a small glass-fronted office on the left and a two-bay garage on the right. Below the name, JIM'S GARAGE, a smaller sign read "Wrecker Service," even though there was no tow truck in evidence.

"That will be fine. What do I owe you?" she asked, opening her purse.

He waved her off. "Glad to be of service. Good luck," he said as she hopped out. "Jim Johnson will take care of you. He's a good fella."

"Thanks."

She walked into the office. "Hello?" she said at the door. "Anyone here?"

She started into the garage part and came face to face with the man who'd been on the bear hunt. They'd called him Jimbo.

He gave her a deadpan nod, acknowledging her presence, but said nothing.

It *would* be one of them, she thought. *A good fella.* Sure. "Your sign says you have a wrecker service and I need one. A deer ran out in front of me on the highway north of town and I lost control. Do you suppose you could tow it in? The fender is bent against the wheel."

He nodded.

"When?" she asked. This man made taciturnity into an art.

He shrugged, dropping his mouth open, and scratched his cheek. "Well, we can put you on the list." He studied a clipboard he took from a nail by the door. "Maybe by tonight, maybe not."

"Is there another wrecker service in town?"

He nodded slowly. "But they won't be any faster. We're all backed up. The snow. People off the roads."

"Well, put me on your list." She gave him her name, the location of the car, and the key, then walked out into the cold air again.

There was a small white stucco motel across the street. It formed a semicircle around an expanse of snow-covered lawn. Under the eye of the sun, a red-tile roof was emerging quickly from its blanket of snow and made the piece look as if it should be called the Hacienda or the Tropicana and should have palm trees in front. Instead its red neon sign read AURORA MOTEL, and it had pines.

Sandy registered, wishing she had her suitcase, but it would have been too heavy to carry when she set out from the car looking for help.

From her room, she made a long distance call to the car rental agency in Minneapolis. The woman there told her to go to the Chrysler dealer in town and he would give her a different car, then would take care of the other one.

"Heard you got some surprise weather up there," the woman said.

"We sure did," Sandy replied. "How is it in Minneapolis?"

The woman told her they hadn't gotten any snow at all. They talked a moment more, than Sandy hung up. She looked up the number for the car dealer and dialed. No one answered. She glanced at her watch. It was only three-thirty. Maybe they hadn't opened because of the weather. She put the receiver down, went over, and turned on the television. A little mindlessness seemed inviting. So did the bed, which was covered with a red and orange jacquard bedspread to coordinate with the well-worn orange shag carpet which spelled *seventies*.

The evening news was on when she woke up, her eyes dry from sleeping in her contacts. She pulled back the drape and looked across the street at the garage, but she couldn't see whether her car was there or not. There didn't seem to be any activity.

Her breakfast was wearing thin, so she put on her coat, stepped out into the brisk evening, and headed for a Dairy Queen several doors down the street. As she sat eating a hamburger, a tow truck came down the highway with her car behind it. It turned into the garage and she watched as they backed it into an empty bay, then lowered the door.

After eating she went over and knocked on the office door. A man, not Jim Johnson, came to the door and spoke to her through the glass. "We're closed," he shouted.

"That's my car," she said, pointing toward the bay.

He unlocked the door and let her in. "We won't have a body man here until the morning. He can pull that fender out so it's driveable."

"It's a rental, so I'm supposed to go to the Chrysler dealer here and get another one. Then they'll take care of it. But I need to get my luggage out."

"Sure, go ahead."

She took the suitcase out of the back seat, slammed the door, and went back into the office. "Thanks," she told the man.

"Where you luggin' that to? Can you manage?"

She nodded. "I'm just going across the street. I have a room at the Aurora."

17

To Sandy the motel seemed very remote. It was as if she were wrapped in a cocoon for the night, waiting for real life to resume. The unexpected snow had cost her over twenty-four hours now.

The next morning, she closed her bag, then began looking for the map of the lakes.

Damn! It must be in the car. She glanced at her watch. It was eight-thirty. Someone would probably be at the garage. They surely started by eight.

She put on her coat and went to the motel office. A loud buzzer sounded when she entered, and after a few moments a door in the back of the office opened and a woman in an apron came out, wiping her hands.

"Sorry to bother you," Sandy said, "but have you heard if the power is back on north of town?"

"No, I haven't, but you might call the electric company. You want to use this phone?"

"Yes, please." Sandy made the call and was told that electricity and phone service had been restored to the area around the Senator's house. Other areas were not so fortunate.

The woman had disappeared into the other room, so

Sandy took the liberty of calling the car dealership, too. They were open for business. Sandy explained the situation and the woman said they'd provide a car.

"Do you have someone who could pick me up? I'm at the Aurora Motel."

"I'm sorry, hon. We're short-handed today. Bill is snowed in."

Bill? Such familiarity.

"And we're only open till noon on Saturday."

Sandy had lost track of the days. She couldn't believe it was already Saturday. "Is there a cab service in town?"

The woman laughed. "In Northlake? You've got to be kidding."

There was nothing to do but walk.

Sandy stepped to the door behind the counter, which apparently led to living quarters, and knocked. Soon the woman appeared.

"I'm going to be back later to get my bag," Sandy said. "I left it in the room."

"Checkout time is eleven."

Sandy patted herself on the back for not rolling her eyes. There was only one car at the motel, so unless everyone else had walked in as she had, that meant rooms were not at a premium. "I'll be out by then. And thanks for letting me use the phone."

It was a sinus-clearing crisp day. The evergreens in front were snow-frosted and the smell of Christmas trees hung in the air. Sandy drank in a deep breath as she walked out of the motel driveway. There was no fragrance anything like this at home. Her street had a token tree or two, framed by cement. The predominant aroma seemed to be exhaust fumes.

The highway through town was clear of snow, but wet

from the melt. The snow plow deposits along the side were now spattered with road grime. More like home.

Sandy jumped back a few feet as a car went past, its tires throwing up a spume of dirt, then hastened across to Jim's Garage. There was no one in the office area, so she went on into the service bay and opened the car door. She found the map on the passenger-side floorboard.

A phone rang in the office as she was closing the car door. She started back toward the office just as someone answered it.

She hesitated, not wanting to startle whoever it was by her sudden appearance from the garage area. She didn't intend to eavesdrop, but it was impossible not to at first, and after a moment, she wanted to.

Jim Johnson was on the phone, much more talkative now, apparently speaking with one of his cronies; "He told me that a guy named Dave Hale works for Fish and Wildlife, but he can't be reached . . . coincidence, ha! . . . Carl got a driver's license picture of this Dave Hale faxed up here. It's Kevin all right . . . yeah . . . some guy he knows works in motor vehicles. Remember how Anderson appeared and started cozyin' up to you? . . . Shit, you shoulda never . . . yeah, I blame you, you're damn right . . . Forget it. Carl says the shipment's going out this weekend and we gotta deal with this . . . Yeah . . . Okay, that's fine with me." He hung up and she heard him moving around in the office.

Sandy's heart started to pound. Johnson mustn't find her here. He would know she'd overheard. She darted to the back of the garage, and there, sheltered by her car, ducked down and waited. There was a side door, but it could be seen from the office if anyone was looking that way. Carefully, she sneaked in front of the car adjacent to the rental, then along the far side, between it and a workbench, peeking up through the car's windows. No sign of Johnson, but she heard him open the front door and greet someone. Their voices indicated they were coming her way.

Several oil drums sat at one end of the workbench near the side door. She slid in behind them. The door was only a couple of feet away, but there was no way she could get to it now, not with the two men so close.

"See? Fender against the wheel," Johnson said. He thumped it. "It's a rental and the gal who brought it in is going to get another car, so she isn't going to be hollerin' for it. You might as well work on the Buick."

"I can't do any more without those parts," the other man said.

"Well, shit. Not much chance of getting 'em on Saturday. Let's roll it out, so you can work on something else. Get the door."

Sandy could see the man as he pressed a switch and the door began rumbling upward. She pulled her head back and crouched even lower.

One of them opened the driver's door, released the brake, and put the car in gear. When she heard the car moving, Sandy dared peek out again.

Lord! Johnson was right there, running forward to help push. He was within touching distance. She instinctively flinched and the map she was holding rattled. She waited an endless moment, but Johnson was occupied; he didn't hear anything.

They were halfway across the lot now, leaning into their work, their attention on the direction in which they were pushing. It was now or never. She edged out of her hiding place, keeping her eyes fixed on the two men. One of them was going to jump in the car and start steering it into a parking place any moment now. She ran out of the bay, crouching behind a car parked to one side, running its width, stopping to reconnoiter when she reached the other side. She prayed no one was watching from across the street.

She darted around the corner of the building and between two cars which were angled in toward the side wall of the garage. She ran, crouched down, taking one last look toward the front of the building before breaking into the open toward the back of the lot. Once she reached it, she jogged down the alley toward town, not slowing down till she was a block away from the garage. She leaned against a telephone pole to catch her breath.

She returned to the main street and continued west, trying to look nonchalant, and feeling anything but. She'd had too many close calls. Now she had to tell Dave Hale that they knew who he really was. She felt she owed it to him for blowing his cover.

At the Laundromat she found a telephone sign. The air inside felt like a tropical rain forest. Dryers whirled their loads and a man stood, arms folded, and stared into one as if he were watching television. He didn't look up, even when Sandy walked by him. An old man and woman were sitting in plastic chairs at the back, waiting. A very young woman in blue jeans, her hair frizzed wildly around her face, pulled clothes out of a washer, while a toddler careened around the corner of a machine, pushing a wheeled basket.

"You quit that, Zack," the mother shrilled as Sandy grabbed the basket to keep it from smacking into her. "Get back over there and sit down. Leave that cart alone."

Sandy spotted the phone at the back. She sidestepped the cart and dug around in her purse and found a quarter. Fortunately the phone book hadn't been pilfered, although it was in a sorry state. The back was half gone—probably someone had torn it off as a notepad—the pages curled and frayed. She balanced it against the wall and turned the pages, looking for a Kevin Anderson. There were several columns of Andersons—and another of Andersens. There were three Kevins with various initials, and six with just the initial K. None looked like the downtown address. There was one Kevin Anderson without any address, and she dialed that one.

A child answered.

Sandy covered one ear to hear better and stood facing the corner formed by the phone and the wall. "Is Kevin there?" she asked. She heard the child yell, "It's for Daddy." She hung up. Kevin Anderson/Dave Hale hadn't had time for that.

A dead end.

It was probably less than a mile to the heart of town. She would walk it—go to the apartment on the alley behind the taxidermy shop. Maybe he would be there.

Twenty minutes later she turned into the alley. A car was parked in back. She hurried up the stairs to the apartment and knocked but no one answered. She peered into the living room through the uncurtained glass panel in the door. No one seemed to be around. She tried the handle. It was unlocked and she went in. "Dave?" she called. No one answered.

She quietly moved out of the living room into the kitchen. There was no one there either. Beyond it, through a curtained doorway, lay another room. She edged toward the opening, reaching out tentatively to pull back the curtains. A squeamish feeling roiled through her, the memory of Gus Skaar's bloated body still too fresh.

Quit it, she ordered herself. You don't know if Gus's death was connected with the poachers. Nevertheless, her hand was trembling when she parted the fabric to scan the room.

The closed window shades gave a dim, yellowish cast to

the room. There were no curtains. An unmade bed dominated the room; clothes lay draped on a straight wooden chair. A pair of boots stood next to it, the laces dangling. A four-drawer dresser sat adjacent to where she stood.

She relaxed. There was no sign of Dave. Another door lay to one side, and she caught her breath again and held it. How much more of this could her heart take? She approached it, opening it cautiously, afraid again, but the bathroom was empty, too.

Her knees were shaking and she leaned on the washbasin regaining her composure. Just then she heard footsteps. She retraced her steps to the curtain between the rooms.

"What are you doing here?" he asked after his initial shock at seeing her step out of his bedroom. "You're white as a sheet."

"I came to tell you that they know who you are."

"What are you talking about?"

She told him about the accident with her car and what she'd overheard at the garage. "They got a picture of you from the motor vehicle department and they know you're with Fish and Wildlife. They also said there's a shipment going out this weekend."

He seemed concerned at first, then at the last tidbit, he became excited. He paced across the floor, his eyes aglow. "Now that I'm known, it may be our last chance to run them to ground. It took me a year to get in tight enough with them to go out like you saw the other day. And now—" He shook his head. "Maybe it can be salvaged. If we could just—" He strode back across the room. "See? Carl Hurd is small potatoes. What we want is to get the big guys, the ones taking this stuff out of the country to the Asian markets. We've got a covert operation going on in four states trying to bust this up. I don't know if you know it, but there's a big black market for bear gall bladders in the Orient. Hell," he said, "you can sell about all of a bear somewhere, the paws, the skin, the claws, but the big bucks are in galls. These guys can afford to waste the rest."

The big guys. The memory of the Senator's trade mission to Korea was like a haymaker to her stomach. It left her feeling queasy.

"And what does my brother have to do with it?" she asked weakly.

"Your brother?"

"You didn't overhear what Hurd was telling me at the trading post?"

"I was kind of preoccupied—you just recognizing me and all."

"It's my brother the police are looking for in connection with the taxidermist's death."

"Jeez. You mean Jerry Cochran is your brother?"

She nodded. "Wilson is my married name."

"Jerry was working with Gus Skaar."

"I know that. But was he involved in the poaching?"

"Not that I know of. Jerry was dating Hurd's daughter, so I suppose he could have been, but—Listen, I've got some business to attend to. I need to get out of here."

"May I use your bathroom?"

"Yeah, sure."

"I'll be quick," she said.

"It's off the bedroom." He pointed.

"I know," she said sheepishly. "I should apologize for being in here when you came home, but I wasn't just snooping. I was afraid—"

"It's okay. I'm not working today because of the weather and I went around to get a newspaper. You surprised me, but"—for a moment his eyes looked wicked—"damn it, your intentions were honorable." He smiled. It was the first evidence she'd seen of a sense of humor.

18

T HE damn toilet wouldn't flush. Sandy pulled on the handle and shook it, but nothing happened. There had to be a trick to it, but she didn't have time for this. She zipped her jeans and opened the door.

She headed for the living room, but just as she reached out to open the curtain, she heard the low murmur of a man's voice. Something made her hesitate and she was glad she did, because another voice answered the first.

They were here: Jim Johnson and his cohort. Was Dave okay? Or had they—? Sweat broke out on Sandy's forehead. She looked around for a weapon. There was nothing, not even a lamp. Dave lived a stark existence.

Would they search in here to see if there was any incriminating evidence? Prickles of alarm shot up her arms, standing the hairs on end. Frantic, she looked for a place to hide. As in many old apartments there wasn't even a closet. She dropped to the floor and went snaking under the bed, mopping up dustballs and cobwebs. There, she waited, praying the two intruders would leave, knowing this was no kind of a hiding place at all if they really thought someone was in the apartment.

The smell of her fear mingled with the odor of mildew from the mattress as the moments ticked away. When at last the silence seemed definitive, she wormed her way out. Cautiously she went into the kitchen, her heartbeat driving into her chest wall. Next the living room.

Dave was lying on the floor in a pool of blood. He'd been brutalized in much the same way as the bear, but without the benefit of a bullet first.

Sandy retched, and turned away from the gruesome sight, grabbing the back of a chair to stay upright as her legs buckled under her. Everything went dark, but she didn't pass out. After a moment, her vision cleared.

My God! Jim Johnson had said on the phone he needed to take care of the situation. How dense did she have to be?

There was clearly no help for Dave. She grabbed her coat and purse and staggered toward the door, tears blinding her. She tried to put the thought of Mildred Hale, his mother, out of her mind, but it kept rising to the surface. If only she hadn't stopped to call from the Laundromat, she and Dave would have been safely out of there.

But no, she reminded herself, he had been out when she arrived. Well, if she hadn't gone to the bathroom. If, if, if. She pressed her temples. She couldn't think like that.

Dave's car keys caught her attention. They lay on a little mahogany table by the door. She grabbed them. She needed transportation and there was no way she could go to the car dealership now. She was in no shape for it.

She stumbled down the stairs, her guilt choking her. The killers must have been coming up the stairs when she left the room, to have accomplished their task in so short a time. Her trip to the bathroom had saved her life.

Shaking all over, she somehow managed to fit the key in the ignition. She jerked the gear lever into reverse, her eyes blurred with tears, then put it into drive, and with a screech of tires that sent gravel flying up into the fender well, she fled down the alley. At the end of the alley she almost hit a passing car. Her head was thrown back against the headrest as she jammed on the brakes. The woman in the other car glared at her.

She sat there a moment, thinking. *I'd better get hold of myself. This is the second murder where I've been on the scene.* She remembered that she hadn't stopped to worry about fingerprints this time. Her eyes widened. Should she go back? But no, there wasn't time. She had to find Jerry before the same thing happened to him. He had something, or knew something, which made him a threat to these people.

She made a right turn, then another, out onto the main thoroughfare.

Try to act normal, she told herself. She drove slowly down the street, past the Laundromat, past the motel and Jim's Garage. She glanced at her watch. It was after eleven, so she couldn't go to the motel room to gather her wits. Her mind skittered through her options, regarding and discarding. The convenience store where she'd stopped the first night she was in town came up on her left. She pulled off the highway and up to the call-from-your-car phone.

She stretched out the window and pressed the buttons for information in the Twin Cities and asked for the U.S. Fish and Wildlife Service. After more punching of buttons and putting in her credit card number, she reached the agency and asked for the person in charge.

"This is Melvin Trumball. Can I help you?"

"You have a Dave Hale working undercover as Kevin Anderson in Northlake."

"No ma'am." She could hear the wariness in his voice; he didn't lie well. "We do have a Dave Hale, but he's working on a project in Arizona at this time."

"Listen to me. Dave Hale is in Northlake and has been murdered. Two men came into his apartment. I was in the bathroom. When I came out, he was dead."

"Who is this?"

"This is Sandy—" She stopped herself. "I can't tell you that. But I can tell you that a man named Jim Johnson either did it or was an accomplice. He has a garage across from the Aurora Motel in Northlake. There were two of them."

"Have you called the police?"

"No. I was afraid to. I don't know who's involved in this."

"Where are you?"

"I'm at a pay phone in front of a convenience store."

"As I said, Dave Hale is in Arizona, but I'd like to let you talk to someone. Where can I reach you?"

"You can't. I have to go." She had to find Jerry before Carl Hurd did. She settled the receiver in its cradle, not waiting for a response.

She went back into town and pulled into an empty space in front of the café, determined to speak to Brigitte. If Carl Hurd wasn't there to stop her, she would force the girl to go with her.

But Carl Hurd *was* there, and there was no sign of his daughter. Well, at least Sandy knew where he was. Now if she could locate Brigitte.

She asked to see a phone book and Hurd pulled one from underneath the counter and handed it to her.

Right under your eyes, you sick bastard, she thought as she looked up his name in the phone book. *Damn!* The address was simply "Rt. 1."

She slammed the book down on the counter and left.

Her next stop was the post office, where she found out Route 1 was east of town. The shops she passed were beginning to seem like familiar friends, and enemies too, she thought as she passed the garage again. Jim Johnson was walking out the door. Was it her imagination that he noticed her? She pressed a little harder on the accelerator.

She was out of town now, and she kept her eyes peeled, trying to stay on the road and read mailboxes at the same time, following the directions the post office clerk had been kind enough to give her. It was frustrating; about half of them didn't have names, just box numbers and that didn't help her a bit.

Finally she stopped at a house where a man was in the yard and asked if he knew where the Hurds lived.

He studied her a moment, his eyes suspicious. "Isn't that Kevin Anderson's Bronco?"

He caught her off guard. "No. It's mine," she answered too quickly. She repeated her question.

Again he ignored it. "Listen, lady, I work with Kevin and I know that car." A slow smile began to grow on his face. "You a friend of his?"

"Could you please tell me if you know where the Hurds live?"

"Yeah. They live third house down on the left. The one with the dog pens."

"Can I turn around here?"

"Yeah. Just pull in there." He pointed. "Kevin never mentioned no lady friend," he called after her, a smirk on his face.

She drove by the house at first, then saw the dog pens he'd mentioned. Suddenly she knew how the wolf hybrid had come to be on the Senator's porch. Hadn't Carl Hurd warned her about the dangers out in the woods, hoping to scare her away? He'd made sure those dangers were realized.

She backed down the shoulder, then jerked the car into drive and went toward the house. The dog pens ran alongside a barn, and her arrival was causing a stir there. Several animals—they looked like wolves to her—were jumping against the enclosure, snarling and barking.

The setting for Hurd's place was beautiful. Stately pines ringed the property, although their presence was marred by several broken-down cars, hauled to and abandoned at the edge of the trees, rusting into oblivion. The house itself was a gold and brown double-wide mobile home, skirted, and with a porch built on.

Sandy got out of her car and approached the house warily. Although she'd seen Carl Hurd in town at the café, she felt she was confronting the enemy on his own turf.

Inside, another dog was barking. Clearly no one came to this place unannounced. The curtain at the picture window was thrust roughly aside, and a wolflike dog's head appeared. The barking became more strident when the creature saw her. It disappeared and she could hear it at the door; then it reappeared in a frenzy at the window.

Did she even want to go on the porch?

She took a deep breath for courage and walked up the three steps and rapped on the storm door. She could already hear Brigitte, yelling at the dog to be quiet. The inner door opened.

"I need to talk to you," Sandy said.

The dog was lunging at the storm door now. Dying to get its teeth in her, Sandy thought.

Brigitte grabbed the dog's collar and pulled it back and opened the storm door.

"Shut up, Baby," the girl yelled. "Sorry," she said to Sandy.

Baby?

Sandy stepped into the house and it was as if a faucet had been turned off. The dog's barking stopped and it began to sniff at her feet. The animal looked like a wolf, just like the one that had attacked her, but sure enough, the tail had a definite curl. Its eyes weren't quite wolflike either, and Sandy thought it was the color.

"Once you're inside, Baby thinks you're a friend."

"I'm glad. I hear that you're engaged to my brother."

The girl blushed, turning her bruised cheek a curious color.

Sandy remembered the picture of Brigitte she'd found at Jerry's house. *I'd blush, too,* she thought. "You've got to tell me what he's involved in and how I can find him."

Brigitte seemed to shrink into herself. "I can't." She pulled at her shirttail and looked down at her scuffed running shoes. Her toes were slightly turned in, giving her a little-girl look. "My father'll kill me."

"But Jerry's your fiancé. Don't you owe him something?"

"Well, we weren't exactly engaged. I just told—"

"He's at Early Dawn Lake, isn't he? Isn't that what your note meant?"

Her hand went to her cheek. "My father said I shouldn't help you. Blood ties are the strongest, he said. He raised me after Mama died. I should help him, not some stranger who wants to ruin my life."

"Ruin your life? Brigitte, your father abuses you. That's not the way life's supposed to be."

The girl's bottom lip quivered.

"Brigitte, do you know Dave—I mean, Kevin Anderson?"

She nodded, looking very much like a naughty four-year-old.

"Well, I just left his place. He's been murdered by that hunting buddy of your father's—Jim Johnson."

"Jimbo? He wouldn't do that. He's my godfather."

"Well, he did do it. Now, tell me why they want Jerry, so

I can find him before they do." She had the urge to grab the girl and shake her, but resisted. She couldn't sink to Carl Hurd's level. "What did Jerry do?"

Brigitte was twisting her shirttail now, keeping her hands busy. "Jerry and I were here—he was taking pictures of me—and my father and some other guy came in. Jerry shouldn't have been here because my father, well, he found a picture Jerry had taken and he was pretty mad at him. He told him never to come here. But I brought him out this one time because we thought my dad was going to be busy picking some guy up in Duluth. But he got back early and brought this guy here. We heard the dogs, but before Jerry could—well, before he could get out—they were in here.

"We stayed in my bedroom, but Jerry heard what they were talking about and he got curious. He snuck down the hall and listened. Then he came back and told me he was going to take some pictures."

Blackmail, thought Sandy. Her first instinct was correct.

"Jerry went back down the hall and stood behind that divider there and took some pictures. Well, my father let Baby in about that time, I guess. And Baby loved Jerry. She strained to get away from my father and ran right around the corner and started whining at Jerry to play." Almost as if her name was a cue, Baby jumped up and began to whine now.

"My father came unglued. Jerry didn't wait around; he ran for the back door and hightailed it into the woods. I would have gone to look for him, because he didn't have a way back to town—I'd brought him out in our car—but my father gave me hell." She wrapped her arms around herself and rocked back on her heels. "By the time he was through with me, Jerry would have been long gone."

Baby's whine had turned to a bark and she had ducked under the curtain again to look out the window.

Brigitte stood up and told her to be quiet. "Someone's here," she said to Sandy.

Sandy went to the door and looked out the little window. "Damn! It's Jim Johnson. I'll get out of here quickly. But first tell me: is Jerry at Early Dawn Lake?"

"I don't know for sure. But he took me to this abandoned cabin out there once. Said it belonged to Gus Skaar."

"Could you help me find it?"

She shook her head just as the door opened and Jim Johnson stepped in. He was carrying a bundle, and his look was dark.

"You've kind of gotten in over your head," he said.

"Pardon me," Sandy said. "I'm just leaving."

She tried to step by him, but he grabbed her by the arm, the injured one. She winced at the pain that shot through it.

Johnson pushed her onto the couch. She struggled to get up, but he shoved her back again. "Just sit still till Carl gets here."

Brigitte looked alarmed. "My father's coming out?"

Johnson nodded.

Brigitte started to leave, but Johnson told her to stay put.

It was only minutes before Baby started getting excited again.

Johnson looked out the window. "There he is."

Hurd burst in, a scowl on his face. "You just can't quit, can you?" he said, addressing Sandy.

"I'm not going to quit looking for my brother, if that's what you mean."

"Your brother's no good. You should have washed your hands of him."

"He's not a murderer."

"That's not what the police think. And it seems to run in the family."

"What do you mean?"

"I mean that you're driving Kevin Anderson's car. In fact, you were seen speeding away from his place. And can you feature it? A short time ago he turned up dead. The police are going to find your fingerprints on the murder weapon. Show her, Jim."

Johnson unwrapped his package. Inside was a hunting knife.

Sandy averted her gaze and Hurd laughed. "She's squeamish, you can tell."

"You'd better think twice about what you're doing," Sandy said.

He interrupted her with a laugh. "You gonna tell your boss on us? Now if you'll just kindly cooperate, this'll be a lot easier."

Sandy made no move to comply.

"Help her along there, Jimbo."

She struggled, but wasn't strong enough to keep Johnson from pressing her fingers into a grip on the knife. If only she could turn it on him—but he was squeezing her wrist too tightly.

Hurd turned his attention to his daughter. "What have you told this lady here, Brigitte?"

"Nothing, Daddy." Her voice quavered.

Sandy had never seen anyone cower better than Brigitte. The beatings had done their work.

He interrupted with a snort. "She just came out here for her health?"

Guilt showed on the girl's face. She looked down and didn't see her father's blow coming. His hand struck her face and she fell back against a lamp table, upsetting the lamp. She straightened up and he hit her again. She slid to the floor and he kicked her solidly on the leg.

"Don't lie to me. Tell me. What did you tell her? Where's your boyfriend?"

"Stop, Daddy," the girl pleaded, her hands over her face in a protective gesture.

The dog was dancing around, barking.

Carl grabbed Brigitte's hair and pulled. She struggled upward to release the tension, but he kept pulling. Her face was twisted in pain and she made a tiny, whimpering sound.

Sandy couldn't take it. She threw herself toward Carl, beating on him. "Leave her alone, you bastard!"

The dog jumped up against Sandy, barking wildly.

Hurd whirled around, fending off her blows with some of his own. He grabbed her wrists. "God, Jimbo, she's a tiger!" He was laughing.

She tried to get her knee up into his groin, but he twisted away.

"Grab this broad, Jim," Hurd said. "Let me get the damn dog outside."

The contest was over, as Johnson enveloped her from behind. If Brigitte could have helped . . . but she sat on the floor, her arms around her legs, whimpering.

Hurd disappeared, dragging the dog with him into the other room. Sandy heard a door open and close, then the sound of a drawer scraping open.

She gave up her struggling, and Johnson threw her face first onto the couch. By the time she turned over, Hurd had returned carrying a gun. He put it under her chin.

He looked over at his daughter. "Now tell me, Brigitte, where's your boyfriend or this woman gets it."

"Maybe he's at Early Dawn Lake," Brigitte said, so softly he made her repeat it.

"Where at Early Dawn?" he asked.

She hesitated and he cocked the gun.

Sweat rolled down Sandy's sides and a lump formed in her throat. She was afraid to breathe.

"Maybe at Gus Skaar's." Her voice was timid.

"Of course. Skaar had that old place out where I baited bears. I should have thought of that." He turned his attention to Sandy. "Where's the key to Anderson's car?"

"In the ignition."

"C'mon," he said, jerking her up by the hair. "Brigitte, you come with me and drive Anderson's Bronco. Jimbo, you follow us. We're going to Mattingly's. We got a buy going down and I don't want to make my man wait."

He pushed and prodded her down the stairs, following behind Brigitte. She winced at the pain when he reached out and grasped her injured arm, pulling her to the car. He forced her into the back seat, then climbed in next to her.

"You thought you were so smart, coming out here while I was at the café," he said. "But Jimbo saw you go by the garage in the Bronco. He'd just seen it over at Anderson's. So he calls me. No sooner had I hung up than my neighbor calls and says you're driving Anderson's car, saying it's yours. Says your lookin' for my house. He tried Kevin—gonna razz him, but Kevin doesn't answer. So he calls me.

"And now," Hurd continued, "we have us a murderer here. Murder. It's bad business. Makes you real depressed, so depressed you might just decide to kill yourself. Sad."

Odd thoughts jumped into Sandy's mind, not the least of which was how awful it would be for Mildred Hale to think Sandy had killed her son Dave.

19

Sandy was surprised to see a strange car parked in front of the Senator's house. Brigitte braked to a stop and Hurd climbed out, then waved the barrel of the gun at Sandy. "C'mon, don't take all day."

Behind them, Jim Johnson appeared in the truck. Hurd motioned him to wait there, then walked Sandy up to the front door, letting go long enough to try the knob. It was locked. He punched the doorbell.

She felt rather than heard footsteps. They set up some vibration in the porch. When the door opened, her mouth dropped.

"Troy."

He smiled his political grin, then took in Hurd's gun, and the smile faded.

"Cat's out of the bag," Hurd said. "The little lady has gotten in deeper than shit."

Troy winced. "I was afraid of that. Why couldn't you have taken my advice, Sandy?"

"You're really involved with this man?"

Troy had the good taste to color slightly. "We're associates, yes."

"And the Senator?"

Troy laughed. "You know better than that. Good ol' Jim Mattingly, an honest Abe for the nineties."

So it was *Troy* Jerry had seen with Hurd. Her brother recognized him from his Washington visit. "And this was all over a roll of film? That's Jerry's only involvement?"

He snorted. "He's a blackmailer. Sent me a letter. You see, my friend and I here, we have a little trade agreement"—he smiled—"with some Koreans, and your brother was threatening to expose it. He's a nuisance, Sandy, a real nuisance. But you know that."

While Troy's recital was going on, Hurd had pushed her into the house. Sandy noticed the power was back on, and the place was warm. Brigitte came in behind them. Troy didn't acknowledge her presence.

"You had someone ransack my mother's house first," Sandy said to Troy. "And when the film wasn't there, mine."

"Yes. Unfortunately when Carl and—who was it? Jim Johnson?"

Carl nodded.

"—when they visited Skaar, he admitted Jerry had mailed the film for safety, but he didn't know where. To himself, maybe? Or his next of kin?" Troy smirked. "We got some nice pictures of your mother's vacation developed. Then I saw the film on the table the night I visited you, but I couldn't just take it. So I—I subcontracted the job. Your odd little neighbor—the one who leers at you all the time—he was eager to get a look at your things."

Ray Champion. She pictured him fingering her lingerie.

"Your brother has put me in the unfortunate position of having to exercise"—he flashed a quick smile at her—"you know, damage control."

Yes, she knew. It was a phrase they used in the office

when something happened that might hurt the Senator's image, like the time when he told what might have been construed as a sexist joke at a party.

She knew what "damage control" implied in this instance. She and Jerry would have to be killed.

He turned to Hurd. "Have you located Cochran yet?"

"No, but I think I know where he is," Hurd said.

"You think?" Troy dropped his cool façade, his tight control gone. "Christ Almighty, what have you been doing? I don't have forever to take care of this." He ran his hand through his hair and paced toward the windows.

"I told you I could handle it," Hurd said.

Troy turned back toward them, his eyes narrow slits. "And I told you this bastard is mine. He's caused me so much time and trouble—"

She'd known Troy didn't like to be crossed, but she had never seen him like this. His eyes had a strange glow as if he were relishing the thought of taking care of Jerry once and for all.

Hurd acquiesced. "Brigitte here says he might be holed up at Early Dawn Lake."

"Might be? Is that the best you can do? Our whole operation is resting on this." Troy was obviously wound tight.

"Don't get bent out of shape. I've been occupied. We had another problem I had to take care of."

"What do you mean?" Troy asked.

"I found out there's been a Fish and Wildlife undercover guy breathing down our necks."

Sandy saw an opportunity to put them at odds. She snorted. "More than that."

Hurd glowered at her. "Shut up!"

"What's she talking about?" Troy asked.

Before Hurd could say anything, Sandy answered. "He

was one of their buddies. He'd been hunting with them. Part of the group. And now they've killed him. If you don't think that's going to bring them swooping down on you—''

Troy looked at Hurd. "Is that true?" he asked, his voice tight with anger.

Hurd looked sheepish; the wind seemed to go out of him under Troy's scrutiny. Then he straightened slightly. "We caught on to him before he did any damage, that's what matters. And that little problem has been eliminated."

Damage control again.

He went on. "But we have that taken care of, too. See, we've got her fingerprints on the weapon. And she was seen driving this guy's car. That's it out in front. I'm going to park it in the Senator's boathouse with the weapon under the seat for the cops to find. They'll think she killed him, then drove the car out here. Then I was planning to take her out in the canoe and make it look like she'd committed suicide—you know, depressed about what she'd done. I've got it figured out."

Troy scowled at him. "You're a jerk. What is her motive supposed to be for killing him? Did you ever think of that?''

Hurd scowled. "Of course I did. What I figured was—''

Troy interrupted. "What we're going to do with Sandy is take her along when we go after her brother. She'll be an incentive for him not to resist."

"And then?" Hurd asked.

"We'll worry about that when we have the brother taken care of.''

The phone rang, and Sandy looked questioningly at Troy.

"Answer it," he said, "but be careful what you say."

It was Pauline Cochran. "I thought you were going to call me. I've been worried sick."

"I'm sorry I haven't called, Mother," she said, trying to keep her voice even. "I've just been occupied."

"Well, you might want to know this. I got a letter from a lawyer. It seems Gus Skaar—that was your father's friend—he died this last week. The lawyer says that you and Jerry are his heirs and his estate includes property in Northlake and a piece of land on some lake up there. There's a legal description."

Too bad Sandy didn't have this information earlier. She could have tracked down the land and might have found Jerry before it was too late.

"Sandy, are you there?"

"Yes, Mother, but I have to go. I have an appointment." Tears welled up in her eyes. Could this really be the last time she would speak to her mother? Unless she did something very quickly, her mother was going to lose both her children. The responsibility made Sandy feel sick. Death didn't seem nearly as frightening as thinking about Pauline being left to face that kind of grief.

"Sandy, are you okay?"

"Yes. Yes. Mother, I—"

Troy grabbed Sandy's arm.

"What is it?" her mother asked.

"Nothing. I just want to say—"

Troy's grip tightened.

"I—I love you," Sandy said as she hung up the phone.

"You're breaking my heart, Sandy," Troy said acerbically.

She narrowed her eyes and glared at him.

Troy turned to Hurd. "Do you have everything ready to go? The plane is coming in when the moon comes up."

"I got to go back to get dry ice, so we can pack the rest of the coolers. Did you bring some more?"

Troy nodded. "Why didn't you get the ice on the way out?"

"I had her with me. Jimbo's out there. You want him to help you here while I make a run into town?"

"I don't want to do business with anyone but you; I've told you that. You haven't been spreading my name around among your cronies, have you?"

"No, keep your pants on. If you don't want Jimbo here, he can drive me and Brigitte back into town. I'll get my truck and the ice, then be back. What about her?" He pointed to Sandy.

"We'll go after her brother later."

"Not tonight. We can drive up before daybreak and get on the water at sunrise." He was eyeing Troy's gray flannel slacks and sport coat. "You got any outdoor clothes?"

"Yes. I just haven't had time to change."

"Do you have a gun?" Hurd asked Troy.

"No."

"Here, take this. You may need it." He handed over his revolver.

Troy hesitated a moment.

"Go on," Hurd said. "You'll have a hard time with her otherwise." He grinned. "She's a tiger."

Troy took the gun and followed Hurd and Brigitte to the door. "And get that Bronco out of sight. We don't want any interference."

"Don't worry. I'll drive it into the boathouse," Carl said.

After the Hurds left, Troy settled down onto the couch. "Go ahead," he said, gesturing with his gun. "Sit down and relax."

"Tell me," she said acidly, ignoring his suggestion. "was your little visit to my place the other night simply to find out about my brother?"

How could a smile be so unfriendly? "I'm afraid so," he said. "I really lost interest in you some time ago, Sandy, but it takes time to break those things off gracefully—you know, when you have to continue to work together. Besides, I didn't have anyone else to replace you.''

She would have liked to wipe the smug look off his face, but he had the gun in his lap. So she just glared at him.

"A man has to be careful in my position. A young lady created quite a problem for me several years ago. I broke it off and she continued to harass me for a long time. Ultimately she committed suicide.''

"Over you?" she blurted out as she sat down in the easy chair across from Troy. "Don't flatter yourself." But she knew it was probably true. His assets looked great; his liabilities were hidden.

Fifteen minutes later the doorbell rang.

Troy jumped, then glanced at his watch. Hurd could not possibly be back so soon. "Do you know who that could be?''

Sandy shook her head.

Troy gave her instructions as she went to the door. He stationed himself just behind it with Hurd's gun.

It was Niles. Her heart constricted as she looked out at him through an opening just wide enough for her face.

"Hi." He caught his bottom lip with his teeth and held it there a minute, waiting, but Sandy didn't say anything, so he continued. "I called the motels in town to find you, and the lady at the Aurora said you'd been there but checked out—asked me to remind you about your suitcase.''

"Oh, right. I forgot it. Thanks. And thanks for clearing the path to the highway." She spoke very quietly.

"You're welcome. Listen, I have to go to the Cities and I came by to see if you needed anything.''

"No, I'm fine.''

"Whose car?" He glanced back at the car Troy was driving.

"I—uh—had an accident with the rental I had, so I traded.''

His brows drew together. "What kind of accident? Were you hurt?"

"A deer ran in front of the car and I put on the brakes, hit a slick patch. But I'm fine."

"Thank goodness. Sandy, I want to apologize for the other day. May I come in?"

"I'm kind of busy."

"Well, okay then." He looked disappointed. "See you around."

Not likely, she thought as she closed the door and leaned against it. Not likely.

20

"Sounds like Sandy found herself a new boyfriend," Troy said sarcastically as he gestured for her to move back to the living room.

She detected a note of jealousy in his voice and wondered how she could use that to her advantage. He might not want her, but he definitely liked to think she still wanted him. Sandy sat down on the couch and looked at him indulgently. "Actually, he's one of your employees."

Troy looked perplexed.

"One of your poachers."

"Oh."

They sat there silently a few moments. This evening was going to last an eternity, she thought, then amended the notion with an *if only*. Considering what might come next, she should be relishing every moment of it.

Troy was fidgety. He finally said, "I'm going to fix myself a drink. Do you want one?"

She nodded. "Why not? I don't have anything better to do." Actually she had something much better to do. As soon as he had turned his back she took her opportunity and bolted for the door.

"Stop, Sandy," she heard him call, "I don't want to shoot you."

But he did want to kill her, she knew that. Only he wanted it to look like an accident, and on his own timetable. She was banking on his not wanting to shoot the Senator's house full of holes. She hurled the door open and plunged outside, hearing his voice become more shrill behind her.

Across the porch, down the steps. His reservations would be diminished now that she was out in the open. She hit a patch of ice, protected from the sun by the shadow of the steps. She danced, trying to maintain her balance, but then as if in slow motion she fell onto the muddy ground beside the walk, to the rhythm of Troy's footsteps trotting behind her.

He grabbed her arm—her vulnerable one—and yanked her up, prodding her with the gun. "Where did you think you were going, Sandy? You didn't have any keys. Were you just going to run into the woods?"

Good question. But it was better to try something— anything—than be docile.

"Sit here," he said, shoving her down onto a straight wooden chair. You're too muddy to sit on the couch." He kept his eye on her this time and the gun at hand. "I still want a drink," he said. "You want a gin and tonic?"

"Fine."

Troy went over to the bar and looked in the small refrigerator. "There's no ice," he said.

"The power's been off."

"Christ Almighty!" He slammed the refrigerator door and charged toward her, motioning broadly with the gun. "Get up," he ordered.

He took her by the arm and shoved her toward the utility room. "How long was the electricity off?"

She calculated for a moment, then answered. "Over

forty-eight hours. It's probably only been back on a little while if that ice hasn't refrozen.''

He ran his hand through his hair. ''Jesus. Turn that light on and open the freezer.''

She obeyed and wasn't surprised to see that the entire freezer was packed with bear gall bladders.

He poked several of the wrappings, then sighed with relief.

''Your plunder is safe,'' she said. ''Too bad.''

''Shut up.''

When they returned to the living room, he mixed two drinks and brought one over to her, then sat down across from her in an easy chair and put his feet on the coffee table. He sighed. ''Too bad I don't find you very attractive anymore. We could find something to do while we wait.'' He smirked.

She nursed her drink; he fixed himself a second one. Outside they heard the sound of a truck. Troy put his drink down and hid behind the door, gripping the gun. In a few minutes, Hurd knocked on the door and announced, ''It's Carl.''

Troy let him in. ''You didn't tell me the power had been off.''

''So? Why—?'' Hurd stammered.

''The power, you jerkoff. We've got a whole freezer full of product in there that could have gone bad.''

Carl wisely kept quiet.

''Do you have a rope or something to tie her up?'' Troy asked, gesturing toward Sandy.

''Yeah, in the truck,'' Hurd said. He disappeared for a few minutes, then came back with a rope and began tying her wrists behind the chair.

''You been mud wrestling?'' he asked Sandy when he noticed the condition of her clothes.

Troy was watching. "She tried to make a getaway. A rather ineffectual one." He snorted. "Where's your daughter?"

"I gave her reason to stay home."

"Beat her up again, Carl?" Sandy asked. He had just finished lashing her ankles to the front legs of the chair, and at her words, he jerked the rope tighter. It cut in like a knife, and she wondered if she would pass out at the pain. Then it slacked off a little, and she breathed again.

When he was finished, he and Troy went outside.

Later Carl returned with a cooler, disappeared toward the utility room, then reappeared a few minutes later. She could tell the cooler was heavier by the way Carl lugged it, so she assumed he was unloading the freezer. How many gall bladders did they have? There must have been several hundred. Quite a haul. Quite a lot of dead bears.

The men made several trips to the utility room as the shadows in the room began to deepen. Sandy twisted her wrists, testing the ropes, hoping to loosen them enough to slip her hands out, but there was no give and after several minutes she had only rope burns to show for the strain. She sat there disconsolate, waiting.

The men eventually returned empty handed, turned the lights on, and sat in the dining area and drank several of the beers that Carl had brought. They told jokes, the alcohol erasing their dissimilar backgrounds. Apparently they had everything ready and were now just waiting for the airplane.

It wasn't a long wait. "There he is," Carl said, dropping the front two legs of his chair back to the floor with a sharp click. Sandy strained her ears and could make out the drone of an engine.

The two men went out the sliding glass door, letting in a brief burst of cold air.

They would be occupied for a while now, Sandy thought.

Maybe she could work her way over to the phone. She pressed her feet hard to the floor and heaved, straining against the ropes. The chair barely wriggled, then settled back in its original spot. The carpet was too deep, her center of gravity too stationary. She tried once more, but the effort exhausted her and she was out of breath. It was no use. She should save her strength for later.

She heard the roar of the plane as it gathered speed and lifted off; then the receding hum as it flew into the night. Shortly after that, the truck started, and she thought she heard the car as well. The fact that Troy didn't come inside seemed to be confirmation of that.

For a while she occupied herself by trying to imagine what would happen if she turned the chair over. Her best guess was that she would be on her side, with her arm trapped under her, as helpless as a turtle on its back.

Several times her head lolled forward as she dropped off to sleep. Then she would jerk alert, wondering how she could drift off at a time like this, particularly as uncomfortable as she was. Her joints ached from her restraints. She longed to stretch.

It seemed hours before Troy returned, but maybe it hadn't been that long. It was hard to tell. Finally she heard a car.

He didn't speak when he came in, but he did come over and test the ropes. He smelled of cigarettes and liquor.

"Untie me, please, Troy. Let me move around. I promise I won't try anything. Let me take my contacts out."

He gave a lazy smile and held his finger up, moving it back and forth, out of sync with shaking his head. Then he passed out on the couch and she had to listen to him snore.

She must have slept because a knock at the door wrestled her from somewhere else. Troy came awake with an expletive. Hurd yelled, "It's me. Hurd. Let me in. Time to go."

• • •

The eastern sky glowed rosy by the time Sandy and the two men reached Early Dawn Lake. Soon the sun would be up.

It had been an uncomfortable ride, but at least they'd untied her legs. She was sandwiched between Troy and Hurd, wrists bound behind her, so she was virtually sitting on her hands, which were numb. Her eyes were scratchy and dry.

Hurd bounced off the track and into a small clearing near the shore and stopped, leaving the truck in gear as he turned off the ignition. The men climbed out, and Sandy struggled across the seat to follow.

The setting was lovely. A light mist blanketed the lake, broken by several islands. It hardly seemed a day for death.

Only the swish of Troy's synthetic parka broke the tranquillity as they took the canoe off the truck. He was wearing blue jeans and rubber boots. It was the first time Sandy had ever seen him dressed this casually, even after dating him for half a year.

Their footsteps crunched on the small rocks as they plodded down to the shore. The boat made a hollow plop as the two men turned it over and set it in the water.

Sandy followed and watched, her shoulders hunched against the morning cold. She wriggled her fingers to warm them.

"Throw those life jackets in," Hurd said, "and I'll get my rifle."

When he returned from the truck, Hurd took Sandy by the upper arm and helped her into the center of the canoe. "You take the bow," he told Troy, "and I'll take the stern."

Troy waded ankle-deep into the water, then climbed in. Hurd had on taller boots and he pushed them off, then climbed in and used his paddle to shove them into deeper water.

Sandy sucked in a cleansing breath of the crisp air. She

was feeling rather philosophical. It seemed appropriate to what might be one's last few hours on earth. It was better than becoming hysterical. Not that she hadn't been thinking of escape. But with her hands tied, it didn't seem very possible. And she really couldn't think of one good reason why they might let her live after they found Jerry.

Dawn slid into morning as Hurd and Troy paddled across the lake. The mist lifted and the lake stretched out lazily lengthwise in the sun. Straight ahead the islands restricted the view of the opposite shore. A slight breeze rose and bit Sandy's nose and cheeks and blew loose wisps of hair into her face. It tickled, but with her hands tied, there was little she could do but try to ignore it.

She wondered what Jerry was doing now. Probably still asleep, not knowing what was quietly, but relentlessly, moving his way. He'd always slept late as a child and teenager. Was that still his habit? Would they move in on him silently and catch him off-guard?

There was one hope she still entertained—that Jerry wasn't at Early Dawn, that Brigitte was mistaken. There was little else for which to wish. Her mother had been placated; she wouldn't be looking for Sandy. The Senator's concern for her had been quieted. The only other person who might have been remotely interested in her well-being was sitting in front of her and she'd been dead wrong about him. Really dead wrong. She smiled at the thought. It was a comfort to know she still had a sense of humor.

The paddles dipped and pulled, dipped and pulled. A vee of geese flew overhead, their faint honking riding the morning air. It was a sound that brought back other autumns.

What did she regret, looking back on her life? That she hadn't had one passionate fling with Niles Benson? What did it matter really, if he wasn't good for the long haul? It would have been fun. Of course, it hadn't been simply up to her. He'd backed away. So she wouldn't even count that. *Don't regret what you can't control.*

She regretted that she had spent too long with Charlie. The divorce had sealed eight years of memories into a barrel she no longer wanted to tap. It was as if the contents were contaminated. Eight lost years and the memories locked away. Of course, it didn't matter much now.

She stared at Troy's back, watching him wield the paddle. He seemed to be managing his share of the work with a certain amount of skill. It surprised her. Probably took a course in canoeing in college, she thought. He'd certainly never shown any interest in the outdoors. There was a regret: that she'd spent any time at all with him!

And she supposed she regretted not knowing her father. Her hurt feelings—essentially that's what they were—had squelched any curiosity about him over the years, till she'd finally convinced herself she didn't care. But not caring sealed another bunch of memories away. Where was her affective life? Abandoned? Tucked away? How many years had really been hers?

The canoe glided around the south end of the largest island and she could see the opposite shore now. The snowstorm had stripped most of the leaves off the trees and the shoreline was bordered by a dull wash of gray slashed by the bleached trunks of the birch and aspen. Above the deciduous skeletons, evergreens edged the skyline. Off to the north a snake of smoke drifted above the trees.

Hurd noticed it, too. "Must be the cabin," he said, "over there where that smoke is."

Troy nodded.

Except for Hurd's remark, the silence was broken only by the drip of the water off their paddles.

The sun beat down on Sandy's back and she began

sweating inside her coat, even though her nose was still cold.

The canoe slid in close to the shoreline and Hurd maneuvered it northward, skirting the bank about ten yards out.

They glided toward the clearing where the cabin stood. As it came into full view, Hurd quietly laid his dripping paddle in the boat and Sandy felt a cold finger of water touch her jeans. Lord, it was icy! She shifted her weight slightly, but the water followed.

Something else moved against her leg. She glanced down. Hurd was picking up the rifle that had been lying in the bottom of the canoe. Why?

Sandy searched the clearing and saw Jerry coming out of the woods, carrying a bow. He was still quite a distance away and his features were indistinct, but she would recognize that walk anywhere. How many times had she waited for him, always late; then along he would come, taking his own sweet time, wrapped up in his own little world.

He was in his own little world now. He was a sitting duck.

Sandy sensed rather than saw Hurd raise his gun.

Her scream echoed through the woods and, with energy she didn't know she had, she propelled herself upward and to the side, against the barrel of the gun which was leveled at her brother. It went off, but there was no time to see if it hit its mark—the world around her turned over. She heard Troy swear just as she hit the icy water. Its cold took her breath and she knew death would be imminent in its grip. She rolled downward, choking. Her lungs felt as if they would burst. She needed air. Her feet touched bottom and she bent her knees and pushed up, shooting toward the sunlight.

She surfaced and turned on her back, coughing and sputtering. *God! She'd never felt such cold.* Her heartbeat seemed suspended, but her earlier, philosophical acceptance of death was gone. She was charged now with a powerful desire to survive. Maybe this was her opportunity to get away. She tried to see where the canoe was through her watery eyes, but she was sinking again. If only her arms were free she might have more of a chance. But they weren't, and she had to depend on her legs. She rolled over, face down, gave a butterfly kick, and was propelled closer to the shore. Her new coat seemed almost buoyant, but her shoes wanted to drag her down.

Had she upset the canoe when she lunged for the gun and fell out? A gurgling cry for help behind her seemed to answer her question, but she didn't lift her head out of the water to look.

Another kick with her legs. It propelled her forward again. It wasn't much farther to the shore, but the freezing cold was sapping her strength and her ability to think clearly.

Her air was gone and her lungs burned. Once again, she rolled onto her back and drank in some air. She tucked her chin against her chest, but her body wanted to sink with her arms behind her back. She tried a sculling movement with her tied hands; her legs treaded water. Her eyes stung and she briefly wondered if her contacts were still in place, but she couldn't tell. Her vision was too blurred by the water.

There was no sign of Troy, but the canoe was sitting in the water as if nothing had happened. Then it moved toward her, and she saw that Hurd was shoving it.

Have to get out of this water, she thought. The cold was an increasing torment.

She twisted toward the shore, dropped her legs down, struggling to touch bottom, but it wasn't there. Again she lay face down in the water and kicked, calling on all the strength she had left in her legs.

One more kick. The shore was so close now. She let her legs drop again, and this time she felt the bottom. *The cold. Unbearable.*

The canoe floated past. Hurd struggled upright beside her. "You damn bitch," he said, his voice quavering. His face was blue-gray, his lips purple.

Sandy's teeth began to chatter as she emerged from the water. Her knees shook. Her whole body seemed to be running down. Hurd didn't matter. Warmth. She had to have warmth. She hobbled toward the cabin.

Behind her the canoe rasped on the pebbly shoreline as Hurd shoved it out of the water.

She got to the cabin door, and had turned to grapple with the latch with her tied hands, when Hurd came up, pushed her away, unlatched the door, and ran in. For a moment she was afraid he was going to slam the door in her face, so she rammed against it with her shoulder. But he was already heading for the pot-bellied woodstove in the corner. She followed, shoving the door closed with her hip. Neither had paused to see if Troy was anywhere nearby. And what about Jerry?

She glanced around the primitive, one-room cabin; there was no sign of him. Had he been shot? Or did he get away? For the moment, both questions would have to remain unanswered. She and Hurd were preoccupied with getting warm.

The stove was sending off heat like a blast furnace. She'd never felt anything more welcome. If only she could get her wet clothes off.

Hurd began stripping his own clothes off his bull-like body, cold beyond self-consciousness. Sandy wished she could do the same, but with her hands tied, she was helpless and felt so in more ways than one. Then an unintentional glance at the naked Hurd reassured her; the cold seemed to have rendered him fairly harmless. She crouched down as close to the stove as possible.

He pulled a blanket off the bed and wrapped it around himself.

"Will you untie me so I can get out of these clothes?" she asked, her teeth clacking together. She could tell by the way he looked at her that the answer was about to be no. He would just as soon she'd freeze to death. "I won't be bait for my brother if I'm dead," she told him.

He seemed to think about it a moment, then with one finger sticking out of his blanket motioned for her to turn around. Uneasily, she turned her back to him as he extended his arm, letting his cover fall partly open. He began to untie the knot, but before he loosened the rope, he managed to brush his penis up against her hands. She lurched from him as if burned by the stove, but he pulled her back by the rope and finished undoing it. He laughed close to her ear. "You could warm me up real fast," he said.

A new kind of fear hung over her now. She pulled her shoes and socks off, looking for someplace to retreat from his eyes. But there was no place. She moved away from the stove to the far corner of the room.

"You could turn your head," she said, glancing back at him, her teeth still chattering.

He chortled. "Shit, lady. It's not often I get a private show like this." He stood to one side of the stove and he opened his blanket to its warm air, and not incidentally to her.

As miserable and fearful as she was, she nevertheless gave him a dirty look. He just laughed and continued to watch her.

Regardless of him, she had to get her cold, wet clothes off. She grabbed a sweatshirt from a peg and after she stripped her coat, sweatshirt, and bra off with her back to Hurd, she quickly put on the dry sweatshirt. It was long enough to cover her as she peeled off her jeans. It was difficult. The heavy, wet denim refused to cooperate. She lost her balance, stumbled backwards, caught herself, and tried again.

Suddenly, she felt him behind her. *God!* He threw his arm around her, pulling the blanket with it. The other end of the blanket was over his opposite shoulder. He ran his other hand along the elastic of her underwear, reached around in front, then pulled her off balance so that she fell against him. He was no longer harmless.

He had almost drowned, and he was already thinking of sex. She couldn't believe it.

The jeans were around her ankles now and she couldn't get away. She made her hands into fists and, twisting around, began to pummel his head and shoulders, whatever she could reach. She tried to jam her fingers in his eyes, but couldn't get a shot at them. The heat of her rage warmed her body like the stove couldn't.

Hurd raised one arm to ward off the blows and the blanket fell to the floor. His left hand insinuated itself between her thighs and she grabbed his wrist to stop him. Just as she did so, the door opened, letting in a cold blast of air.

"You son of a bitch." It was Troy. He stood in the door, shoeless, dripping wet. His voice was quavering. "I'm out there drowning and you're in here—Jesus Christ! You're an animal."

Troy, that exemplar of self-control, was being beaten down by the wilderness.

"Well, damn me to hell, I thought you drowned," Hurd said, falling away from Sandy and grabbing his blanket.

"Well, I didn't, no thanks to you." Troy staggered over to the stove. "God, I'm freezing."

Sandy was thankful Troy had appeared. Even though it raised the odds against her again, for the moment his presence had protected her. Shaken, she sat down on the floor and wrestled the jeans off.

Hurd was rummaging around the cabin, looking for things to wear. "Well, get your damn clothes off," he said. "That'll help. Here, lady"—he threw a pair of jeans Sandy's way—"these look like they'll fit you."

Sandy grabbed them and slipped them on.

Troy's hands were shaking so much he had difficulty getting his clothes off, but finally managed.

In an act of compassion she found hard to understand considering what the man had planned for her, Sandy pulled a second blanket off the bed and gave it to Troy.

He trembled convulsively. "I think I'm gonna die of the cold," he said, hunching up under the cover.

Hurd gave a snort. "You'll make it. You've got the shivers. That's a good sign." He had pulled on a T-shirt and a pair of sweat pants that were a size too small, and was checking out a rifle he'd taken from a rack on the wall. "What happened to you, anyway? I didn't see you when surfaced."

Haltingly Troy told them how he'd managed to stay in the boat when the canoe first tipped, then fell out backward when it tilted in the other direction. "I was doing fine, till my damn boots filled with water and took me down. They were like anchors. I had to get them off. When I surfaced you two were heading inside. I thought I'd never make it to shore."

"Do you have my gun?"

"I got rid of it. It was like a lead sinker on a fishing line."

"That's great," Hurd said, disgruntled. "Why didn't you holler?"

"Holler? I could hardly breathe, you backwoods ape."

"Look, city boy, I'm about fed up to here"—he tapped the underside of his chin—"with your name-calling."

"You think I give a good goddamn if you're fed up?

You're working for me and don't forget it." He turned to Sandy. "Find me some clothes," he said, then turned toward the stove to warm his front side.

She folded her arms to show she was ignoring him, but he wasn't paying any attention. Her gesture made her appreciate what a luxury it was to be untied. And to be able to see clearly. Her contacts, she realized, *were* still in place.

Hurd threw him some camouflage pants. "Try these." He'd just put on a down-filled vest over the T-shirt and was snapping it shut.

"We've got to go after Cochran," Troy said, stepping into the cammies. His voice quivered as he spoke, and Sandy had to admire his determination. But it was just like him, when she thought about it. When he sank his teeth into an adversary, even a staffer who failed to please him, he hung on.

She'd almost forgotten about Jerry. Now Troy's words raised her hopes about her brother.

"Did you see him before you fell in?" Hurd asked.

"Yeah. He took off into the woods. What happened anyway? How'd you manage to tip the damn canoe over?"

"Me! Your girlfriend here did it. She came up under the gun barrel."

"Well, I think you wounded him. He jumped like he was hit."

"Sounds like you managed to keep your piss-ant brother in the game, lady," Hurd said. He snickered. "Now we'll have us a real hunt."

Sandy was reminded of Niles's comment so long ago—that he hunted humans. Had their little group done this sort of thing before?

Sandy dreaded leaving the warmth of the cabin. She put on two pair of dry socks, but then had to put her wet shoes back on, and in only moments the dampness seeped through and the cold began to penetrate her body again. She took a navy blue wool watch cap off a hook and pulled it over her wet hair.

Troy sat down and was putting on a pair of Jerry's boots that Hurd had unearthed. Hurd had found another pair that he could wear. They made quite a picture in their ill-fitting outfits. Hurd was preoccupied, stuffing his vest pockets with ammunition he'd found in a drawer.

Sandy edged toward the door. Hurd hadn't loaded the rifle; she'd noticed that. Was it already loaded? She'd have to risk it. Maybe she could get to the door without attracting attention, then make it to the canoe. She had to take advantage of having her hands untied.

She was almost there, when Troy noticed her.

"Stop her," he said in warning.

Hurd swiveled and started toward her. She lunged toward the door and got it halfway open before Hurd slammed against it, sideswiping her leg. He grabbed her by the upper arm and lifted it high, so that she had to stand on tiptoe while he bullied her to the other side of the room. He moved so quickly it kept her off balance, and she did well to stay upright, let alone try to retaliate.

He threw her down on the bed, then slapped her across the cheek.

The blow stung, bringing tears to her eyes. But she looked at him defiantly. At least she had tried.

"Put this on," Hurd ordered, handing her a wool jacket. She sat up and did as she was told, taking her time, until Hurd slapped her again. She didn't want to press her luck too far.

As soon as she had the jacket on, he once again tied her hands behind her back with the wet rope.

"I feel like a clown," Troy said, looking down at his boots. He was swimming in Jerry's size elevens.

"So which way did he go?" Hurd asked Troy when they got outside.

"Over there, just where he first came out of the woods."

Hurd set out, giving a little jump-start to Sandy by pulling her arm. She could hear the plod of Troy's oversized boots behind her.

Hurd looked for trail sign, anything to show the way Jerry had gone. The early snow had left the ground mushy and there was an occasional footprint to follow. In other places, trampled plants or broken-off twigs pointed the way. Once when he thought he'd lost the track, Hurd crouched down and examined the leaves and found fresh blood. It worried Sandy. How badly wounded was her brother?

Physical discomfort overshadowed the worry. The layers of clothing would have probably been enough to keep her warm had her feet not been wet. But they ramrodded the cold deep into her bones.

The woods were so dense here that the sun hardly penetrated them. A drear hush prevailed, broken only by the crack of the brush underfoot as they traipsed along. The haunting cry of a loon cut through the wilderness from the lake, which was dropping farther and farther away as they began to climb.

The incline had Sandy huffing and puffing, but at least there was more sunlight as they went up out of the cedars. Hurd kept a fast pace; he was used to tramping in the woods. But finally Troy, breathlessly, insisted on stopping for a moment. Sandy was glad for the breather. The muscles in her legs were knotting into cramps.

"Can't we slow down?" Troy asked, his breath coming out unevenly. He leaned against a tree.

"We got to run him to ground," Hurd said. "I don't want him to double back to the cabin and take off."

"Well, hell, why don't I go back there and stay and watch the canoe? It'd be better than my clumping along in these." Troy looked down at Jerry's boots.

"Because we only got this one gun. And he has a bow

with him. Besides, you were so hot to take him out yourself.''

"Okay. You made your point. But if he's injured, he isn't going to be making very good time. We can take it a little slower. Time didn't seem so all-fired important, back there, when you were trying to hump Sandy.''

Hurd snorted. "Listen, you can't hold his nature against a man. I saw that sweet little white ass and—Jee-sus.'' He ran his hand through his hair.

Troy growled, "You son of a bitch,'' and Sandy recognized the tone.

Even in the midst of this, she thought, he feels proprietary about me. It was incredible.

Sandy took a long, incredulous look at him. She would never understand men, if she lived to be a hundred, which didn't look like a serious possibility right now.

Troy's face was flushed, and sweat glistened along his browline.

"I think Troy is ill,'' she told Hurd.

"I'm not ill,'' Troy said.

"I bet you've got a fever.'' She was beyond caring about his health, but maybe Hurd would send him back. It would make the odds more in her favor. "You look pretty bad.''

"I'm just hot from this walking.''

"You may be having a heart attack from all this unaccustomed exertion,'' she said.

"Shut up, Sandy,'' Troy said from between clenched teeth. She could see the veins standing out in his temples.

"C'mon, let's go, Miss Nursemaid,'' Hurd said, wrenching the ropes at her wrists.

If they kept her in tow, she would be their bargaining chip for bringing Jerry out in the open. Escape still seemed to be the only way to help him. She kept her eyes peeled for opportunities, but nothing presented itself.

A granite escarpment rose to one side of them now. They picked their way along a rocky path along its base. Troy was muttering, and from time to time a curse reached Sandy. It was hard walking in her own shoes, so she could imagine how he was faring in Jerry's oversized boots. Hurd, too, who was up ahead of her, was having trouble with his ill-fitting footgear. Once he seemed to turn his ankle, but he didn't complain. Not him. Sandy figured he would sooner die than destroy his macho image.

She couldn't imagine how there had been any sign to follow, but it had led them here and now there weren't any other choices. The trail had narrowed and there was just one way along this outcrop. The other side rolled down toward the lake rather steeply. Here and there were the seasonal remains of blueberry patches clinging to the breast of the hill.

Hurd had developed a limp, and he called them to a halt while he knelt down and unlaced his boot. A blister had risen on his heel. He reached for a fuzzy plant growing in a crevice, ripped some of its leaves off, and stuffed them in his sock. Sandy watched, but Troy passed and went around a bend.

He had barely disappeared when a cry of "Goddamn!" reached them.

Hurd grabbed his rifle and jumped up, hobbling awkwardly across the rocky surface, one shoe off, to see what was going on.

Troy's boot was caught in the steel jaws of a trap. The red flush had drained from his face.

"Get me out of this goddamn thing."

Hurd leaned the gun against a rock and bent to see what he could do. "You're lucky you had on those 'clown' boots."

Sandy quit paying attention to them. The gun was sitting

there unattended. Hurd had his back to it and both men were focused on the trap.

She eased forward, then in a sudden movement, she twisted around and shot her tied hands out toward the rifle. She felt the cold metal, then seized it by the barrel.

"Hey," she heard Troy say. Her sudden movement had attracted his attention. But she had the gun. Hurd reached out to grab her but she danced away and he missed. She stepped over to the edge of the path where it dropped steeply away and she drew her arms to one side as far as she could, then hurled the rifle out into the air. She put everything she had into it, and when the rifle left her hand, she realized she'd given it too much. Her body followed in a slow-motion arc. One foot landed a few feet down the hillside, bulldozing a path below it as it slid downward. Her leg gave out under her and she began an uncontrolled fall down the rocky surface.

Desperately she tried to stop herself with her heels, digging them in. Her shoulders flexed as she instinctively tried to throw her hands out to break the fall. Her wrists strained against the rope, and she pitched forward as she gathered momentum, then threw herself sideways to protect her head. Her shoulder scraped against a rocky outcrop, throwing her onto her back. She tried to grab something with her hands, but then the steep terrain threw her into another roll and she plunged on down through a scraggly patch of blueberry bushes, the twigs scratching and stabbing at her as she dragged through them. For a moment she thought they would save her, but the steep surface gave way again and she slid downward, unearthing the fragile plants that clung to the slope. Her eyes widened. Nothing lay in front of her except blue sky, but she was powerless to stop herself.

21

SANDY plunged over a ledge and down a steeper version of what she'd just slid down. Finally, she came to rest in a bog of unmelted snow and mud amid a garden of boulders.

Now she lay there a moment getting a grip on herself. At least she wasn't dead, although she wondered momentarily if it would be better. Every part of her body hurt. If she were dead, it would all be over now.

She heard a voice overhead. It was Hurd. "Go after her while I get this boot on. The gun's down there on the rocks."

They were coming—after her, after the gun. She struggled to get up and look for the rifle. Her head throbbed as she rose and the world went dark. She fought to stay upright, leaning toward the hill and bracing her legs to steady herself. After a moment, her vision cleared.

She scanned her surroundings. There was no sign of the gun, but unlike her pursuers, she hadn't been in a position to see where it landed. She needed to get out of there.

She turned away from the voices and slogged through the mud and rocks. The mud sucked at her feet, and an insistent pain in her left leg made it difficult to muster the strength to take another step. She could taste blood and wondered where it was coming from. But without the use of her arms, she couldn't investigate. She heard the clatter of pebbles as Troy descended. Then a thump and a groan as he must have dropped over the rim.

"Hold it, Sandy."

She kept going, trying to hurry.

After a moment and closer: "You heard me. I've got the gun. I'll use it." And something in his voice made her realize he meant it. Their shared experiences, nothing from their past would deter him. He would kill her. She turned slowly and faced her former friend. A great sorrow came over her when she looked at him in the clothes that didn't fit, holding the muddy gun, a grim look freezing his face into ugliness.

Only his eyes arrested her sadness. They glinted with something akin to madness. Sandy locked on them, curiously fascinated. In her peripheral vision she saw Hurd struggling down the hill toward them, trying to keep a controlled descent. A trickle of pebbles spilled over the ledge.

"Wait," he said, throwing his arm out in a halting gesture just as Troy pulled the trigger. "Is that gun—"

Sandy flinched at the blast, expecting to feel the bullet, but instead Troy's face flew apart before her eyes. The gun had blown up.

Shock riveted her to the spot for a moment as a sound of terror came screaming out of her soul to join the reverberations of the explosion echoing in the rocks. Hurd landed beside Troy's slumped body, stringing curses together against his surprise.

Sandy's shoulders rose and her chin dropped against her chest vainly trying to suppress the sound. She turned and began to limp away. As silence returned, reality did, too, and she realized Hurd would be after her. She glanced around. He was still kneeling by the body.

She had no idea where Jerry was, but she had to get back to the cabin and the canoe. From there she could go for help.

She hobbled into a grove of cedars and looked for any sort of a rudimentary trail to give her direction. The ground underfoot was mushy, quivering when she stepped on it. All around her there was devastation, a maze of fallen limbs and tree trunks from the storm earlier in the week. She picked her way along, shoving through the branches with her shoulders. Limbs sprang back and stung her face with scratches.

She found an overgrown trail and followed it until it disappeared under the splayed branches of a downed tree. She couldn't hoist herself across it, so she began to work her way along its length.

The ground had grown spongier, and she realized she must be in a bog just as her foot broke through the surface to water below. She leaped forward to a hummock, hoping it would hold her and that it wasn't another illusion of solid ground. She stumbled awkwardly to catch her balance before she toppled forward. The sharp conifer needles stabbed her as she tangled with a tree limb. The sudden movement tormented her aching muscles. But she couldn't give in to the pain; she had to keep going.

Now, worried that she might sink without warning, she tested each step before putting her weight down, going carefully back along the other side of the downed tree and locating the trail again. It began to rise, leaving the swamp behind.

Overhead, atop another bluff, she could hear the soothing voices of the pines. They seemed to urge her on. Boulders left behind by some long-ago glacier as if they were small stones emerged to the right of the path and she became certain this was the same bluff she'd fallen down. It had the same look. She stopped and scanned the sky. Had she made a big curve? And could Carl Hurd have already passed by here?

No, he would have followed her footsteps through the mud into the swamp—unless he was hightailing it straight back to the cabin and had better bearings than she did.

She decided she'd keep to the rocks; it would be harder for him to follow. That decision made, she started upward. Having her hands tied made it tedious, and time and time again she fell forward. She would be lucky to get out of this without a twisted ankle or a broken leg, or even a broken nose. Her heart pounded fiercely from the climbing and she stopped to rest on a ledge.

A sound from below caught her attention. It was Hurd. He was coming along the same way she had. His limp was more pronounced.

She froze momentarily. So far he hadn't looked up, but he might at any moment. She was reluctant to move for fear of catching his attention, but if he happened to look anyway, she was in plain view. Slowly, she thawed and sank as flat as she could, bellying behind the cover of a scraggly shrub. She could hear the crunch of his footsteps on the rocks below and she held her breath.

An eternity seemed to pass before the sound vanished and once again she heard only the whispering of the pines up above. Still she didn't move, afraid he might come back. Finally, she thought it had been long enough. She rolled to one side and pushed herself up with her shoulder, then stood and started up the next slope. The sun felt good on her back as she drove herself to keep going, thinking it would be easier to just hide out. Carl Hurd was still out there somewhere looking for her. Or he would get back to the cabin, take the canoe, and get away. She hoped for the latter. Then she could find Jerry and together they could set out for help, wherever that might be. This possibility seemed rather unlikely. It was crucial that Carl Hurd get rid of the two of them.

She started up the brow of the hill and was preoccupied when a loose patch of rocks slid out from under her foot. Caught off guard, she slipped downward, falling onto her knees. She blinked back tears at the new assault of pain and wriggled her way upright again. She'd landed near a narrow fissure in the rock. A sanctuary. She struggled into a squatting position and waddled to the opening. The crack would be an ideal hiding place—if there wasn't a bear denned up in it. *Horrible thought.* She peered into the darkness.

A deep voice said, "Don't move a muscle."

She was staring down the shaft of an arrow.

22

"**J**ERRY," Sandy said. "It's me." She'd recognized her brother's voice.

The arrow pointing at her dropped with a clatter. "Sandy? Oh, my God, I almost shot you. Was that you who yelled this morning?"

She nodded as her eyes adjusted to the darkness. Jerry was slumped against the back of the shallow rock cavity.

"What are you doing here?" he asked, almost casual surprise in his voice.

Her temper flared at his tone. What did he think? That he could just send out his mysterious little package of film and she wouldn't try to contact him? She squelched her anger. This was no time to lecture him.

"Carl Hurd brought me out here to find you," she said. "He's the one who shot at you. And he's out there looking for both of us now."

"It figures."

"Did he hit you?"

"Yeah. I got it in the leg, but it just grazed me, took a hunk of flesh, but it didn't hit any major arteries or anything."

"Can you get this rope off my wrists? Then I can take a look at it." Still squatting, she turned and, avoiding his legs, crowded backwards holding out her hands.

"I'm okay," he said gruffly.

"Well, I want to take a look anyway. And I definitely want to be untied."

"Who else was with you?" Jerry asked as he fiddled with the knot. "I caught a glimpse just before I was hit and I thought there were three people in the canoe."

"Troy Gunderson was with us."

"Damn. They're really serious about all this."

She was incredulous. "Did you think you could do your blackmail number and no one would get excited? What's wrong with you? They're involved in big-time stuff."

"Blackmail? What are you talking about?"

"This is no time for your lies, Jerry." The rope dropped free and she turned back toward him, flexing her fingers and wrists.

"I didn't try to blackmail anyone. Don't you think you taught me better than that?"

She chose to ignore that. She hadn't taught him to do drugs either, but that hadn't stopped him. Her shadow blocked the light and she shifted around awkwardly so she could examine his wound. "I don't know how you made it up here on this leg."

"The same way you did. Naked fear snapping at my butt."

"If you weren't trying to blackmail Troy, then what was that film you sent me?" She pulled the shredded fabric of his jeans away. A quiver inside her chest made her wonder if she was going to faint, but she willed herself to look at the injury. He'd torn a piece of cloth from his shirt and tied it around his thigh as a tourniquet. She loosened it and watched to see if the bleeding resumed.

"Photographs of him and Carl. I overheard them talking one night and when I saw who it was, I just about freaked. Man, like I figured this was hot stuff with the Senator's aide involved. I managed to snap off a few pictures. With them and a little snooping around for the whole story, I could have written my ticket. But they saw me and I had to like, split, in the interest of survival.'' He gave a short chuckle.

"That sounds like blackmail to me,'' Sandy said.

"Jeez, you really trust me, don't you?''

"Well, what do you mean?''

"San, if I had pictures and a story like that, I could sell it to about any magazine in the country. They'd take me seriously.''

"But Troy told me that you'd sent him a letter asking for money in exchange for the pictures. Let me have another strip of your shirt and I'll wrap this up.''

Jerry gave her an exasperated look as he lifted his jacket, caught hold of his shirt, and began to rip it. "Not true. Who are you going to believe? Him or me?''

Sandy wanted to believe her brother; she always did. But if Jerry hadn't sent the letter to Troy, who had? She thought about it a moment, then said, "You're lucky you got away alive. They killed Dave Hale.''

"Who's that?''

"Kevin Anderson. Maybe you know him by that name.''

Jerry's mouth dropped. "No shit. He's dead?''

Sandy nodded. "He was a Fish and Wildlife agent, working undercover.''

"That's a bummer.''

"And,'' she said reluctantly, "Gus Skaar is dead.'' She tied off the improvised bandage and sat back on her heels.

"Oh, shit. Don't tell me that.'' Jerry's voice quavered

and she could tell this news had hit him hard. "Poor Gus. What happened?"

"He was murdered. Actually the police are looking for you. They think you did it."

"Me?" He sounded incredulous.

"Well, he turned up dead and you had disappeared. But Hurd and one of his friends visited Gus to try to find the film and—"

"Oh, God!" Jerry put his hands over his face, and they were silent for a moment. Finally he looked up at Sandy. "Do you know who Gus was?"

"What do you mean?"

"He was a friend of our father's."

"Yes, I know that." Briefly she told him about coming to Northlake and what she knew about Gus Skaar.

"Then you know that he and our father were—uh— companions."

She nodded. "You say, *were*. Does that mean—?" Her voice choked a little and she couldn't continue.

Jerry nodded. "He's been dead a couple of years. I went to the cemetery and visited his grave. Gus showed it to me."

"He must have only been in his fifties."

"He died of cancer."

"How did you feel when you found out Dad was gay?"

He shrugged. "Surprised, I guess. Not too much, though, because Mom was so uptight about telling me anything. I think maybe I suspected. It kind of explains a lot of things."

"Like what?"

"How she freaked out once when I got into her makeup and put it on. You remember?"

Sandy hadn't thought about this incident in years, but the vision of her mother's anger came back in a flash now.

Jerry'd only been four at the time and just naturally curious about all the bright-colored "paints" in his mom's vanity.

"Another time, I brought this kid home—you remember Teddy Brown?"

Sandy nodded.

"He *was* kind of effeminate, I guess. Well, Mom wouldn't leave us alone. Teddy thought she was nutso. I guess she thought, like father, like son, and was afraid if we were alone Teddy would jump my bones. Or vice versa."

"But not if she could help it." Sandy gave a brief laugh, then sobered. "It must have really kept her uptight, watching you for *signs*."

"San, I wish you'd met Gus. He was such a cool dude, I can see why our father—well, I mean, not like that, but—you know. He made me understand about Dad. How long have you known?"

"Mother just told me."

"I was about to be pissed off that you didn't tell me."

She held her hands up in a placating gesture. "Listen, I just learned it."

"What a crock, for her to keep this from us."

"She was just trying to protect us—that's what she thought. I can forgive that, but I'm not sure I can forgive him."

"C'mon, Sandy. It's not like he chose to be gay."

"That's not what I mean. What I've had trouble with is that he just left when she told him to. He didn't put up a fight; he didn't even try to see us. He walked away and never gave us another thought." She surprised herself at being so honest with Jerry about her feelings. It was a first. In the past she'd always couched her conversation in generalities or euphemisms, as if talking to a child.

"That isn't true. Gus said our father was always tormented about having left us. He wasn't a happy man. He just didn't want to disturb our new life.''

''That's a cop-out. Torment is an overdramatic excuse for not doing anything.''

''God, Sandy. Let up. He was a human being.''

Jerry was right, and maybe eventually, if she got the chance, she could work through her child's-eye view of her father. She sighed and was starting to say something, when Jerry touched her arm and put his fingers to his lips. He cocked his head, listening.

All this talk, Sandy thought. *Where do we think we are?* She listened too, and heard nothing.

Finally, Jerry broke the silence, but kept his voice at a whisper. ''I thought I heard something. False alarm, I guess.''

''What do you think we should do?''

''Wait till night.''

''I don't think we can afford to. You've lost blood and I—'' She shivered at how cold she was. ''—I think we need to get out of here and get help.''

''I'm not going anywhere very fast on this.'' He indicated his leg. ''I think if we leave here in daylight, Hurd will catch us easy.''

''You could lean on me.''

He gave her a crooked grin. ''I've always done that.'' He paused, then continued, ''Let's face it. There's no way we could take any kind of evasive action with me leaning on you. So, if you're not going to listen to me, and I don't suppose you are, then you've got to go alone, back to the cabin. There's a revolver under the mattress. It's loaded. You'll have to take care of Carl Hurd.''

She would have liked to wait until night, but she was feeling so cold. By tomorrow morning hypothermia could set in, saving Hurd the trouble of killing her. "I hate to leave you alone," she said. Why did she have such a sense of foreboding that she'd never see Jerry again if she left him?

"I've got the bow," he told her. "If Carl looks in here I'll—" He left the rest unspoken.

23

The sun had crested the sky now. Sandy had no idea what time it was, but it must be past noon. She needed a drink desperately, and when she came to a slab of rock from which snow melt was dripping, she put her face under it and drank the cold water.

The only sounds around her were quiet ones. The gentle drip of the water, the soft caress of the wind in the pines high above. Suddenly, the raucous call of a jay disturbed the peace, startling her.

Jerry had suggested she return to the cabin in a roundabout way, approaching from the west, and she was following his instructions, but she felt uneasy. Hurd was out there somewhere, perhaps stalking her. She'd seen his tracking skills. At least he wasn't armed.

The sight of the cabin in the clearing was like a homecoming, but she didn't dare rush over to it. Instead, she stayed under cover, watching, reconnoitering, looking for signs of Carl Hurd. There was his canoe by the water where it bobbed on the ripples washing into shore. There was Jerry's canoe upside down beside the cabin. There was no sign of smoke from the chimney.

When at last it seemed safe, she made a dash to the near side of the cabin, where she stood on tiptoe and peeked in. No one there. Cautiously she crept around to the front and went in, closing the door solidly behind her.

The fire had died, but the cabin had retained enough heat to feel good to her cold bones. The four walls felt so safe.

She darted to the bed and snaked her hand between the frame and the mattress, running it sideways. She felt no gun, so she heaved the mattress up with a grunt, ignoring the pain that stabbed through her arm. There was no gun to be seen. Only then did she notice that the cabin was in disarray. Carl Hurd had been there. He had searched very thoroughly and he had found the gun.

Since both canoes were outside, Hurd was still in the woods. Was he watching the cabin? If so, why didn't he just walk over and come in? He had the gun.

Maybe he still wants me for his bargaining chip in drawing Jerry out. Or maybe by now he'd found him. The thought scared her. Jerry was so trapped up there in that crevice.

She found a pair of dry socks and put them on, then put the damp shoes back on, while she tried to make a decision.

The best course seemed to be to go for help. She could paddle across the lake, take the truck—she'd watched Hurd put the keys on top of the rear wheel—and find the man who'd picked her up when she'd had the accident on the icy road. Red Feather Inn? Lodge? Something like that. His place had to be somewhere near the logging road. Within miles. *Oh, God! It was so far.* A feeling of panic seemed to have taken up permanent residence in her chest.

She reluctantly stepped out the door after scanning the woods across from the cabin. She went around to the north side of the cabin to Jerry's canoe. She would sink it so that

Hurd couldn't follow her. Even setting it afloat would at least slow him down.

She picked up one end of the boat, thinking she would walk under it and hoist it up as she'd seen people—men—do, but it was too heavy, so she settled for dragging it. Even that was difficult, draining her and making all her aches and pains much worse. She rested the bow on her thighs and squeezed her upper arm for a moment. The throbbing in it felt as if the stitches were going to break open. She released the pressure and pulled the canoe another several yards, then gave up.

It was taking too long. She had to get out of there. No sooner had she thought it than she heard Carl Hurd's gravelly voice and felt a gun being shoved against her back. "Put it down and let's head into the woods, you and me, and we'll find that brother of yours."

He marched her, prodding with the revolver, back the way she'd come, her recent passage a guide for him to trace the way to Jerry. Her little brother had been right. They should have waited till night.

She tried to think, but her brain was lethargic, incapable of figuring anything out. She shook her head to clear it. *Don't give up now. Lead him the wrong way, anything.*

They came to the outcrop where she'd stopped for water earlier. Hurd went a little ahead, bent down, and drank from the same place, keeping an eye on her. It was picture-perfect, she thought. The woodsman getting a drink from the melt water dripping off the granite, framed overhead by evergreens, a dense stand of alders on either side of the path. Clouds scudded across the blue sky.

As Hurd straightened up to face her, she saw a movement behind him. A bear was lumbering toward him, treading softly on the blanket of pine needles. She started to gasp, then choked it back. As she watched, the beast rose majestically to its full height. Niles had told her there were no grizzlies in Minnesota, but the size of this! It came closer, silently, man-fashion, stealing in behind Carl Hurd.

She tried to control her expression so as not to reflect the danger, but it was hard not to rivet her attention on the bear. It had definitely spotted them.

"You've been a hell of a nuisance ever since you came to town," Hurd said, wiping his mouth with the back of his hand. "A little longer and—" He drew his finger across his neck and laughed.

She had trouble acting as if she were listening to him, but her instinctive reaction to back away satisfied him that she was paying attention to his aggressive gesture.

The bear had hesitated at the sound of a human voice, but now it moved forward again. It was so close Sandy could see the pieces of leaves and twigs clinging to its shaggy coat. It reminded her of a muscle-bound jock, weight slightly forward, mighty chest puffed, arms slightly away from the body. But so silent. The water had completely masked its approach if there was any sound at all.

It was cinnamon-colored and Sandy remembered Hurd's tale of the bear carrying his slug. Hadn't he said it was a cinnamon? And hadn't he baited in this area? Had the animal been stalking the man? Had it remembered the smell of the enemy? She prayed for some kind of primordial justice to be carried out right there before her.

"Well, c'mon. Get up here," Hurd said, motioning with the gun. "Don't get any idea of running off."

The animal hesitated again at the voice, turned its head as if to catch a scent, its Roman nose slightly upward, then resumed its quiet approach.

Keep coming, she begged silently. *Keep coming.* Hurd mustn't realize the danger until it was too late, until the predator became the prey.

But Carl must have finally heard something, because he turned his head slightly just before one of the bear's massive front paws swept out and grabbed him by the neck. The curved claws so coveted by Hurd and his buddies hooked into his throat, and Sandy saw blood begin to spurt out, dappling the leaves at his feet.

The man's gun hand shot up, but before he could pull the trigger, the fingers opened and the revolver dropped with a dull thud to the soft earth. His head lolled and the eyes bulged.

The bear turned, sweeping Hurd against its chest. His body went limp and slipped to the ground as the animal released its grip, then dropped down on all fours, put its long maw around Hurd's shoulder, and began to drag him away into the devouring forest as the birds continued their incessant gossip high overhead.

24

THE gun seemed irrelevant now, but Sandy picked it up anyway, looked it over and pulled back what she thought was the safety, then stuck it in her waistband. She went beyond the tamaracks and peered into the woods. She could see the disturbed undergrowth where the bear had dragged Hurd. Bent twigs and upturned humus marked the way.

She returned to the path and carefully chose an alternate route, refusing to think about what might be happening out there in the forest. She hoped Hurd died at the first blow as she suspected he had.

It took two hours for her to reach Jerry and for the two of them to make it back to the cabin shortly before sunset. The sun had dropped behind the trees and a new chill was coming on the air.

They'd almost made it to the clearing when they heard a small plane buzzing the lake.

"It landed," Jerry said, attuned to the different sound.

"Let's get into the cabin," Sandy said.

He moaned as they hurried to the door.

"I'm sorry," she said. The trip down had been tortuous

on his leg and she was amazed at her own endurance. But now was no time to fret over a little more pain.

"Never mind," he said through gritted teeth. "Let's get inside."

"Who is it? Do you have any idea?"

"Probably one of Hurd's cronies."

No more, please God. No more.

He took his arm from around her neck and collapsed on the bed. "Let me rest a moment, then give me the gun and you get over behind the door."

She took a long look at Jerry. Sweat had broken out on his upper lip and temples, and his mouth had a white ring around it. He was in no condition to defend them.

So there was to be more.

"Lie down. I'll take care of it," she said. She went to the window and looked toward the lake. A single-engine floatplane had come into sight and was taxiing into shore. The engine was cut off and in a moment a man stepped out on one float, steadying himself by holding onto a strut. Then he leaped to shore with a rope for securing the bobbing plane.

Sandy's heart stopped. It was Niles.

A flood of emotions poured through her, but she knew she had to deal with things as they happened. She drew the gun out from her waistband, undid the safety and cocked it, then stood back from the entrance. He came up silently, but she could sense his presence on the other side of the door.

All at once, the door flew open. She saw his foot withdrawing from a kick; he was off to one side. She jumped at the suddenness of the intrusion and the gun went off. The explosion echoed through the small cabin. She heard Jerry behind her, diving for cover. Niles leaped into view, his gun aimed.

"Freeze!" he said, then shocked: "Sandy!"

"I'll shoot you," she shrieked, although she didn't even know if there was another bullet. "I will. I really will." It was so stupid. He would also shoot her, but she was primed to say the words.

Niles raised his arms, pointing the gun skyward. She was amazed at his docility. "Don't shoot me, Sandy. I give up. I'm not—"

She heard a woman's voice from behind him. "It's okay. He's a Fish and Wildlife guy." It was Brigitte. Her face and arms had fresh bruises.

Could she be trusted? This was Carl Hurd's daughter talking.

"Did you find Jerry?" The girl saw him as she asked the question. She ignored Sandy's gun, went around Niles, and zeroed in on Jerry.

Sandy dropped her hands. This was Jerry's girlfriend talking. She hadn't even asked about her father.

The minute the gun went down, Niles was inside. He took it from her. "I'd feel more comfortable if it were on the table," he said.

She was shaking. She'd come very close to blowing him away. A Fish and Wildlife guy.

Niles began throwing questions at her, but Sandy shook her head and went over and knelt down by Brigitte. Gently she told her about her father. The girl's eyes looked troubled as she heard the story, and Jerry kept hold of her hand until Sandy had finished, ending with "I'm sorry."

Brigitte sighed deeply and put her head down against Jerry, who was back on the bed again. He put his hand on her hair and stroked it.

Sandy stood up and said to Niles, "Someone will need to go up and find him." Troy, too, but she didn't mention it yet. Jerry's leg needed attention.

"My brother was shot in the leg. Can you take a look at it? Do you know anything about—?"

"I've got a first-aid kit in the plane." He sprinted out the door to get it.

"Did you contact Niles?" Sandy asked after he'd left.

Brigitte shook her head. "No. He came and got me."

Niles returned a few minutes later and he examined Jerry's wound and treated it as well as he could. Then he turned to Sandy. "Sit down over here," he ordered.

"Is it bad?" she asked, touching her cheek.

"It looks kind of deep. Let me put some peroxide on it, then we'll put a butterfly across it, hold it together. When was your last tetanus shot?" he asked.

"Just the other day." It seemed longer than that. She flinched as he cleaned the wound.

He looked puzzled, but said, "Good. You won't need another." He cleaned her other wounds, then snapped the kit shut. "Let's get you two to town."

"Why did you come looking for me? I thought you went to the Cities?"

"My boss called me yesterday, just before I came by the Senator's place. He told me Kevin—I mean, Dave—had been found dead and that I should get out of here."

"You and Dave were both working undercover?"

"Yes. Backup," he said bitterly.

"I think I'm the one who caused his death."

"We both knew the risks going in. He told me you had recognized him, and, with hindsight, we should have pulled out then, but we discussed it and decided to go for the prize. We were so close to pulling in the big guy."

"You did."

He tilted his head. "What?"

"Troy Gunderson. Senator Mattingly's aide. He's up in the woods dead."

"He was working with Carl Hurd."

"She nodded. "I was in Dave's apartment when he was killed, so they came after me and then planned to use me as bait to get Jerry. You still haven't told me how you came to be here."

"Like I said, I went to the Cities, and this morning my boss was filling me in—said a woman had called in to report Dave's murder. He said she identified herself as Sandy. Just that. I was out of there. When I got back up here, I went to the Senator's. When you weren't there, I went directly to Carl Hurd's. He wasn't there, but Brigitte was. She told me what she knew. I got hold of a plane from the department and—" He spread his hands. "Let's get out of here. I'll get some help, come back later to tie things up."

She still didn't know who had sent the blackmail letter to Troy. Jerry denied it and, as usual, she believed him. This time, though, it seemed different. He seemed older, sobered. Tracking down their father, meeting Gus Skaar, or maybe getting shot at—he was changed. Somehow she thought maybe it would come out that Carl Hurd had seen a way to go for the sweepstakes. Maybe Brigitte knew. And maybe it would never come out at all. She really didn't care.

A short time later the four of them were in the floatplane, taxiing up the lake, into the wind. After an initial glance into the back where Brigitte and Jerry were, Sandy decided to keep her eyes to the front.

Now Niles pulled back on the stick; the floats lifted, sending up a spray behind them. She craned her neck at the novelty of it. She'd never been in a floatplane before.

They were planing along on the surface of the lake as if it were a runway, gaining speed. Then all at once they were airborne. The steady drone of the engine was comforting, almost like a lullaby, and Sandy felt safe, wrapped in a cocoon. It felt good to be leaving Early Dawn and the death that lingered there.

She turned slightly so she could study Niles, a Fish and Wildlife investigator, as it turned out. That sounded a little more stable than a trapper. And he had come to rescue her. Of course, she hadn't needed to be rescued, but that didn't matter. A smile tickled her insides.

She watched his hands on the yoke and remembered him sharpening his knife the first night she'd met him, his brachioradialis flexing, looking up from under his eyelashes occasionally. Sexy, but vaguely sinister. She was tired, but even now she could feel something stirring in her. As if he read her thoughts, he glanced over at her, nothing sinister about him.

"There's something I need to tell you," Niles said.

Sandy looked at him speculatively, a frown drawing her eyebrows together. He was going to tell her he was married. She felt it coming.

"My name isn't Niles Benson. It's Michael Taylor. And I'm not a Minnesotan. I live in Pennsylvania and—"

"—and you're married." *Subtle, Sandy. Very subtle.*

He looked at her and a smile flickered across his face. It looked as if he was stifling it, and she could feel her color rise.

He looked worried. "Well, as a matter of fact—" he paused, drawing his words out "—I'm single."

"Really?"

He nodded. "Pennsylvania's not all that far from Washington."

"No, it isn't." She looked outside. They weren't at a high altitude, but she was having trouble getting enough oxygen.

"How did you get involved in all this?" he asked.

A slow smile began to soften her face, and she watched the endless necklace of lakes strung out below. "It all started with what I thought was a sample vole. It's a long story,'' she said, rather breathlessly. "Maybe there'll be time to tell you later.'' She was suddenly very self-conscious about her hair, which was all mashed down by the watch cap. And she was muddy and bloody and bruised.

Niles—Michael—that would take some getting used to—Michael didn't seem to mind. He reached out and put his hand on the back of her neck and kept it there till he had to bank for a final approach.